SECRET ADDICTION- COLLATERAL DAMAGE

THE FORGOTTEN VICTIMS

JOSEPH FLYE

Copyright © 2023 by Joseph Flye

All Rights Reserved.

ISBN: 978-0-578-72814-8

No part of this publication may be reproduced, distributed, or transmitted in any form or by any means, including photocopying, recording, or other electronic or mechanical methods, or by any information storage and retrieval system without the prior written permission of the publisher.

This is a work of fiction. Names, characters, businesses, places, events, and incidents are either the products of the author's imagination or used in a fictitious manner. Any resemblance to actual persons, living or dead, or actual events is purely coincidental.

Published by: Divine Intervention Publications

Other books written by Joseph Flye:

40 Moments Of Divine Intervention: My Personal Journey, Journal, and Bible Study

www.divineinpub.com

DEDICATION

I express my appreciation to God for breathing into me the words to write in this book. I dedicate it to my wife Bernita, my two daughters, Crystal and Nicole, and their spouses Bryan and Jacquail, respectively. I also dedicate this book to my awesome grands- Bryan, Jaidyn, Micah, Milaya, and Jordan. Finally, last but not least I dedicate this book to the rest of my family members who have always encouraged me to pray and ask God for direction. Your prayers have helped me complete a timely and God-given assignment that I believe will be used as a tool for spiritual, physical, and emotional healing.

CHAPTER 1
FROM RICHES TO RAGS

Carl Forester spent many sleepless nights and tireless days planning and eventually building up his small-town cosmetics business. After he and his wife Beverly were married, they lived a simple, ordinary, and financially disciplined life. Beverly, who worked the second shift at a twenty-four-hour grocery store, was also a Christian mother who was very involved in the women's group at her church. Carl, on the other hand, refused to step inside a church. After years of faithful church attendance and service, he quit attending because he felt as though he was cheated out of a leadership position he deserved.

About a year after Carl opened his cosmetics business, their frugal and restrained life, and the peace and contentment that came with it faded away. Carl's change in appetite for bigger and better possessions altered their lives forever. Maybe working in the cosmetics business created his appetite for indulgence, but he believed he deserved the best home, the best car, the best appliances, and even the best wardrobe. He would settle for no less than the newest and most expensive products on the market, often spending well beyond what he and Beverly could financially afford.

Carl's obsession with stylish clothing created personal problems for their fifteen-year-old son, John. He spent more time working in his cosmetics business than spending time with his son, who loved baseball, soccer, watching superhero videos, and playing video games. Carl was excessively absorbed in what John wore to school, buying him expensive designer clothing, and demanding that he wear them. He was unconcerned and uninterested in what John wanted to wear. John had no interest in wearing expensive designer clothing, especially to school; he preferred dressing simple and modest.

Carl's demands exposed John to constant bullying at his school by a group of classmates who accused him of thinking he was better than them because of his expensive and fashionable attire. Because of this perception, John had no friends, distancing himself from associating with any of his classmates.

Beverly would practically beg Carl to talk to John about the bullying at his school. She consistently made an emotional appeal to him to stop demanding that he wear expensive clothing to school and to quit running the charge cards up on items they couldn't afford. His response would make her feel as though her words meant nothing to him.

"I know what I'm doing. If I want my son to think sharp and be the best dressed at his school, he needs to look sharp, and that requires dressing like he's the best. You worry about taking care of things at home. I'll deal with what our son wears to school."

Usually, Beverly wouldn't respond to Carl's arrogance, but this time, she couldn't hold back.

"Yes, that's the total sum of what you do with your son. You are more concerned about him making a fashion statement at his school than spending quality time with him at home. Wow! That makes you the greatest dad in the world."

Beverly touched a nerve in Carl. Her comment permanently altered their relationship and threatened their marriage. He began intentionally distancing himself away from her. His isolation from her became a form of emotional abuse. She was forced to endure this abuse every time she was around him.

Contrary to Carl's opinion of her, Beverly was one of the most humble, hardworking, and thrifty Christian wives you could ever meet. She was raised in a family where three meals a day was a luxury. She missed the country life she grew up in as a child, every day praying that one day she would return to it.

Beverly couldn't bring herself to enjoy extravagant living as much as Carl enjoyed it; this was his lifestyle, his comfort zone, not hers. As it was with their son, she was a modest dresser. She wasn't into having the best possessions, nor dressing in stylish clothing. She was content with wearing plain dresses, pants, and outfits.

Although Beverly's wardrobe was no different than any other woman's wardrobe, other than the rich and famous, Carl often scorned her for how she dressed, making known to her that he was ashamed to go out in public with her. One afternoon, his distaste for her style of clothing hit a boiling point as they made their way out the door to go grocery shopping.

"This is not happening, it's just not. I've been looking at you wearing the same old style of clothes for years, and I'm tired of it. I refuse to be seen walking down the grocery store aisles with you looking like a despicable old-fashioned goat. I can't do this anymore."

That insult was a low blow from Carl that greatly embarrassed and hurt Beverly, but she hid it from him. There was no way she was going to let him know how much his malicious verbal abuse hurt her. She turned away from him and with her head lifted high, walked up the stairs and into the bedroom, falling on her knees praying for Carl while he was left to do the grocery shopping alone, which he hated doing.

Carl's insults towards Beverly did little to ease the financial stress the family was going through; financial stress that was getting worse. Although Carl loved his job and the hefty salary he was making, as the big city competition released new lines of cosmetic products, his sales began to slide. There was only one best-selling product that helped his business stay profitable. When a major cosmetics chain released a similar product comparable to Carl's best-selling product, sales at his business fell flat; he couldn't compete.

Despite Carl's efforts to keep his cosmetics business afloat, sales never rebounded; he had no other choice than to go out of business. Facing a huge amount of debt, all of it due to his appetite for the most expensive and top-of-the-line items, Carl's business closure had a devastating effect on the family, marking the end of bringing home a large salary. Meeting their financial obligations became difficult, almost impossible.

While he worked odd jobs here and there, Carl insisted that Beverly pick up some overtime hours to help pay for their astronomical credit card bills. She refused to work herself to death due to his negligent spending habits, especially when he consistently rejected her plea to tone down the spending.

"I've already put blood, sweat, and tears into this marriage, and you expect more. There's no more to give. I refuse to kill myself trying to hold on to stuff you irresponsibly bought on credit and can't afford to make the payments. The way it looks, we're going to lose everything anyway."

Fuming at her response, Carl charged at Beverly like an out-of-control angry bull, and for the first time in their marriage, lifted his hand poised to strike her. The only thing that interrupted his swing and Beverly being the intended recipient of physical abuse was their son who walked in and unfortunately, witnessed what was about to take place. Carl lowered his hand, and with eyes full of rage, verbally threatened Beverly.

"I've had enough of you and your insensitive attitude. I'll get through this, even if I have to do it alone, but if you cross me or smart off to me again, I don't care who walks into the room, nothing's going to stop me from finishing what I started to do a moment ago and give you what you deserve."

After Carl stormed out of the room, Beverly sat paralyzed at what had just taken place. Carl had raised his hand to strike her and threatened to do it again. Beverly Forester, who up until this night, stood her ground when challenged by her husband, was now a fearful wife in unchartered territory. His threat of physical abuse created a new level of anxiety in her. He had won a significant victory over her, and after that distressing victory, he took advantage of it.

Carl worked twelve hours a day, determined to prove Beverly wrong about them losing everything. Every effort he made in an attempt to work their way out of debt failed. They lost nearly everything they had accumulated. The only big-ticket item they were able to hold on to was their Mercedes, on which they owed no debt.

The severity of the Forester's financial collapse hit home when their dream home, or Carl's dream home, was foreclosed on because they defaulted on their mortgage payments. The Forester's found that they had turned to a humbling page of a new chapter in their no longer luxurious, but soon, turbulent lives.

With the family facing homelessness, through Beverly's prayers, God supplied their need as she sought Him for help. She wasn't waiting on Carl to get his act together. Despite all that had transpired and how fearful she was of him, she still loved him. She was looking forward to a change, ready to move forward, refusing to stoop low and let Carl's anger and bitterness rise in her towards him.

If there was any good that came out of the Forester's downfall, it was Beverly having her prayer to move back to the country answered. While Carl was grieving over the loss of their home and all of his prized possessions, she remembered her deceased parents left her the deed to their farmhouse in a rural area down south.

Beverly grew up in this farmhouse, and for her, their financial calamity was a ticket back home. Although the farmhouse was a crumbling structure in need of repairs, it was sound enough for them to occupy. Their massive amount of debt and bad credit left them with no other option than to move down south into the farmhouse. The truth is, the Forester's couldn't afford to go anywhere else.

Beverly's excitement about their move down south escalated Carl's displeasure and anger towards her. He had a delusional idea in his mind that she was reveling in their financial and material loss because for years, she had constantly bugged him about moving down south. Because of his false perception of her, there was less communication and companionship between them. They slept in separate bedrooms; there was no intimacy nor romance whatsoever. Predictably, Carl blamed Beverly for their inability to recover from their financial downfall.

Carl's view was that if Beverly had worked more overtime hours on her job as he insisted, they wouldn't be living in what he viewed the farmhouse as, "a miserable dump." The farmhouse was a total downgrade because it was half the size of their previous home. It was dated and hadn't been worked on since Beverly's parents lived in it.

Shortly after settling into the farmhouse, Beverly was hired at the local twenty-four-hour grocery store working as a second shift cashier, the same hours and position she had worked at the grocery store in their previous hometown. Carl was hired as a cosmetics salesman, but he was determined to continue working on restarting his cosmetics business. Deciding to work as a salesman was the best he could do at the time, but that decision negatively impacted the Forester's lives for years to come.

Every day during the week, Carl would take an hour-long drive to his office downtown, then after work, arrive home retreating into his garage where he would spend the rest of the evening alone. Whenever Beverly would ask him why he spent so much time in the garage than with his family, he would tell her that he was working on design plans to remodel the house and restart his business and that the garage was his private "man-cave" to relax and do some thinking. The garage was off-limits to Beverly and John, and while he was in there, he wasn't to be disturbed.

Soon after Carl began his salesman job, Beverly was beginning to feel more isolated and lonelier than she had already been feeling. John noticed her loneliness and how Carl neglected her when she was at home. He never saw him spending quality time alone with her, but it was her loneliness that created a robust mother-son relationship between him and her.

The most fun John would ever have at home was with Beverly when they would hit baseballs together in the middle of the dusty road outside their farmhouse. They would pretend they were hitting a home run with the bases loaded in a capacity-filled major league stadium with the crowd cheering as they ran the bases home to victory. John's goal in life was to play baseball in college and move on to the pros.

John loved going to church with Beverly, especially Sunday school, and helping her with the women's group at the church and around the house. The only time Carl would interact with John was to discipline him for something he did wrong, never complimenting him for anything he did right. Sometimes he would yell at him even if he did nothing wrong. He never played football, baseball, or basketball with John. At times, he would go fishing with some co-workers from work, but John was never invited.

Carl refused to allow John to get up close and personal with him; they never had a down-to-earth father-to-son conversation. John was more concerned about Carl's isolation from Beverly than his isolation from him. He was also worried about his safety and Beverly's safety, especially after the day he saw Carl lifting his hand to strike her, something he had never seen him do. John and Beverly became the subjects of verbal and emotional abuse from Carl that unfortunately led to physical abuse.

CHAPTER 2
THE OBSESSION

The women who worked at the office where Carl worked as a salesman outnumbered the men. All of these women dressed stylishly and faithfully used the makeup and other beauty products the company sold; they were walking advertising billboards for the company. Some of the women intentionally, and some of them unintentionally, attracted the attention of the men in the office. Carl became highly obsessed with their beauty. Based solely upon the outward appearance of these women, he practically reverenced them as beauty queens, and the way a real woman should physically look and dress.

When Carl married Beverly, he was aware that she was a modest dresser and never wore anything flattering or seductive that would attract another man's attention. She never wore makeup. She had such a natural beauty on her face and soft skin that there was no need for her to cover that beauty with makeup. She also carried her weight well. Her natural beauty on the outside did not define her, but it was her loving and caring Christ-like spirit on the inside that prompted other women to admire her. Beverly was all that a man could desire in a wife, but her inner beauty wasn't satisfying enough for Carl, and strangely, her outer beauty was even less appealing.

One day while working at his desk in the office, Carl's friend Bob's wife, who was a mail clerk in the office, stopped at Carl's desk to make a delivery. They engaged in a long conversation as John asked her:

"Susan, I've noticed that you are the best-dressed woman in the office. How do you manage to look so good and fresh every morning, and what does Bob think about you coming to work looking like a model?"

"Carl, there's a lot you don't know about me and Bob. He could care less about what I wear to work, it's just been that way between us lately. He's so beside himself that he pays me no attention whatsoever. We've been at odds with one another for a long time. I feel so lonely in my own home, even when he's home."

"Susan, you know Amanda in accounting, right?"

"Yes, we're best friends."

"Well, the other day at lunch, she shared with me how she was going through sort of the same thing you're going through with Bob. I tried to encourage her, but I think I sent her the wrong message. Ever since that conversation, I try to avoid her because I think she has feelings for me, even though she knows I'm married."

"Carl, whether she wants a relationship or not, she's lonely and doesn't know how to deal with that loneliness. She's craving companionship and simply wants to be noticed. Every woman in this office wears what they wear to be noticed. Look around. You may have noticed that every female wears the same style of clothing because they feel uncomfortable wearing anything different. Peer pressure won't allow them to wear anything different. Although they want to be noticed, they don't want to be noticed as someone who doesn't fit in.

"Whenever I'm at work, I have a sense of confidence when I get attention because of the way I dress. I love to dress nice, but I also want to be loved and respected for who I am. If a man comments on my outer beauty, I don't want to be disrespected for who I am on the inside. On many occasions, I have caught you looking at me from top to bottom, but I don't mind because it makes me feel good. I wish Bob looked at me the way you do."

"Susan, I didn't realize you knew I was admiring you. I just know a woman who dresses nice has a sense of pride in the way she looks. If I were you, if the other women in this office got noticed and I didn't, I'd feel left out. But, you don't have to worry about that, you have them all beat by a mile.

"I know some women here are intentionally sending a message by the clothing they wear. I know some men in this office are driven by what these women are wearing, but they look at them as sex objects based on what they are wearing. In your case, that's not me. Whenever I look at you, I see more than just a beautiful body. The way you dress shows me that you are confident and intelligent, and I admire that.

After eighteen years of marriage, I've never seen that in Beverly."

"What do you mean Carl? Beverly is a smart and good person. Are you guy's having marriage problems also?"

"Well, Susan, just between me and you, I have considered the D-word."

"What do you mean Carl, divorce?"

"A few days ago, when I got home, I decided to give Beverly the news. I know she didn't want to hear it, or maybe she did due to the direction our marriage was going. I had no idea how I was going to say it, but I wanted to let her know I was thinking about getting a divorce. When I finally got the nerve to tell her, the only words that came out of her weeping mouth were, 'Is that what you want, a divorce? This is not just about me and you. I've practically raised our son all by myself, now you want to abandon him. Is that what you want to do?'

"I didn't give her an answer, then she just walked away. That night, we didn't talk to each other. I thought to myself, what do I want? I'm not happy in our marriage and I don't know how to fix it other than get out of it. Ever since then, for some reason, divorce hasn't been mentioned."

"John, I have to finish my deliveries, but let me leave this thought with you. All the women here in this office know you are a man who knows what he wants. If Beverly doesn't see that, that's her problem. Amanda and, who knows, maybe even myself, would love to be where Brenda is; if you know what I mean."

While Carl was driving home from work, the conversation he had with Susan, and the mere thought of the beauty and classy dress style of the women at the office fascinated him, but when his thoughts compared Susan and the other women in the office to Beverly, his fascination quickly turned into repulsion.

The next morning, while Beverly was cooking breakfast, Carl walked up to the kitchen doorway without her noticing. He stood in the doorway, staring at her for about a minute with a disgusted and unhappy look on his face. When she turned around, she caught a glimpse of his unappealing facial expression before he sat down at the table, but ignored it, thinking that maybe he didn't sleep well. She sat down at the table with her plate, preparing to eat breakfast.

Usually, in the mornings at breakfast time, Carl would complain about anything he thought was wrong or not being taken care of around the house. On this morning, she noticed that there was something different about him; he was quiet and more distant than usual. After about five minutes, Beverly had enough of Carl's silence. For a brief moment, she set her fear of him aside.

"Alright, that's it. I worked hard last night, haven't been to bed, cooked you breakfast with hot coffee on the side, and you have the nerve to sit here silent and for whatever reason, walk in here looking at me as if I disgust you. Yes, I saw how you were looking at me before you walked in. I've had enough of this. Why would you even think I deserve this kind of treatment?"

Carl was shocked at her boldness, shouting at her as if this was his way of proving who was in control.

"What you deserve? It's not all about what you deserve! If I gave you what you deserve, you wouldn't be sitting in that chair right now, and I would be in jail!"

After getting up to get a cup of coffee, Carl sat down, throwing insult after insult at Beverly.

"You talk about deserving, what about what I deserve? I deserve a wife who looks like a woman who respects herself and her beauty. We have been married for eighteen years and I have never seen you in makeup. When you go shopping, you buy the same type of out-of-style clothing.

"The women I work with at the office have a sense of pride in how they look and what they wear, but then I look at you and I can honestly say that I get turned off at the sight of you. I look at our friend Bob's wife, Susan, who is just a mail clerk at the office. It perplexes me that this man works as a stocker in a bookstore, but his wife, a mail clerk, dresses and looks like a supermodel. Why can't my wife look the same?"

Beverly couldn't hold back her tears and anger as she sat wondering what possessed her husband to come at her in the way he just did. She wouldn't let him get off humiliating her without saying a word.

"Are you serious? I can't believe you just said that to me. I am not the least bit interested in looking like a supermodel for you or myself. Sadly, you have the nerve to sit there and say I turn you off because you are obsessed with how the women in your office at work look and dress. It's insulting and wrong for you to say something like that to my face.

"Right now, I think you need to quit that job and get your mind where it needs to be, on respecting and loving your wife, not admiring women who intentionally dress provocatively to mess you all up. Don't bring that lustful junk you have allowed to fester in your mind into my home and to this table. If I turn you off, leave. I'll give you that divorce you asked for if that's what things have come to. John and I will survive without you just like we've been doing. Otherwise, get your act together and deal with it because I'm not changing the way I am to satisfy your fantasies."

Beverly stood up with a sense of pride in herself, throwing her dirty plate in the kitchen sink, the plate shattering just as their marriage was shattering. Beverly was simply demanding that Carl treat her with respect.

"Start getting your act together washing these dishes and helping your wife around the house as a real husband would do rather than complaining to her every morning, criticizing, and isolating her. That's why you need to come to church with me, or whoever it may be that dresses to fulfill your depraved illusions, since you have something negative to say about the way I dress. You've been bitter for years about how you feel you were cheated out of a position even I don't think you deserved, and how you treated me this morning proves it. Before you even think about being a church leader, you need to learn how to respect and honor your wife."

Carl had no other words to say to her because he had a plan of action on his mind. He cleaned up the broken plate and reluctantly washed the dishes, then headed off to work confident that whether Beverly wanted to or not, she was going to change; he was going to demand and force it.

The next day, Carl's devious plan was put into action. Beverly had worked a double shift at the grocery store due to sick calls and was on her way home. Carl was on his way to work, and John had just left the house for school when Beverly arrived and went into the bedroom, discovering that her entire wardrobe was missing from her closet. She was shocked and bewildered at first, but after considering the conversation she had with Carl at the kitchen table the day before, she knew he had something to do with her missing clothing.

She searched all over the house for her clothing, but could not find them. The thought came to her to check the trash bins outside. After noticing an unusually large number of garbage bags sitting next to the trash bins, she opened one of the bags.

Inside the bag were some of her items of clothing. Upset and frustrated at the fact that Carl would go this far in an attempt to force her to change, she gathered all the bags containing her clothing, taking them back inside. As she was hanging them inside her closet, she became more frustrated each time she rehung a garment as thoughts of revenge raced through her mind. She felt a need to talk to someone before doing anything she would later regret.

Beverly would call her best friend Carmen when she was going through with Carl. Carmen experienced some of the same types of abuse from her former husband that Beverly was experiencing with Carl, except Carl was more outspoken and humiliating. Beverly was troubled and afraid when she shared with Carmen the details of some of the verbal and emotional abuse she was experiencing in her marriage. While talking with Beverly on the phone, Carmen gave her some encouraging advice.

"Ever since I have known you Beverly, you have never run from a fight. You know I have never been comfortable with you marrying Carl, but for now, I'll leave that alone. You are still my best friend and you always will be, no matter what. In adversity, you have held yourself together, no matter how big and strong the opponent is.

"I have loved you as a friend and I will always back you up for doing what is right. Believe it or not, during my marriage, there were many times when I had to fight to maintain my sanity, even when I felt I didn't have the strength to do so. Even though we have had slightly different battles with spouses to fight, I see you in me, a real fighter. During your battles, you have to take time to watch every move the enemy makes, and every inch he moves. You need to find out who or what is fueling his rage.

"Study your enemy so that you know where to strike that single and most effective blow that will take him down. God will only allow your enemy to advance toward you inch by inch, but He will also allow you to stay a mile ahead of him so you can see him coming. I know you feel pain right now, but if I could, I would bear that pain for you. You are beautiful and unique, don't let anyone take that away from you.

"Don't let anyone manipulate you and take your kindness for granted, even those close to you. As long as you try your best to make your marriage work, don't ever blame yourself if things don't work out. Whatever the outcome, don't sit and drown in a sea of self-pity; don't ever allow anyone to take you there. If by chance you find yourself drowning in misery, rise to the occasion, pick yourself up, and move forward, even if you have to do it alone."

Beverly's phone rang immediately after she ended her conversation with Carmen; it was Carl calling. She was confused at the excitement in his voice when he told her he had a surprise for her, especially after his threats and insults, and then finding her wardrobe in the garbage. There was not a hint of excitement in her voice when she responded to his unsettling exhilaration.

"Surprise? I found your ignorant and immature surprise. Do you think all of this is a game? I am not the least bit surprised at what you did, and right now, another surprise from you is far from what I want. Why in the world would you throw all my clothes in the garbage? Have you lost your obsessed mind?"

Carl's exhilaration quickly turned into anger.

"Let's get things straight right now. I don't play games and don't ever call me ignorant and obsessed again. The clothes in the garbage weren't the surprise I was talking about, but since you mentioned it, I told you the other day that I was tired of seeing you in the same old boring clothes. I am not impressed by them. The clothes you wear make you look fat and distasteful.

"I'm to the point where I've gotten to be more and more embarrassed to be around you whenever we go out in public. This weekend, that's all going to change. After how you talked to me at breakfast yesterday and just now, I'm going to give you a chance to redeem yourself." Beverly slammed the phone down, still steaming about Carl throwing her entire wardrobe in the garbage, and acting like a deranged dictator.

When Carl arrived home from work, he was the last person Beverly wanted to see. After hearing his car door shut, she ran up the stairs and into the bathroom, closing and locking the door. She sat on the sink counter still puzzled and asking herself why Carl would resort to throwing her clothes out as if they were garbage.

"Is his obsession with how those women on his job dress that deep and captivating? God, I'm trying to be humble, but it's getting to be more and more difficult. I don't know how much more of this I can take. I need you to help me get through this foolishness."

After Beverly was in the bathroom for about a half-hour, she heard Carl calling her name as he banged on the door, but she refused to answer him. He called her name again, but there was still no response from her as he continued to bang on the door, yelling for her to open it. She became fed up with Carl's yelling and banging.

"There is no need for you to stand out there yelling at me and banging on the door. You are the last one in the world I want to see or talk to right now."

Carl waited outside the bathroom door for about thirty seconds more, then kicked the door open. He stood in front of Beverly, angry and upset with an armful of new women's clothing. After throwing the clothing on the bathroom floor, he ran up to her and put his fist in front of her face threatening her.

"If you want to know, that's your surprise down there on the floor. Don't ever make me have to kick a door open again in my own home, ever!" I told you before, don't cross me. You can fight this losing battle all you want, but you will not disrespect me. I have the right to choose how my wife should look, and that is not like a sloppy peasant. You will do what I say because one way or another, I'm going to break your stubbornness, beginning right now."

Beverly was afraid to say anything to Carl. For the second time in as many days, he had put his hand up threatening to strike her. Bit by bit, he was chipping at her emotions, trying to break her. Carl backed away from Beverly, speaking to her with slightly less anger in his voice.

"The president of the company has invited all the employees to an awards dinner Saturday night. Whether you care or not, I was surprised to find out that I'm going to receive an award and you will go to this dinner with me. You don't have to act surprised, but I bought you those dresses lying on the floor and you will wear one of them to the dinner. You will show me the respect I deserve, and you will not embarrass me at this dinner."

Carl's obsession with the women at the office, and the way Beverly dressed were rising to new levels moment by moment. It was getting so scary that Beverly did not know who this man was living in her house. She remembered the advice her friend Carmen had given her during their conversation on the phone.

"During your battles, you have to take time to watch every move the enemy makes, and every inch he moves. You need to find out who or what is fueling his rage. Study your enemy so that you know where to strike that powerful blow that will take him down."

Reluctantly, Beverly agreed to wear one of the new dresses Carl had bought her to the dinner. He found a little success in forcing her to yield to his plan, but she had a plan of her own. If she wanted to know who her competition was, she had to attend the dinner. She knew the woman or women Carl was so obsessed with at his office would be there. The time had come, as her friend Carmen advised, for her to know who or what was fueling the destructive obsession that had overtaken her husband and was destroying their marriage.

When Carl and Beverly arrived at the dinner, he left her alone to mingle with the crowd while he socialized with some of his co-workers. Although Beverly was dressed as elegant as all the other women that were at the dinner, she felt out of place. It wasn't the way she was dressed that made her feel out of place, nor did she feel as though the women were a special breed of women that would fuel an obsession.

Beverly felt as though she was in a place where she did not belong after conversing with a few of the women. She concluded that the forced smiles were just as false as the makeup they were wearing. She also felt as though she was in a room full of people who cared less about actually knowing an individual for who they were. Yes, they were co-workers, knowing of one another, but knowing very little about one another.

She sat down at Carl's assigned table, alone for about fifteen minutes, waiting for him to finish socializing. She was bored and didn't want to be at this dinner. Although the dinner was an awards dinner, the majority of the recipients, for one reason or another, could care less about receiving an award.

None of the women she conversed with had a good word to say about the female president of the company who was preparing to hand out the awards. A few of them confessed that they were only working at the company to receive a paycheck and to pick up dates and that picking up dates was not a problem with the men at the office.

Before the awards were presented, Beverly noticed that sitting at a table on the opposite side of the room from her and Carl's table was Bob's wife, Susan, the mailroom clerk with whose dress style Carl was overly obsessed. Susan was sitting talking to Carl, her friend Amanda, and a group of other female co-workers when Beverly caught Susan glancing at her. She waved for Susan and Carl to come over to her table and talk a little bit before the ceremony began. Susan turned her head in the other direction, pretending as though she didn't see Beverly waving at her. Beverly thought this reaction was strange since they had become close neighborhood friends after Susan helped them settle into their farmhouse. She also thought the hug Susan and her friend Amanda gave Carl as he was leaving their table was too close and inappropriately affectionate.

While Beverly sat puzzled about Susan's reaction towards her, and Susan and Amanda's flirtatious behavior, she felt Carl put his hand on her shoulder as he sat down next to her along with some of his male co-workers. With his hand on her shoulder and his eyes fixed on the group of female co-workers sitting across the way, Carl quietly insulted her.

"Look at those women over there, especially Susan, that's how beautiful I want you to look."

Beverly shoved Carl's hand off her shoulder, making him aware that she was surprised at how far he would go to prove his point.

"I'm struggling to understand why you are doing all of this and what has gotten into you. You have the nerve to sit next to your wife, lusting after those fake women over there, even your best friend's wife. Tonight, more than ever, you sicken me."

In his usual sarcastic way and with just a few words, Carl expressed what he wanted out of Beverly.

"You don't have to be jealous, just change."

While dinner was being served, in a joking manner, one of Carl's single male co-workers complimented Beverly on how elegant and beautiful she looked.

"Beverly, you look exceptionally elegant tonight. If Carl doesn't treat you right, I'm available, just give me a call."

From the look on Carl's face, it was apparent that he was irritated at what his co-worker said to Beverly, but instead of directing his anger and frustration at his co-worker, he directed it towards Beverly instead.

"That's an off-the-wall invitation Tim, but if you find my wife elegant and beautiful, the credit goes to me, I made her that way tonight. She insists on wearing clothes that reflect who she is, out-of-style. If you're serious about taking her home with you, that's fine with me. If you do take her home with you, I guarantee that you will find that under all those elegant clothes I bought her, there's an unattractive and homely individual who will leave you desperately desiring to bring her back."

Carl needed to say no more. As far as Beverly was concerned, his insults ended the night; the dinner was over. She had felt enough of his hateful and fiery darts. He admired the beauty of his female co-workers and her friend right in front of her, then verbally insulted her in front of his male co-workers. Beverly expressed her displeasure with his tasteless actions as she stood up to leave, preparing to call her friend Carmen to come and pick her up and take her back home.

"God knows, I've thought about leaving you many times. If it weren't for our son who cries to me every night about wanting to spend time with you, I would be gone. You won't win this. I've seen another side of you, and I've seen the fake women at this dinner who are motivating and fueling you to do what you do to me."

Carl tried to hide his embarrassment as he grabbed Beverly's hand, pulling on her and laughing at the same time.

"Sit down and take a chill pill, I was just joking."

Beverly pulled her hand away from him and walked out the door after responding to his insensitivity.

"There's nothing funny about this. If you sit there thinking that there is, then the jokes on you. Shaming me and throwing hurtful words at me in front of your co-workers in an attempt to beat me down to submission won't work, but if you want to take me there, you'll quickly find out that with God, I'm stronger than you think. Until you change and treat me with respect, I'll keep praying for you, but I'll be a praying wife from a distance."

Beverly left the dinner after being picked up by Carmen. As she was lying in bed thinking about how Carl humiliated her at the dinner, she was convinced that he had drawn a battle line. He had made her his enemy and declared war, but she wasn't going to retreat. If there was going to be any peace in their home, he must want it and be willing to change. She wasn't going to surrender, lower her standards, or beg him to change. After the incident at the awards dinner, Carl and Beverly drew further apart from one another. She said she was going to pray for him at a distance, and she followed through on that promise.

Carl felt as though he was highly embarrassed by Beverly in front of his co-workers when she took a stand against his insults at the dinner. He conceded that his plan to force Beverly to change was not working. He gave up trying, but his obsession with the women on his job remained strong and intimidating for her. His obsession and isolation from Beverly continued to plague them, creating more problems for them that unfortunately, negatively affected their son.

CHAPTER 3

SUPERHERO

During summer school break on Saturdays, if he weren't helping Beverly around the house, outside catching baseballs with her, or playing soccer with her, you would find John in his bedroom watching superhero videos or playing video games. While most sons can look to their fathers as a type of superhero, John didn't have that luxury. Beverly would buy him his superhero videos and action figures, but Carl, in a not-so-nice way, expressed to John his feelings about him watching too many videos about things he considered too far from reality for kids to spend time watching.

"It's ridiculous how much money your mom wastes buying you all that fantasy stuff, games, and videos. Just keep all of that junk in your bedroom and away from me. One day you'll grow up and find out that life is a harsh reality, not games and weird imaginations."

John could care less about how Carl felt about his games, videos, and action figures. As long as Beverly bought them for him, he was satisfied. Superhero videos, games, and action figures weren't automatic gifts from Beverly; John earned them by helping her around the house. Beverly would often sit with John in his bedroom watching his superhero videos with him, and because of that, to him, she was a superhero.

Whenever he found himself in a difficult situation, Beverly was the superhero who would step in and save the day. For example, one particular instance occurred when Beverly left to go on a camping trip with the church women's group.

Before she left, she instructed John, as she always did when he was playing outside, to stay out of the woods that bordered their backyard. While she was gone, as expected, Carl spent the majority of the time in the garage. On the final day of Beverly's camping trip, John was in the backyard playing with his soccer set when he kicked his soccer ball so hard that it flew past the goal and deep into the woods. He wanted to tell Carl, but he would have yelled at him and put him on punishment, and left the ball in the woods.

John figured that since Carl was preoccupied in the garage, and he usually was for hours, he would quickly run into the woods to get his soccer ball. He had to get in and out of the woods before Beverly returned home; she was expected to be back home within the next half hour. Against the rules, and for the first time going into the woods, he ran inside, carrying a thick stick for protection.

As he treaded further into the woods, fear and hesitation came upon him when he heard the sounds of all kinds of wildlife, sounds he had heard before outside of the woods but seemed creepier on the inside. He clutched his stick and slowly advanced. Willing to fight lions if necessary, he was determined and confident that he was going to get his ball. He said to himself, "A superhero never runs from a fight."

After he was about five minutes into the woods, John heard a loud and heavy panting sound. He slowed his pace and cautiously walked towards the sound. As he brushed away the branches of a row of tall shrubs, he noticed a large stray dog playing with his ball. The dog had found his ball and taken it deeper into the woods. It seemed to be a friendly dog, unaware of John's presence while continuing to play with the ball. Hearing John moving through the shrubs, the dog quickly ran away.

John made a final push through the tall shrubs and ran to retrieve his soccer ball. As he was running to retrieve it, he stumbled and fell over a tree trunk that was hidden under a pile of leaves and overgrown brush. After landing, he felt an excruciating pain in his left leg.

When he looked down to investigate what was causing the pain, he noticed that a sharp branch protruding from the tree trunk had partially pierced into his leg. He yelled for help, but no one heard his yelling except the stray dog. The dog came back to where John was lying, afraid to approach him until it realized he was not a threat, so it walked over to him.

Sensing John was in danger, the dog began barking as loud as it could. While the dog was barking, unwilling to leave John alone in the woods, Beverly pulled into the driveway and stepped out of her car.

Assuming John was inside the house, she called his name at least three times for him to come out and help her with her camping gear, but he didn't answer. She thought it was strange that he didn't answer because she would always get a quick response whenever she called him.

Beverly walked over to the garage and banged on the garage door, yelling for Carl to come out. When he came out, she asked him, "Where's John, I called him at least three times and he's not answering."

Carl had been so caught up in what he was doing in the garage that he had no clue of John's whereabouts, nor did it seem like he cared.

"Why are you asking me where he is? If he's not in the house, most likely he's in the backyard, did you think about checking back there before bothering me?"

"Bothering you? I'm bothering you? Any other husband would greet their wife with love and compassion after she has been away for a week, but you greet me saying I'm bothering you. I'm the one who's bothered by your nasty attitude. Just retreat into that garage and do what you do. I'll find out where John is by myself."

After hearing Beverly calling for John and shouting at Carl, the stray dog came barking and continuously running back and forth to where Carl and Beverly stood, then back to the woods. Carl wasn't a dog lover. He felt that having a dog as a pet was a waste of money, time, and energy. He became frustrated and irritated at the dogs barking and running back and forth.

"Whose dog is this? People should keep their mangy dogs off other people's property."

Observing the dog barking and running back and forth, Beverly sensed that it was telling them something was wrong.

"You need to quit being so mean. That dog is not mangy, it's telling us something is wrong and it's trying to lead us somewhere. Maybe it knows where John is. Stop thinking about yourself and come help me find John."

After she convinced Carl to follow the dog with her, the dog led them into the woods to where John was lying hurt with blood profusely flowing from his leg. Beverly ran to him, lifting his head and cradling him in her arms, assuring him that everything was going to be alright.

She asked Carl to give her his belt to use as a tourniquet to stop the bleeding from John's leg. Although the question entered her mind, her compassion for her injured son was more important than asking him why he was in the woods. On the other hand, while Carl was taking off his belt and giving it to Beverly, not once did he ask John how he was doing nor did he say any comforting or reassuring words to him. He was good at scolding John, and this time was no exception.

"What were you doing out here in the woods when you have been told many times to stay out? Whose crazy dog is this? Did you steal it?"

Whenever Carl showed his lack of compassion towards John, Beverly had no problem rebuking him.

"Our son is lying here in the middle of the woods seriously hurt, and you're more interested in whose dog that is. You're worried about whether or not he stole the dog rather than concentrating on helping him. Get focused and help me get him up."

After giving Beverly his belt and helping John get up, Carl refocused his attention on the dog, running towards it to chase it away. The dog stood its ground until Carl picked up a rock and threw it, hitting and injuring the dog that possibly saved his son's life. The dog quickly ran away in pain and whimpering.

Beverly had enough of Carl's anger towards the dog and lack of concern for John.

"That dog wasn't bothering you at all. Why would you do such an ungrateful thing? Why would you hurt that dog after he led us to our injured son? That wasn't necessary, and you're wasting time. We need to get John to the hospital right now!"

From the moment Carl and Beverly carried John out of the woods up until arriving at the hospital, Carl furiously made it clear that going to the hospital was not on his agenda for the day.

"If you hadn't been on that so-called women's camping trip, this would not have happened. I've never heard of women going on a camping trip. What was I thinking? I should have never agreed to let you go. I can find a lot more interesting things to do than wasting time taking my hard-headed son to the emergency room." Although she wanted to respond, Beverly focused her attention on John's injury, ignoring what she considered Carl's selfish comments.

Carl was in the hospital restroom while John was treated, bandaged up, and preparing to be discharged. His injury was not as severe as it looked in the woods. While Beverly was sitting by his side, she gave him a surprising answer when he asked her where she learned to tie a tourniquet the way she did out in the woods.

"It's interesting that you would ask that question. Up until yesterday, I didn't know how to tie a tourniquet, but tying a tourniquet was one of the last things we learned at our women's camp meeting yesterday; it looks like that knowledge paid off right on time."

John looked at Beverly as though he was in the presence of a genuine superhero. When he was in danger, she detected the danger and came running to the rescue. She didn't inquire about the cause of the danger or panic out there in the woods; and most of all, she stood up to the villain, Carl. John knew he had messed up by going into the woods, and he was apologetic for doing so.

"Mom, I'm sorry for disobeying you. I guess there will be consequences. I messed things up. It looks like we probably won't be throwing baseballs to one another or playing soccer for a while."

Beverly gave John a motherly hug and reassured him that everything would be alright.

"You were severely injured out in those woods because of your disobedience, I just hope you learned from it. You might be right about being out of action for a while, but your life is not just about playing soccer, throwing baseballs, or playing professional baseball, which I know playing in the pros is your dream.

"Life is about working together as a team so that one day, someone will hit a home run, and then the whole team wins. You and I are a team, and we will always be. You will be the one that hits the home run one day that will help the whole team win."

Although John knew what Beverly was asking of him, he

questioned her desire anyway.

"So you're counting on me to hit a home run other than in baseball?" "Yes, I am. I'm not just looking forward to you becoming a professional baseball player, but you don't know how much I'm counting on you to grow up as a man who faces life's difficulties. I want you to be a man who makes me proud.

"I'm counting on you becoming a man who stands up and faces his challenges head-on, rather than running away and isolating himself from them. I don't want you to fail, I want you to be a winner, and every time you win, I win. A winning home run is what your life is waiting on you to hit."

After Beverly and John ended their chat, they grabbed hands and began praying for one another. Carl interrupted their prayer, rushing into the room talking loudly, extremely short-tempered, and impatient.

"What are you guys doing? It's time to get out of here. Other than cemeteries, hospitals are the most depressing place in the world. I've got too many other things to do other than waste my time here, shouldn't have been here in the first place."

The conversation John had with his mother in his hospital room challenging him to face life's difficulties head-on proved to be one of the most significant challenges he would ever face in life. Beverly didn't want to see John travel down the same uncompassionate, isolated, and lonely path as Carl. Isolated by Carl, John and Beverly became a team of two.

John was determined to one day stand at life's home plate, ready to hit a winning home run that would make his mother proud. He wanted success, and his mother wanted it as well. If success was to become a reality for him, there were many barriers along the way that would test his faith and resilience.

CHAPTER 4
THE OLD OAK TREE

Beverly tried as best as she possibly could to hide her feelings of loneliness from John. She would laugh whenever she interacted with him, but on the inside, she was silently crying. Carl had built a wall of separation between himself, her, and John, and she could not figure out how to get around it. Her spirit was heavy when she called her friend Carmen. While Carl was in the garage, she emptied herself out to Carmen over the phone.

"Carmen, this marriage hasn't been easy. I have felt so lonely that it hurts on the inside. I know you warned me about marrying Carl, but just the fact that he isolates me brings so much agonizing pain. I have tried so hard to bring happiness and joy into this marriage, but I can't do it alone. Whenever I try, I run into a brick wall of anger and humiliation Carl has built around me.

"I feel as though I'm held prisoner in my own home. My mother told me that sometimes before you see the good, you may have to experience the bad, and sometimes, before you are lifted, you may have to fall. Now that I have gotten older and a little bit wiser, I'm finding some truth in what my mother said.

"Bad times are full of eye-opening experiences. In bad times you learn who your real friends are and who you can count on, and that person may not be your spouse. Bad times will humble you, show you your weaknesses, and at the same time, help you fulfill your purpose in life. But at this very moment, I feel as though I'm a rejected woman with many unfulfilled needs and wants.

"I need to feel that I belong. I want to experience joy again, and I want to be loved. I know I can be happy in the good times as well as the bad, God knows I try, but Carl doesn't make it easy. I don't want to have happiness in the good times only, but if Carl shows he loves me and doesn't shut me out, I can be happy with him in the bad times.

"I've always heard and read about wives who live in daily fear of their abusive husbands, constantly praying for God's deliverance. You can never actually understand what painful reality these women are going through until it lands on your doorstep."

After listening to Beverly's frustration with Carl, Carmen gave her some encouraging advice.

"What you need to remember is that no matter who neglects or rejects you, whether Carl, a family member, a friend, or an enemy, God wants you to allow Him to break you free from your prison of loneliness. He wants you to move forward and fulfill your purpose in life. He patiently waits at the prison doors that confine us and restricts us from being free to move when and where He tells us to move.

"God stands waiting for us to let Him in, but we tend to open every other door except the one where He stands. God will never force Himself into our lives; although He could, He never will. When you open and expose your vulnerabilities to those who are trying to destroy you instead of leaving those vulnerabilities at the altar, you will never make a difference to anyone who might be going through the same thing you are experiencing."

Beverly said to Carmen, "You are so right. Sometimes we think the loneliness and pain we feel is greater than the loneliness and pain others might be feeling. We seem to forget that Jesus persevered through a crushing pain for us that we will never experience. We would never survive the torture and humiliation He endured for all humanity. He was severely beaten on His way to the cross, proving to the world that He was willing to turn His back towards flesh-ripping lashes struck against it rather than turn His back on us.

"I know God is calling for me to be strong for myself, John, and Carl. Showing weakness will not win Carl over. If my faith in God is strong throughout our marriage, He will guide us both through the bad times, and when the bad times are over, He will rejoice with us. If God can use you to reach me, I believe He can use me to reach someone as well. I know that I cannot reach anyone while sitting in self-pity, loneliness, bitterness, and fear. No one can see me, nor the God who guides me as long as I hide my face behind a mountain of difficulty."

While Beverly was struggling to deal with her loneliness, John was struggling to deal with his loneliness as well. Carmen was only a phone call away from Beverly, but John felt as though he had no one to call for a word of encouragement. There were times when he would talk to Beverly about issues at his school and church, but he never felt comfortable talking to her about his loneliness at home. Sometimes she could detect when he was feeling lonely, taking him into her arms and holding him close, hoping he would open up, but he never would.

John eventually found a place he could go to leave all his feelings of loneliness behind. He didn't find this place of refuge in a person or friend he could confide in and possibly get some good advice from, but he found it as he was thinking about how Jesus spoke in parables or short stories in the Bible. He loved the lessons Jesus taught through the use of these stories because they would change His listener's attitudes, way of thinking, and the way they would live after hearing them.

John recalled learning in Sunday school that Jesus would tell his short stories using earthly people, places, and things to teach a spiritual and life-changing message. He decided to try creating his own life-changing short story. John was ready for a change, and he believed that creating a story related to what he was experiencing at home was the first step.

He decided that he was going to go to his bedroom window, pick out an earthly object, and observe the challenges the object faced in life. He was going to use the object as a learning tool that would teach him how to deal with his problems. He believed that observing and learning from the object would take his mind off his feelings of loneliness.

John knew that creating his short story would be new to him and take him out of his comfort zone of playing video games and watching superhero videos. He felt as though he needed to find a place to escape from being tormented on the inside. Whenever tormenting feelings of loneliness would come upon him, John would always emotionally curl up in a corner, but he was tired of giving in to his feelings. He wanted to try something he had never tried before.

One of Jesus's stories John loved so well and remembered writing about for a class project was the parable of the fig tree that failed to produce fruit.

"Before I write my short story today, I think I need to read the story I wrote about the parable of the fig tree a long time ago. That story has always inspired me, and right now, I need some inspiration."

John went to his closet and grabbed a box containing many of the projects he completed in Sunday school. After a short time of digging through his projects, he found his fig tree project, sat on his bed, and began to read:

"There was an owner of a vineyard, the owner representing God, who had a fig tree planted in his vineyard. The fig tree represented those who have heard the gospel of Christ. The fig tree was planted in the same vineyard where you would find grapes and other fruit trees. It would take the fig tree at least three years to mature and bear fruit. If the fig tree failed to produce fruit, it would be unwise to allow it to remain in the vineyard, taking up valuable soil and space where a tree that does produce fruit could be planted.

"The vineyard would be better off without the fruitless fig tree. A fruitless fig tree in the vineyard would subject the other grapevines and fruit trees planted in the vineyard to being crowded out and their fertile soil being overtaken by the fig tree's deep roots. Crowded out and restricted, the vines and branches of the fruit trees would fail to produce delicious fruit.

"Three years after planting the fig tree, which represented the number of years of Jesus's ministry on earth, the owner of the vineyard traveled to inspect his vineyard. Expecting fruit, he found that the fig tree branches didn't have any figs; it was fruitless. Having no fruit was unusual for the fig tree because it was given plenty of time to bear fruit. The owner of the vineyard lost his patience with the tree. He decided that for the sake of saving his vineyard or other vines and trees from being destroyed by a fruitless and damaging fig tree, the fig tree must be cut down.

"The parable also mentioned another key player, the vineyard keeper, or the gardener, who represented Jesus. The vineyard keeper begged the owner for one more year to nourish and cultivate the unproductive fig tree. If the tree remained unfruitful after the additional year expired, it would be cut down.

"After the owner gave the fig tree a measure of grace, the vinedresser continued to cultivate it for another year, looking for a miracle of complete transformation and regeneration to take place, but the fig tree had to respond to the cultivation if it was to experience that miracle; it failed to respond.

"Although there is much to learn from this parable, I have learned how the fig tree symbolizes those who need to repent. John the Baptist preached to the Jews that they needed to repent, but because of their unbelief and unfaithfulness, they rejected his message and Jesus, the Messiah. Because of this rejection, John the Baptist warned the Jews that the ax was already at the root due to their unfruitfulness.

"Understanding the meaning of John the Baptist's warning and the significance of where the ax was placed is important. The use of an ax signifies lining it up against a specific point on the tree whereas, when the ax comes down, it hits that specific point dead on target. In the parable of the fig tree, that specific point was the root. The corrupt religious system of the Jewish nation was the root of the problem with the nation of Israel's belief system, and that system was going to be cut down to make room for new growth, the Messiah.

"After three years, it seemed that it would be impossible for the fig tree to bear any fruit, but that's when the vinedresser does his work as a cultivator or mediator. Jesus is the mediator between God and man. He intercedes and pleads for grace and mercy, and time to cultivate us on our behalf. God will grant that measure of grace and mercy, up to a point.

"As the vinedresser, Jesus is also a servant who came from on high to serve in a low position on earth. We need Jesus, our intercessor, to cultivate us and feed us the nutrients of His Word. His Word will keep us rooted and grounded, and then we will be found fruitful when fruit inspection time comes. If God finds us barren, His grace will turn to judgment, and we will be cut down. He will be patient with us until there is no more hope or time left for us to bear fruit.

"God will go the third mile or whatever it takes to save us, but there is a limit on how much time we have to repent before the opportunity to respond to God's call is forever lost. Once the fruitless fig tree was cut down, there was no coming back to life for that tree. Once we leave this earth, there is no coming back. Therefore, there should be no delay in producing good spiritual fruit.

"Nothing is impossible with God. When it seems as though all hope is lost and we are in a dead situation, even in our sinful state, His grace and mercy will bring us life, and call us out of sin so that we might fulfill our godly purpose. How we respond to that call determines whether a fruit-bearing miracle will take place in our lives or whether we are the recipient of God's judgment."

After reading his fig tree story, inspired by it, John got up from his bed and stood looking out his bedroom window at an old oak tree that stood very close to his house. His fascination with how commanding the oak tree stood against all the other trees fueled his inspiration and excitement about writing his story.

"That's it! That oak tree will be used in my story. I will let it take my imagination away from everything that surrounds me that is not right. I will observe it and what goes on around it, and learn a spiritual lesson from it."

John was captivated by the large size of the oak tree and how it stood with a purpose and dominated everything that surrounded it. As he was admiring the tree, he noticed the actions of two butterflies. One butterfly was flying freely around the perimeter of the base of the oak tree, enjoying its freedom and seemingly having no care in the world. The other butterfly was busy, laying its eggs on the leaves of the tree.

John grabbed his binoculars out of his drawer and ran outside to get a closer look. As he looked through his binoculars and up at the butterfly laying its eggs, he noticed at least a hundred eggs on the bottom of some of the oak tree leaves. The other butterfly landed to rest on a leaf, then flew away out of the shade of the oak tree and into the bright sunshine without leaving any eggs.

The oak tree, enjoying a life of thirty years, was providing a place of rest and a place to bring forth new life for the butterfly that was laying eggs. John thought of the fact that a butterfly is a species whose life span is very short-lived compared to that of the oak tree. Unlike the frolicking butterfly, who seemed unconcerned about time, the busy butterflies actions proved that it was very aware that its life was limited in how much time it had to lay its eggs.

For a long time, the busy butterfly proudly danced against the shade of the oak tree laying its eggs. It waved its wings back and forth as if it were saying to the oak tree, "I wish my life was as long as yours, but very soon, my life will end. Thanks for not rejecting me and providing a place for me to lay my eggs so that new life can be brought into the world."

John was astonished that in a brief moment, after watching the activities of the butterflies and the oak tree, he had all the inspiration he needed for his story. He laid on his bed that night and began to write.

"There was an oak tree that offered a place of rest and provision for two butterflies, a place where they can lay their eggs, bringing forth new life. The oak tree displayed one of the characteristics of what it was created to be. It knew it wasn't created to reject the butterflies, but to be a place of provision. It was up to the butterflies to take advantage of that provision while they had the opportunity and the time.

"One butterfly kept busy laying eggs, knowing it had a short amount of time to do so. The other butterfly was busy, but busy enjoying life. It assumed it had plenty of time to lay eggs, but in the end, time caught up with it, and it failed to produce and bring forth new life, just like the fig tree in the parable. It failed to carry out its role in producing a new generation of butterflies."

After observing all that had just taken place around the oak tree, creating a story about these events, and retelling the story to himself, John understood how much the story was related to what he was going through. He believed that God will treat him like the oak tree treated the butterflies; He will not reject him. He will give him rest and provision, and bring new life to every dead situation, even his feelings of loneliness. John began to understand how true it is that life has many uncertainties, even how long that life will be. As it was with the two butterflies, he had a limited time to take advantage of the time and provision given to him.

After reminiscing about the parable of the fig tree and creating his story about the oak tree and the two butterflies, John was confident that God would assist him in creating more stories to help him overcome his loneliness, using the window as his schoolhouse, and God and the oak tree as his schoolmaster.

CHAPTER 5
THE ADDICTION

John would spend most evenings alone while Carl was working privately in the garage. This loneliness created a curiosity in John that would take him down a dark road into gross immorality from which he would never return. One night, doubts about what Carl said he was doing in the garage entered John's mind when he looked out his bedroom window before going to bed. He observed a classy-dressed woman with her face covered going into the garage with Carl while Beverly was working double shifts.

He also noticed that shortly after Carl and this woman went into the garage, a black car came down the road, then parked about a half-mile up the road, turning off its headlights. After about ten minutes, the black car drove away.

The next night it was the same routine. After Carl pulled into the driveway, the same mysterious woman as the night before, with her face covered, stepped out of the car and went inside the garage with him. Also, the same black car parked in the same spot with its lights out, then it drove away after about ten minutes.

Like clockwork, every night, while Beverly was at work, Carl would take what appeared to be the same face-covered woman into the garage, then after about an hour, they both would leave. John became curious about these repetitive chains of events that looked very suspicious. Although the garage was a restricted area for John and Beverly, and he knew what the consequences were if Carl found out he had been inside, John had an urge to investigate.

The following day, in an attempt to get into the garage and find out why Carl was spending so much time inside of it, why it was off-limits, and what he and the mysterious woman were up to, John thought about asking Carl if he needed the garage cleaned. He had asked him many times before, but Carl would always say, "The garage doesn't need to be cleaned. Anyway, if I want it to be cleaned, I'll do it myself."

Because Carl had observed him many times helping Beverly

around the house, John felt as though now was as good a time as any to ask Carl once again about cleaning the garage; he was determined to get inside of that garage. He slowly and cautiously walked on the paving stones leading up to the garage.

As John moved closer to the garage, the sound of the door being opened startled him and stopped him dead in his tracks; it was Carl. Before he had a chance to say anything, Carl angrily chastised him.

"Is this all you can find to do today is stand there and look stupid? What's wrong with you? How many times have I told you to stay away from here? Find something to do. I have a lot of work to do, and none of it involves dealing with your stupidity."

John was left standing speechless as Carl walked away, got into his car, and headed up the road. As he looked into his rearview mirror while driving away, watching John standing looking sad and lonely, for the first time a feeling of guilt and loneliness overcame him as well. He drove down the road until John was out of his sight.

Carl pulled over to the side of the road, unusually overcome with remorse concerning his treatment of his family and what he was secretly doing in the garage. "I have felt so empty and unfulfilled for so long that I'm afraid that I have wandered into a place I never thought I would go. It doesn't feel right. Something is missing in my life, and I don't know where to look for it.

"I feel as though my soul is crying out, and no one is listening. I know I have been uncompassionate and heartless towards my son. I once had a vision for my family, but I have serious issues that have turned that vision into an illusion.

"I feel as though I'm injecting a poisonous drug into my mind, body, and spirit. I feel as though there are chains of bondage gripping my soul, and it burdens me. I feel so helpless, drained, and weak in my attempts to fight this battle. I ache physically, and I feel as though I'm at death's doorstep.

"I don't want to do what I'm doing in secret behind closed doors, but I'm human and confused, and I cannot stop. I admit to you God that I have forsaken you and your work, but I also admit that I have a serious sickness. I need spiritual and emotional healing.

"My past haunts me every day. My dad never wanted me, but I find myself walking in his same abusive and corrupt footsteps. Despite my issues, I'm trying to do my best to survive.

"God, as I travel down a lonely road that is taking me further away from my son and my wife, let that road one day lead me back to you. As my feelings for my family grow faint, place your hand inside my wounded soul and force me to feel, please force me to feel something greater than my craving."

After Carl pulled back onto the road and drove away, John felt lonelier and more rejected than ever after Carl had just called him stupid. He stood staring at the garage, questioning himself whether he should risk going inside.

He noticed that Carl had gotten so caught up with scolding him that he forgot to lock the padlock on the garage door. To John, this unlocked door was an invitation to proceed moving forward. As he dried his tears, his sadness turned into curiosity.

He waited until Carl's car was completely out of sight. He waited another ten minutes because Carl had a bad habit of forgetting things and coming back. After the extra ten minutes expired, he felt it was safe to go up to the garage and remove the unlocked padlock from the door.

He opened the garage door and entered in, knowing that entering the garage was breaking a major rule that had significant consequences, but in his mind, there was no turning back. Something in that garage other than working on design plans or wanting his private space provoked Carl into isolating him, and he had to know what it was.

Standing and looking around the garage, John saw nothing out of the ordinary. As he began walking around, he thought it was odd that most of the shelves were draped over with burlap. After noticing he was still carrying the padlock, he placed it on a table to investigate what was so important on the shelves that Carl would cover it up.

He proceeded to lift one of the burlap coverings, and to his surprise, the shelf was stacked with sexually explicit videos. He checked another shelf that was covered, and there were more of the same type of videos. He estimated that there must have been at least two hundred sexually explicit videos on the shelves in Carl's garage.

While backing away from a wall of shelves, John accidentally bumped into the table on which he placed the padlock, knocking the table over and everything else that was sitting on top of it. While picking up the items that had fallen, he saw stacks and stacks of magazines hidden under a desk that was sitting next to the fallen table. Curious, he grabbed one of the magazines and looking at the cover, noticed that it was a sexually explicit magazine, as were all of the other magazines under the desk.

Simply holding one of the magazines in his hand, John trembled in fear, but he was also curious. Surrounded by a garage full of sexually explicit materials was new to him. In Sunday school, he had been taught that looking at pornographic materials was wrong. He was compelled to look at something that he had never seen before. As he flipped through magazine after magazine, he was beginning to experience a feeling inside that he had never felt before, and he was enjoying it.

While he was in the garage looking at the sexually explicit images in the magazines, he heard the sound of Carl's car coming down the gravel and dusty road. He quickly gathered everything together and tried his best to put things back the way he found them. He didn't want to leave the garage because he was overwhelmed with a feeling of satisfaction while flipping through the magazines. He wanted to see more. There were stacks of magazines he hadn't flipped through, and he wanted to view them all.

On his way out of the garage, John could see Carl's car getting closer and closer. While attempting to secure the door, he discovered that he had left the padlock in the garage, but had no time to go back inside to retrieve it. He wanted to go back into the garage again when Carl was not around to flip through more magazines, but he needed a key to get inside. He remembered that there was a spare key to the garage door padlock hidden under an old broken birdbath that was lying on the side of the garage. He quickly grabbed the key before Carl pulled into the driveway, then ran inside the house and up the stairs into his bedroom.

After John made it up the stairs and into his bedroom without being seen, Carl got out of the car and walked towards the garage. He noticed that the padlock on the garage door was missing. As he entered the garage, he noticed right away that someone had been inside.

In his rush to get out, John failed to pick up some items that had fallen off the table. Carl also noticed that the padlock to the garage door was lying on the floor. In his mind, the only suspect was John. Entering the garage without permission, John had violated Carl's private space and was going to suffer the consequences because of his disobedience.

John heard Carl charge angrily inside the house mumbling words he couldn't understand. He continued mumbling as he stood at the bottom of the stairs; then there was complete silence. The thought came to John's mind that if Carl was standing silent at the bottom of the stairs, he must have discovered that he had been in the garage.

"Dad must know or suspect that I was in the garage. I've messed up, but I don't care what dad does to me. He gets on me all the time about the wrong things I do, but in that garage, I discovered his wrong. Yes, I messed up, but I also have a messed-up dad."

Sitting at the bottom of the stairs staring at John's bedroom door, Carl began wondering how much John saw in the garage, and how he should confront him about it.

"If he saw what I think he saw in that garage, what does he think of his dad now? I'm full of so much shame and embarrassment that I can't go up there to discipline him right now; I have to sort this out. I feel as though I'm losing my mind in a desolate place where a determined tempter is always hiding in the shadows waiting for me to slip up, and he always gets his way.

"Every time he raises his head, instead of stomping him down, I yield to his demands, drifting further into a deep sea of immorality. I know I am in a place where God does not want me to be. I feel as though I'm all alone in a cold and dark cave. Lord, if you hear me, help me break free from all of this blackness so that I may find a place of rest."

For the second time in one day, Carl was feeling emotionally lonely and under conviction. Although he never again intended to step inside of a church due to his perception of being shunned by the church, Carl sounded repentant of his wrongdoings. This repentant feeling only lasted for a moment after he began to focus on John failing to follow his commands, rather than on himself failing to follow God's commands concerning his immorality.

He gathered himself together and prepared to confront John about entering the garage. He decided that John needed to be disciplined and that there was no way he was going to allow his son to disrespect him in his home and get away with it. It seems as though the more he thought about what John had done, the more furious he became.

Stirred up and rushing up the stairs and into John's bedroom, Carl stared at John for about a minute with a face full of rage. John jumped off his bed and for a moment, feared for his life.

With a loud and commanding voice, Carl ordered him to sit down on the bed, and then he began verbally scolding him.

"I know your disrespect and disobedience led you into my garage, the only place where I can have some privacy. Whatever you saw in there and whatever you know about me right now, at this point I don't care. But this I do know, you will not disrespect me, my privacy, and my home. Are we clear on that?"

At first, John was intimidated by Carl's loud voice, but as Carl was waiting on an answer, John thought within himself about the day Beverly stood up to him. Although trembling on the inside, John built up enough boldness to confront Carl.

"Are you serious? Are you asking me am I clear? How about we clear things up right now? You have lied to mom and me. You have preached to me so many times about how I'm disrespecting your home. I'm your son. I can't begin to count how many times you have disrespected me. How many times I have tried to speak to you, and you have never taken time out to listen? You say you don't care about what I found out. Well, you have taken me to the point where I don't care what you do.

"You burst in here talking about me disrespecting your home. What home? This is a house, but it is not a home. A home is where you feel free, relaxed, secure, and loved; I don't feel any of that here. A home is where there are no hidden secrets or lies that have the potential to hurt the very ones you are supposed to love. This is just a house where we live. You have not helped make this a home.

"In this house, not home, I'm disciplined continuously for no reason at all. In this house, not home, I'm lonely, but I pretend to be happy when most of the time I'm sad. Yes, dad, I went into your filthy garage. Am I sorry that I disobeyed you? Yes. Am I sorry for what I saw? No. I'm not sorry in the least bit because I have seen another side of you. I'm sorry that what I was exposed to in that garage has now affected me.

"As I was flipping through those magazines, I was enjoying what I was seeing. I'm not sorry for learning that you need some help and because I couldn't control myself in that garage, maybe I need some help as well. Am I going to say anything to mom, probably not, that's your responsibility. But I will pray that you will do the right thing, she's been too good to both of us."

After John finished talking, for a moment he thought he saw tears in Carl's eyes. He thought he was going to get a compassionate and assuring hug that everything was going to be alright. Instead, Carl angrily lunged toward him, pinned him against the wall, and standing inches away from his face, threatened him.

"Pray for me? You just admitted enjoying what you were looking at in those magazines and you dare to say you are going to pray for me? Whether or not you tell your mom what you saw in that garage is your business. What you enjoyed looking at in that garage is on you, you can't blame that on me. You shouldn't have been there in the first place. And don't worry about me, I'm going to do the right thing very soon, but on my terms, not because you prayed for me.

"Let this be a final warning. If you disrespect me one more time and I find out you entered my garage again, there will be no talking. I'll send you away somewhere where you will learn respect. I have just the right place in mind. Don't mess with me."

After Carl stomped out of the room, slamming the door shut behind him, John, who moments ago stood up bold and courageous against his dad's verbal abuse, sat on his bed feeling guilty for disobeying him. He was remorseful for speaking to Carl in the manner in which he did. He reached under his bed to retrieve a box of keepsakes that were very precious and memorable to him. After taking out a photo of Carl, he stared at it, struggling to hold back his tears and words of confession.

"Dad, I'm sorry for disrespecting you. Right now, I feel like locking myself in my bedroom, never coming out. There have been many times that I have felt that you failed me, but at a time when I find out you have an addiction and needed my help and support, I failed you. I think of all the times I wanted to talk to you, and you would not listen.

"Maybe you were in so much pain from the problems you were dealing with that you didn't want me to be a part of that pain. Maybe you felt so bad about the life you were living and the world of misery you were living in that you didn't want me to enter into that world. I pray that we both will find some help and fight this, rather than fight one another."

Later that night, it was apparent that Carl wasn't going to do the right thing soon. While in his bedroom, John heard Carl's car pulling into the driveway and observed the same face-covered mysterious woman from the previous night's following him into the garage. The same black car sat up the road parked in the darkness for a while, then drove off.

John was confused at Carl's intentions. "If dad said he was going to do the right thing, why is he still with this woman? Why would he continue to do this if he knows it's not right?"

Although he felt he needed to, John didn't confront Carl about the woman he was taking into the garage every night. Instead, he became content with satisfying his addiction by keeping everything quiet. If he exposed Carl, the secret pornographic stockpile in the garage would be exposed as well; then there wouldn't be any sexually explicit magazines for him to flip through. He was trapped in his addiction with no intention of getting out.

Night after night while his mom was at work, John watched Carl bring the mysterious woman into the garage, and the black car come and go without Carl or the woman noticing. The craving to flip through the stack of sexually explicit magazines was drawing John into the garage nearly every day whenever Carl was not around. By the end of the summer, he realized that his sexual addiction had risen to the same level as Carl's, maybe even worse.

CHAPTER 6
THE LOSS OF A FRIEND

The start of a new school year had come, and John was hoping that his junior year in high school would be better than the past two years when he practically stayed to himself, having no friends. In his last-period science class, he was assigned a seat next to a classmate named Adrian. Adrian was a quiet and shy boy who all the athletic jocks in the school enjoyed mocking and teasing. It wasn't his shyness that they made fun of, but his speech impairment.

Adrian would stutter whenever he got nervous or frustrated. Whenever he was made fun of because of his stuttering, he would stutter even more when trying to defend himself. The mocking and teasing would be so severe that he would end up on the floor crying, holding his hands on his ears in an attempt to drown out the verbal attacks.

About two months into the school year, John entered his science class, sitting in his seat that was to the left of Adrian. After the teacher had been teaching for about fifteen minutes, John noticed the sad and troubled look Adrian had on his face. He had never talked to Adrian, but like everyone else in the school, he knew about the daily bullying he faced and was concerned about his state of mind.

Having no friends himself, John did not necessarily want a friend. He felt he could relate to what Adrian was feeling after he began thinking of the bullying and verbal abuse he was getting from Carl at home. He felt that if Carl's bullying was affecting him emotionally, the bullying Adrian was getting at school must be emotionally affecting him as well.

He slipped Adrian a note asking him why he was looking so sad. Adrian responded, "Don't worry about me; I'm fine. There's nothing wrong." John wrote him another note. "I am not worried, but concerned because I see you getting bullied every day. I know how that feels because I get it at home. Maybe we can help one another get through it."

For the first time, Adrian felt that at least one person in the school cared about him, and it may be worth establishing a friendship. He sent a note back to John.

"We'll talk about it after school."

Adrian looked over at John with a smile on his face. John thought that if in that brief moment, he could bring a smile to Adrian's face, what more could he do for him if they became friends.

When class ended, John and Adrian formally introduced themselves to one another as they walked home from school. Adrian told him how it upset him when someone teased and made fun of him and that he was feeling so sad that he didn't know how much he could take. He told him that the same group of boys who were bullying him in high school were the same ones doing it when he was in elementary school.

"It hurts when those guys make fun of me. I thought they would stop when I got into high school, but some people never grow up. Sadly, some people get satisfaction out of hurting others, when on the inside, they are hurting themselves and don't realize it." John agreed with what Adrian was saying. He tried his best to encourage him.

"You're right, when people hurt other people, they are hurting on the inside themselves. You are different and because of that, some people will not understand your difference and don't know how to handle it. Jesus was different. His difference made people feel uncomfortable and threatened on the inside, but that didn't give them the right to crucify Him.

"People will make fun of what makes us different. The very thing that makes us different also makes us unique. Although the guys picking on you have athletic abilities, that doesn't permit them to bully you.

"As I said, I can relate to where you are. At the school I use to attend, I was bullied just like you simply because my dad demanded that I wear designer clothes to school. Some of my classmates believed I was trying to be better than they were because of what I wore.

"People like us who are bullied can become real friends, and as friends, we can stand up for ourselves, be strong, and fight together.

Those guys bullying you are not perfect, although they pretend to be. No one down here on earth is perfect.

"We were all born with imperfections. You were created to be who you are, not what someone else wants you to be. Today, you are officially my friend, and as a friend, I'm telling you that you have to confuse the bully because when the bully comes, he expects a specific reaction out of you. Don't react the same way you have been reacting.

"Give those who are bullying you what they don't expect. They don't expect you to stand your ground and be proud of who you are. When you stand up for yourself, you might encourage other individuals who are being bullied into taking a stand. Just stick with me, and you'll be fine."

One morning while John was getting ready for school, Beverly asked him if he and Adrian had become best friends. She heard the excitement in his voice.

"Yes mom, we are best friends. I try to stick close to him because when I do, he doesn't get teased. We eat lunch together and walk home together. At first, I was hesitant because I didn't know how he would receive me, but the more I got to know him, the more I realized that he was like me. He was different and like me because the bullying and everything else he was going through reminded me of myself."

John's excitement was an encouragement to Beverly, knowing that after so many years of loneliness, he finally had a friend with whom he could confide.

"I'm excited for you. It's kind of strange that you would connect with Adrian. He's the son of some friends of myself and your dad, Bob Williams, who works at a bookstore, and his wife Susan, who works with your dad. It's kind of weird how things come together. Anyway, I've noticed that Adrian comes over quite a bit to play video games with you in your room, but it sounds like you guys spend a lot of time talking about what you are personally going through."

"Mom, it's just that I have never had a close friend; neither did he until he met me. After I met him after school, we began talking more, and sharing experiences, finding out that we have a lot in common. Adversity in our lives has brought us together as friends. He was being bullied at school more than once every day, but I refused to be a partaker of it, he needed a friend to come to his rescue."

John headed out to school after Beverly gave him a big hug. She was proud of him and confident that he had found a friend who would help fill the emptiness and loneliness inside him that Carl was not filling. Adrian was committed to going through thick and thin with John until one day when he visited his home as he had done on many occasions to help each other with homework, he discovered that John hadn't shared everything about himself, his newfound sexual addiction.

Adrian expressed to John how bored he had gotten playing video games every night after they completed their homework. He wanted to do something fun and different, anything as long as it didn't involve playing video games.

John thought of a risky idea.

"I have something in mind, but it may not necessarily be something we do, but something I know you'll enjoy seeing. It's risky, but we'll be alright."

What they ultimately decided to do would change their lives dramatically and forever.

John walked to his bedroom window, inviting Adrian to look out of it with him. As they both looked out the window, he directed Adrian's attention towards the garage.

"My dad lied to my mom when he told her he was in that garage working on remodeling plans for the house and plans for restarting his cosmetics business; he considered it his private space. My mom doesn't know what's in there. My dad didn't want anyone going in there, but I went in and discovered something in that garage that I had never seen before, and I know you probably have never seen it before in your life; I almost know you haven't."

While John stood looking out the window with Adrian, Carl pulled up, got out of the car, and entered the garage with his mysterious woman. The same black car as always, also pulled up and hid in the shadows after they were in the garage. Adrian had a surprised and curious look on his face when he asked John, "Who is that woman with your dad? Is that your mom? Why is her face covered? Why are they going in the garage?"

"Adrian, I know you are smarter than that. No, that woman is not my mom. She's covering her face because she doesn't want anyone to see who she is. And do you seriously need me to tell you why they are going in the garage together? It's not to look at remodeling and business plans. They will be gone in about an hour. When they leave, there's something in that garage that I want to show you."

John felt Adrian was getting nervous and panicky because he began stuttering.

"I don't want to do anything that's going to get me in trouble. I have been involved in too many incidents in school because of people teasing me. My dad thinks it's all my fault. He calls me a coward for not sticking up for myself when I get teased, and because I curl up in a ball on the floor stuttering, I encourage people to make fun of me. He told me that the next time I got into an incident or mischief, he was going to send me away to a special boy's school to learn how to be a man."

"Calm down Adrian. We'll be alright. We'll go in and be out in no time."

Adrian seemed a little calmer when he asked, "What if your dad comes back and catches us?"

The question seemed to touch a nerve in John, resulting in a change in his facial appearance. He looked as though someone had done something dreadful and unforgiving to him, and he was out to get revenge. He turned to Adrian and said with a raised voice as if he was offended by what he had just asked, "I could care less what dad does or catches me doing. After I show you what he has been hiding in that garage, you will understand why."

When the mysterious woman and Carl came out of the garage and drove off, John whispered to Adrian to wait until the car was out of sight. They waited another ten minutes before bolting down the stairs, heading towards the garage. Standing in front of the garage with Adrian at his side, John pulled the spare key to the padlock out of his pocket.

Fear and panic came over Adrian again as he begged John to leave with him.

"We need to get out of here while we have a chance. I don't care what your dad is hiding in that garage. I told you what my dad said if I get in trouble again. Please John, let's go back inside the house."

John looked at Adrian, putting his hands on his shoulders, reminding him of what he asked him to do and reassuring him that everything would be alright.

"You said you wanted to do something fun and you didn't care what it was. You will enjoy this. And besides, I'm the only friend you have, why would I get you in trouble? If you run away now, you're going to prove your dad right, that you are a coward."

John took one more look down the road to make sure the coast was clear before unlocking the padlock and entering the garage. Once inside, he swiftly ran to the spot where he had previously discovered the stacks of sexually explicit magazines under the desk. He reached down to pull out a magazine from a stack while prepping Adrian for what he was about to show him.

"As I said, you are about to see something I know you have never seen before, but you can't tell anyone. We have to keep this a secret."

After John pulled a magazine from the stack under the desk, Adrian looked at the cover, shocked at what he was seeing.

"That's a bad magazine, I can't look at that, and you shouldn't look at it either. We learned that in Sunday school. My dad will send me away if I get caught and he finds out I was looking at that. This doesn't feel right. I don't want to be here and I don't want to be sent away. We should go before your dad gets back."

John struggled in his attempt to calm Adrian down and convince him to join him flipping through the magazines.

"Why are you so afraid? There's no one around. We'll look at a couple of pictures, and then we'll go."

He grabbed Adrian's arm, trying to force him to sit down in a desk chair, determined to flip through the magazines, even if Adrian refused to do so. John kept pulling and pulling on Adrian's arm, but Adrian managed to pull away from him.

In the process of pulling away from John, Adrian fell backward. His left shoulder bumped into a lever that lowered down an old and heavy fold-down bed that was against the wall. As the heavy bed was falling, it came down so fast and hard that Adrian didn't have time to get out of its way. A sharp edge of the frame on the bed struck him in his left temple, knocking him to the ground and unconscious as the bed fell on top of him.

As Adrian was lying on the ground with the heavy fold-down bed on top of him, John continued flipping through the magazines, assuming Adrian was playing around with him, pretending to be hurt so they could leave out of the garage. John begged Adrian, "Quit playing around; we're not leaving yet. You have to get up and look at this. This is some good stuff here."

When Adrian didn't respond, with the magazine in his hand, John ran to where he was lying hurt under the bed and yelled his name, "Adrian! Adrian! Are you okay? Quit faking."

Instead of lifting the bed right away to see if Adrian was alright, John ran into the house and stuffed the magazine he had in his hand under his mattress to continue viewing at a later time.

He swiftly returned to the garage, attempting to lift the heavy bed off Adrian. Lifting the bed was difficult, but he managed to lift it and push it back against the wall. Adrian was lying on his stomach, still unconscious. When John turned him over, he panicked at the sight of blood streaming from Adrian's head.

He attempted to lift Adrian and carry him out of the garage, but he couldn't do it alone because Adrian was sixty pounds heavier than he was. Although the next house was half a mile away in either direction, John ran out of the garage and began yelling for help.

"Somebody help! Please, somebody, my friend Adrian is hurt, and I need some help!" He ran back inside the garage to check on Adrian.

While John was sitting inside the garage with Adrian's head in his lap, Carl pulled into the driveway. As he exited his car, he thought he heard John calling for help. When he looked over towards the garage, he became curious as to why the garage door was open, knowing that he had locked it before leaving. After clearly hearing John's call for help coming from inside the garage, he ran towards it and went inside, surprised to see John crying and holding his co-worker Susan's son in his arms, bleeding and unconscious.

Carl stood at the garage entrance for a few seconds, watching John raise his tear-drenched eyes looking at him with a look of desperation and guilt. He ran to John, kneeling and asking him, "Why in the world is Adrian in here with you? He's hurt and in bad shape. Did you call his parents?" Feeling guilty, ashamed, and at the same time concerned for Adrian, John cried, "I'm sorry, it's my fault. I can't get him to wake up."

Carl reprimanded John for bringing Adrian into the garage.

"You ought to be sorry. You and your disobedience have gotten you and your friend in a bad situation. You bring him in here after I told you many times to stay out. Help me get him up. We need to get him to the hospital."

John helped Carl lift Adrian, carrying him out of the garage and into the car. Getting to the hospital was critical because Adrian was going in and out of consciousness. On their way to the hospital, John continued to get a scolding from Carl.

"I don't know what has gotten into you, but one thing I do know is that you need to stay out of my business. You've gotten yourself caught up in something that you should not have, and I don't feel sorry for you. Unfortunately, you've become just like me, and you can't control it. How does it feel being unable to control something you don't want to do?"

John looked at Carl, angry, and frustrated.

"There's no way I'm like you. There's no way I'll ever be like you. Your secrecy and inability to interact with me drew me into this, but I'm going to fight it."

Unfortunately, the only reaction John got out of Carl was a laugh and condemnation.

"I drew you into this? You're going to fight it? That's funny. That's funny. Son, you've already lost the battle and don't realize it. You're addicted just like I am and headed down the same painful path. You know the difference between right and wrong, and you know the consequences of it. I guess you didn't learn that in Sunday school.

"Look at what you've done to Adrian. What you have done is

strictly your fault, not mine. This situation will be dealt with to make sure Adrian won't have to worry about you getting him caught up in this again, and you can count on that."

Adrian gained full consciousness shortly before arriving at the hospital. After he was admitted and began receiving treatment, John wasn't surprised when Carl left him alone at the hospital, saying he had business to take care of. A little while later, Adrian's parents, Bob and Susan walked into the hospital room. They questioned John and Adrian as to what happened and where it happened.

John lied in an attempt to protect Adrian.

"We were at my house tossing a football to one another. Adrian slipped and fell, trying to catch the ball. As he fell, he hit his head on a large fence post and was knocked unconscious."

Adrian heard everything John told his parents but didn't say anything about John's lie because he knew he was trying to protect him. John stayed with Adrian and his parents at the hospital overnight.

The next morning, while Adrian's parents were in the hospital cafeteria eating breakfast, he expressed to John a concern he had about his inappropriate actions in the garage that would sever their relationship as friends.

"John, there was a time when I had no friends, and you were the only one who saw something good in me. Thanks for covering for me when my mom and dad asked what happened. I do want to say something to you as a friend."

John asked, "Sure Adrian, friend to friend, what's on your mind?" Adrian was hesitant to say what he wanted to say, but respecting John as a friend, he said what he needed to say.

"Before I got hurt, and when I saw you looking at those magazines, I thought to myself, that's not my friend, that's not the John Forester I know or thought I knew. It hurt me to see that addiction take you over in that garage where I didn't want to be. You tried to force me to stay in that garage, and I got hurt. If you stay in that ugly place your sexual addiction is forcing you to stay, you will get hurt. Please get some help."

At first, John looked as though he was feeling remorseful, but then he turned defensive.

"You need to understand that just because I'm your only friend, that doesn't give you the right to tell me what to do with my life. When you were hurt, my dad and I picked you up, carried you out of that garage, and drove you here.

"I stayed with you all night, that's what friends do, they don't find fault in one another. You said I'll get hurt if I don't get over my addiction, well guess what, I'm already hurting because my so-called friend is sitting here passing judgment upon me. I guess I'm not good enough to hang out with you anymore."

John walked out of the room and waited in the hospital lobby for his mom and dad. He sat with his head hung down, hurt by what Adrian had said to him. He looked up and saw Beverly walking down the hallway towards him, alone and without Carl. When Beverly questioned him as to why he wasn't in the room with Adrian, he said, "Mom, sometimes you get close to people you think are your friend until they find out intimate things about you that they don't like or agree with. Let's go. I don't want to talk about it anymore."

John's comments only confused Beverly, who up until this point believed John had developed a close friendship with Adrian. She was concerned about him as any mother would be. She figured that she would give him some space and time to work out whatever issues he and Adrian were having.

Adrian was released from the hospital the next day. Other than healing from his injury, he was having a difficult time trying to understand why John would get so upset with him, especially when all he was doing was trying to help him. John had heard nothing from Adrian or about him in days; he hadn't seen him in school either. He assumed he was still at home recovering from his injury.

John desperately wanted to tell Adrian he was sorry for what he said to him in the hospital but didn't know how to do it or if Adrian even wanted to talk to him. He thought Adrian might be upset with him because he hadn't called him since he was released from the hospital.

About two weeks later, after finishing his homework, John heard a knock on his bedroom door, it was Beverly. After entering the room, Beverly sat down next to him on his bed, attempting to console him concerning his broken relationship with Adrian.

"John, I don't know what is going on between you and Adrian, but I know you are hurt by it. We have always been able to talk about things, right?"

"Yes mom, we have, but this time, it's personal and I can't share it with you right now. Maybe one day I will, but not right now."

"Okay John, I understand." Beverly began to cry. "It's just that, I don't like seeing you lose such a good friend and be heartbroken because of it. We both are going through a difficult time. I just want you to be happy."

"Mom, what I'm going through with Adrian is something I need to take care of all by myself. You have always been there for me, more than dad. I'm happy just being around you, talking to you, and doing things with you. No more talk about me. I want you to be happy mom, and this seems to be the right time to give you a good surprise that will bring a smile to your face."

"Okay John. I'll leave you alone about Adrian. I could use a good surprise right now. What is this surprise?" John grabbed Beverly's hand. "Okay mom, just close your eyes and I will lead." John guided Beverly out of his bedroom, down the stairs, and out the front door. "Open your eyes mom." When she opened her eyes, they were standing in front of the oak tree John loved observing through his bedroom window.

Beverly had noticed many times how large and beautiful the oak tree was getting, but this time, something was sitting under it that caught her eye; it was a beautifully crafted bench. She and John proceeded to sit down on the bench. "John, where did you get this beautiful bench, and how could you afford it?"

"Mom, I didn't buy it. It was a project Adrian and I worked on at school, and I wanted you to have it. This oak tree has become an object of inspiration to me, and I want it to become your inspiration every time you sit here on this bench and look at it."

"John, that's very thoughtful of you. I love it. I think I could sit here for the rest of the day enjoying how beautiful it looks under this tree. That reminds me, I think I have just the right thing that will make this area even more beautiful for years to come." "What's that mom?" "Just wait here John, this won't take long if you help me."

Beverly got up to get something out of the shed. She returned to where John was sitting carrying two trays of beautiful ground cover. "John, I love this groundcover. I just bought it the other day and was trying to figure out where to plant it. It will look beautiful around this tree and bench, especially after it spreads out. This is the perfect place for it."

"Okay mom, I think the bench makes things beautiful enough, but if it makes you happy and gives you a place to rest and be at peace, I'm all for it." "Thanks John, you have just made my day. I have a feeling I'm going to spend a lot of time here with God."

After helping Beverly plant the groundcover around the oak tree and bench, they created a pathway with stepping stones leading up to the bench. Exhausted, John returned to his bedroom. While lying on his bed, thinking about the good times he had with Adrian, he wished he could take back what he said to him at the hospital.

"I was wrong for what I said to Adrian. He was right about my addiction, and he was only trying to help. I shouldn't have said what I said to him."

Sometimes we say things out of anger in one moment that ruins a friendship forever.

CHAPTER 7
INEVITABLE

John was awakened late in the evening by the strong wind outside and the sound of Carl's car pulling into the driveway. He got up out of his bed to investigate, standing back far enough to see, but not be seen. Since earlier in the day Carl had parked Beverly's deceased parent's car that was being stored in the garage on the side of the driveway where he usually parked, He parked his car on the other side of the driveway, the side closer to John's bedroom window.

As John had observed many times before, he saw Carl's mystery woman getting out of the car. A strong wind blew away the covering she always wore to hide her face. Also, the outside lamp post shined brighter on the side of the driveway where Carl had parked.

For the first time, John was able to see the face of the mysterious woman Carl had been taking into the garage every night. The woman he saw surprised him more than the first time he discovered Carl's library of sexually explicit material in the garage. John was shocked, angry, and heartbroken to see that the mysterious woman was Adrian's mom and Carl's co-worker, Susan.

Disgusted at what he had just seen, John fell to the floor and sat against the edge of his bed hurt and feeling sorry for everyone affected by Carl's sexual lust and poor judgment.

"I've seen dad say and do some arrogant and low-down things to my mom, but this right here takes the cake. How could he do such a thing to mom and disrespect Adrian and his dad, seeming to have no care in the world? This is not right. Tomorrow, I'm going to go and apologize to Adrian for how I treated him. I'm also going to let him know what's been going on between my dad and his mom. It's going to hurt him, but he needs to know."

John woke up early the next day on a Saturday morning, grabbed his bicycle, and headed towards Adrian's house. When he arrived, he jumped off his bicycle, ran up to the porch, and rang the doorbell. When Susan came to the door, he stood in front of her for a minute with his head hanging down, unable to look her in the face because of what he knew about her and his dad.

Slightly raising his head and looking to the side to avoid looking directly at her, John inquired, "Is Adrian home, there's something he and I need to talk about."

Susan felt disrespected at his refusal to look into her eyes.

"John, raise your head and look at me. Show some respect. I guess you don't know about Adrian?"

Quickly raising his head and looking directly into Susan's eyes, John asked, "Know what about Adrian? Has something bad happened to him? The last time I saw him was at the hospital. When I left him, it wasn't on good terms."

Susan invited him inside. When they sat down at the kitchen table, she turned the conversation into an investigation.

"Nothing seriously bad has happened to Adrian, but there is something I want to ask you. Do you remember when we were at the hospital, you told me that you and Adrian were throwing a football and he fell, hitting his head on a fence post?"

Right away, John had this strange feeling that his lie had been found out. He tried to avoid answering Susan's question.

"I don't mean to be rude, but I just came here to talk to Adrian and..." Before he could get another word out, Susan interrupted, "Hold on, don't say anything else, this is not about Adrian, it's about your untruthfulness. The day before Adrian was to be released from the hospital, Carl came over to tell us what happened that night Adrian got hurt. You lied when you said you and Adrian were tossing a football and he fell and hit his head.

"Carl told us that both of you were in the garage looking at dirty magazines, which we always forbade Adrian to do. He said Adrian had stolen these magazines from the bookstore where my husband works. When Carl came home, he caught both of you in the garage and you both tried to run. In the process of running, Adrian fell, hitting his head."

John began confessing.

"I know I lied, and I'm sorry about that. Adrian told me he would get sent away if he got into trouble again, so I was trying to protect him. When my dad came to talk to you, he lied to you about what happened."

Susan came out of investigative mode, revealing what she already knew and filling John in on the whereabouts of Adrian.

"I'm aware that Carl lied. Bob and I questioned Adrian about what happened. He told us a different version of the story than Carl's version. He said the magazines were Carl's and that he was hit by the frame of a fold-down bed as he was running trying to get out of the garage before being caught. He also told us that you had forced him to go into the garage.

"I believed every word Adrian said about the incident, but Bob didn't believe he was telling the truth, he believed your dad's version. After the incident in the garage, Bob told Adrian that he had used up his last chance. A couple of days after Adrian was discharged from the hospital, Bob sent him away to a special all-boys school that excels in teaching the required subjects for graduation as well as self-defense and discipline."

John enlightened Susan of Carl's intentions and motives,

"Adrian was telling the truth. There is only one reason why my dad came over here and lied to you about Adrian stealing the magazines. On the day Adrian got hurt, while we were taking him to the hospital, my dad looked at me and said he was going to make sure what happened to Adrian wasn't going to happen again. He said he was going to see to it that Adrian wouldn't have to worry about me getting him into trouble anymore.

"My dad knew your husband was going to send Adrian away if he got into trouble. I believe he wanted to send him away because he knew what my dad was secretly hiding in his garage. Although he pretended to be, my dad wasn't concerned about Adrian's well-being; he doesn't even care about mine. His scheme to have Adrian sent away left one less person around who knew the truth about what he was hiding and doing in that garage."

After hearing John refer to what Carl was secretly doing in the garage, Susan suspected that he knew more. She didn't press him on trying to find out what more he knew, else she would expose her secret. She changed the subject.

"I begged Bob not to send Adrian away, but he would not listen. I guess he had enough and figured sending him off to boy's school would do him some good. Adrian will probably be back next summer, but I will miss him, and I know you will too."

John cried as he stood up to leave, "It's all my fault. I told Adrian he wouldn't get in trouble. Because of me and my revengeful dad, he got sent away."

John ran out the door, grabbed his bicycle, and headed down the road towards home. He had only gotten halfway down the road when he decided to turn around and confront Susan about her affair with Carl. When he arrived at her home, Susan came outside to meet him, asking, "Did you forget something?"

John began attacking her infidelity.

"No, I didn't forget anything. What I came back to say is, the reason why you believed Adrian when he told you about the magazines belonging to my dad and the bed falling on him is that you have been in that garage."

A surprised look came on Susan's face as she asked, "Why would you say such a thing?"

John continued his attack.

"I say it because I have seen you go in that garage with my own eyes. You know what and where everything is, the magazines, the videos, the bed, everything. You asked me if I had forgotten something. Are you serious? Have I forgotten something? I wish I could forget all of this happened.

"I wish I could forget going into that garage and finding what I found. I wish I could forget how badly I treated Adrian. I wish I could forget all the nights I saw you and dad going into his garage doing who knows what behind my mom's back. No, I didn't forget any of that, but I wish I could."

Crying profusely with tears of remorse, Susan emotionally fired back at John.

"You are not the only victim here. You are not the only one wanting to forget all this happened. I wish I could forget the day I started working with Carl at the office and agreed to go out with him. Both of us knew it wasn't right, the both of us being married and all, but he wouldn't let me say no.

"Every day at work, he kept pestering me to go out with him until one night I did. After that, things just went too far. Carl wouldn't let me break up the relationship we had started. He threatened to kill me if I told anyone."

Although he began to feel sorry for Susan, John needed her to answer an important question.

"I know how arrogant and evil my dad is, but didn't you think twice about hurting my mom, your friend?"

Apologetic and regaining her composure, Susan answered,

"I'm so sorry I did this behind your mom's back because she is my friend. I wanted to tell her what was going on, but I was afraid for my life, I have been hurting on the inside for a long time. Adrian never found out about your dad and me, nor does Bob know, but he will, soon.

"Before you came back, as I was sitting at the kitchen table thinking about how many people I have hurt. I decided that no matter what happens to me, my relationship with your dad is going to end. I'm going to meet him here tonight for the last time while Bob's away.

"Tonight, you will not see us going into the garage together. I promise you that I'm going to tell your dad that it's all over. Please trust me when I say, I'm sorry."

John was still standing on Susan's porch when he hugged her and said, "I forgive you and trust you when you say you're sorry. Trust me when I say this, I know my dad got you caught up in his sick and corrupt life, just like he got me caught up in it. Do what you need to do; do the right thing for all our sakes."

John left Susan's house emotionally upset, but not surprised at what Carl had done in starting a relationship with her, and threatening her if she tried to get out of it. Because of Carl's lies and deceitful ways, John lost a friend, and he was determined to confront Carl about it.

Later that afternoon, John, Beverly, and Carl were sitting at the kitchen table eating an early dinner before Beverly headed out to work a double shift. John looked over at Carl prepared to confront him about what he did to Adrian right then and there, but decided that it wasn't the time.

Beverly finished eating her dinner, then left out the door and headed for work. John felt that it was an opportune time to confront Carl about Adrian and Susan. Before he could get a word out, Carl looked at him and verbally attacked him.

"I looked over at you and it looked like you wanted to say something to me. I should have reached over and slapped it out of you right then and there. So if you've got something to say, and if something is going on that you don't like, let's get it out in the open right now, man to man."

John stood up as bold as a lion confronting Carl.

"You know there's not much more I can say because you know exactly what's going on. I know more than you think I know. First, it was all the pornographic stuff in the garage, and then I find out you've been cheating on mom with her friend Susan, and then you lied and caused my friend to be sent away.

"You only think about yourself and could care less about the people you hurt, isolating yourself, but in the process, breaking up families. You broke up this family and Adrian's family, and I will never forgive you for that. I lost a dad a long time ago, and now I'm forced to deal with losing my best friend because of you."

John's boldness raised Carl's anger level so high that he jumped out of his chair, grabbed John by the neck, and pushed him against the wall screaming at him.

"I don't know who you think you are rising against me. If you do it again, you'll have to deal with more than losing a friend you lost because of your mistake, not mine. Yes, I wanted Adrian sent away to keep him from being hurt by you and your addictive ways.

"If you keep challenging me, I'll give you the worst beating of your life just to protect myself and everything you think you know about me. If you get any thoughts about telling your mom about all of this, you will regret the day you were ever born. Get a life. Stay in your lane and out of mine."

John stood motionless as he watched Carl storm out the door, get into his car, and speed up the road. As he sped up the road, a cloud of dust and gravel flew into the air, a visual testament of his inner rage and anger towards John. John ran upstairs and sat on his bed. Looking out his bedroom window, he could see the dust settling from when Carl sped away.

For the first time in his life, John was hoping Carl would never come back. A couple of hours later, while sitting at his window finishing up his homework, he heard Carl returning home and his car pulling into the driveway. This time he was alone. As Carl proceeded to get out of his car, John could tell by the look on his face that he was angrier than when he left. He looked as though he had just come from fighting with someone.

The unknown black car passed by and parked farther down the road than usual. After Carl got out of his car, slamming the door shut and mumbling something, within a minute, another car pulled into the driveway. An enraged woman stepped out of the car; it was Susan.

John was shocked to see Carl run towards Susan and violently grab her by the arm while yelling at her. "There is no way I'm going to let you walk out of this as if nothing happened. Coming to work every day dressed as you do, you started this; I'll decide when to end it. You're in this too deep to walk away and leave me hanging."

John assumed this altercation began at Susan's home and overflowed into their driveway. He could hear Susan begging Carl to let go of her arm. After he grabbed her by the neck, throwing her against the trunk of her car, the unknown black car sped out of the shadows towards the house. John could see the fear in Carl's eyes when the car came to a screeching halt in the driveway, nearly pinning him between the two vehicles. He also heard the trembling in Carl's voice when he addressed the individual getting out of the car.

"Bob, what's up with you? What are you doing here? Why are you driving like a mad man into my driveway? Do you realize how close you came to killing me? Or is that what you were trying to accomplish?"

Bob ran up to him with his fist drawn and yelling, "That's exactly what I'm going to do, kill you. I've been right here every night watching a cheat who I thought was a friend stab me in the back. Like a coward and fool, I just sat there watching you destroy my family and me. But when it comes to you laying a hand on my wife, I'm not going to sit back and let that happen."

Bob punched Carl in the face so hard that he was knocked to the ground. Although Carl was big and muscular, Bob was about eighty pounds heavier and more muscular.

John thought about running down to help, but he quickly reconsidered. "I knew this would happen. Sooner or later, the bill comes due. After all the turmoil he's put me and mom through, he's just getting his due punishment and paying for his arrogance, deceit, and deception."

John watched Carl struggling to get up, only to have Bob put his knee into his chest and keep punching him over and over again, knocking him back down to the ground every time he tried to get up. Susan saw enough of the violent beat down. She ran over to Bob, then jumped on his back screaming, "Bob Stop! Stop! He's not worth it. He's not worth going to jail for assault. Come on, let's go. It's just as much my fault as it is his, and I'm sorry for what I've done. I know I made a big mistake. Don't take it all out on him. I ended everything tonight, and it's over between him and me. Let's go home, please."

Bob delivered one more punch before demanding that Susan get back into her car. John saw Carl lying on the ground, bruised and bloody before Bob pulled him by the collar and gave him an ultimatum.

"I trusted you as a friend. A friend doesn't go behind his friend's back and seduce his wife. You are a sick individual. I'm not done with you yet. I'm going to take my wife home, but I'll be back to finish this. You won't do this behind my back and get away with just a few punches. I'm coming back. I advise you, don't be here when I do."

Bob got into his car, slamming the door shut. As he and Susan drove off, John heard Bob yell from his car, "This isn't over you backstabber and cheat! I'll be back to finish this!"

John stepped away from the window so that Carl wouldn't know that he saw everything that went on, but didn't come out to help him. After he closed his bedroom door, he heard Carl run inside the house, slamming the storm door shut so hard that the glass in the door shattered. He heard him run up the stairs. Cracking his bedroom door open, John observed Carl packing a suitcase as if he was going somewhere fast.

John came out of his bedroom. When he looked at Carl carrying a suitcase down the stairs, he couldn't believe how much rage and anger distorted his bloodied face in such a way that he practically looked scary. John had a feeling that this was the last image he would see of Carl. He couldn't think of any words to say, but Carl didn't hold back the last words he wanted to say to him.

"You finally got what you wished for; I'm leaving for a while. I hope you're happy. I know you've had a hard time doing what I told you to do, but I hope you will do this one last thing. I'm asking you to hold back from telling your mom any of the things you have found out about me.

"If you love your mom, you'll keep all of this a secret. Please do what I'm asking you to do this time. I hate for things to end this way, but it was inevitable. My life is in danger and I need to leave fast. Things haven't been right between your mom and me for a long time. Goodbye son, take care of your mom. When things have settled down, I'll be back for the rest of my things and clean up my mess. I believe you know what mess I'm talking about."

As the sun was setting in the western sky, John watched Carl walk down the stairs and out the door for what would be the last time. He ran down the stairs and stood at the door, paralyzed. At the sound of Carl's car door closing, so was a chapter in an isolated and abusive-filled life for John and his Beverly.

Tears began to flow from John's eyes as he ran out the door to tell Carl he was sorry for everything he said, but it was too late. As he stood in the middle of the dusty road watching Carl drive away, it looked as though he was driving straight into the red-orange setting sun.

At around midnight, John was sleeping when he heard Beverly enter the house, returning home from work. Hearing her walking around the house as if she was looking for Carl, he got up out of bed and went downstairs to talk to her. She asked him where Carl was, and what happened to the glass in the storm door. Heeding Carl's last request to keep his sexual addiction and infidelity a secret, John gave Beverly minimal details.

"Dad packed some things and walked out the door. I don't think he's coming back. On his way out he slammed the door shut and the glass shattered. I don't know what to say or how to feel."

Beverly hugged John close and with tears in her eyes said, "I had a feeling this was going to happen one day, even sooner than today. He's not coming back. It's going to be alright; God's got us. We have to believe that things are going to be alright."

Pressing his head against Beverly's shoulder, John thought to himself, "I'm not sure if she knows anything about what dad was secretly doing, but if she doesn't, she won't hear it from me."

The moment Carl walked out the door, as far as Beverly was concerned, his secret went with him.

The next morning while John was sitting looking out his window at the oak tree, thinking about Adrian and Carl leaving, the thought came to him that he hadn't seen the busy butterfly in a while. He stood up, putting his head out the window, trying his best to see if it was flying around the tree.

After seeing no sign of the butterfly, he grabbed his binoculars to go outside to take a closer look at the top of the tree. As he got closer to the tree, he noticed that caught in a spider web among the fresh groundcover he and Beverly had just planted at the base of the tree was the butterfly, slowly flapping its wings. The butterfly was getting weaker and weaker in its desperate attempt to escape; it was facing sudden death.

When John reached down to release the butterfly out of captivity, the owner of the web, a large brown spider was on its way out to claim its catch. Sensing John as a threat, the spider crawled back into the small entrance of its well-spun home. When John looked at the butterfly, it seemed as though it was begging for him to try freeing it again. He leaned forward, putting his right thumb and index finger together, preparing to pluck the butterfly out of the spider's trap, but mid-stride, a thought occurred to him that prompted him to pull back and away from the web.

John began to think of the day he observed the butterfly laying eggs on the oak tree leaves, fulfilling its role in helping bring forth life. Now it's trapped alive, facing death in a place where it doesn't want to die. It has pollinated who knows how many plants and flowers, but it has fulfilled its purpose of extending the life of its species by laying its eggs.

He also thought to himself that when the butterfly died, its corpse, as a source of food, would help extend the life of another species, the spider. He decided to refrain from interfering with nature, stepping back to watch nature in action. After a little while, as the butterfly became more aggressive in its attempt to escape, the spider came out of hiding, coating it in a mesh of silk. With all its strength, the spider carried the butterfly into its silk cave to be seen no more.

Observing the butterfly and the spider under the oak tree and no longer having Adrian and his dad around, John learned a valuable lesson about the nature of things. Taking into consideration the last words he heard from his dad that some things are inevitable, he learned that some things are just bound to happen. The death of the butterfly and the spider building a web to trap it was inevitable; it's the nature of things.

It was ironic that in Carl's presence he never sat down with John to give him lessons that would help him in life, but in his absence, he taught him that there are times and seasons for all things. There is a time to live, and a time to die. There is a time to build, and a time to tear down. There is a time to laugh, and there is a time to cry. There is a time to stay, and a time to go.

In every relationship, there are problems. When relationship problems arise, some decisions inevitably must be made; that's the nature of things. Sometimes we want things to remain as they are, but in the nature of things, our interference is futile, change will always prevail.

CHAPTER 8
BROKEN RELATIONSHIPS

John was in his senior year in high school, and the school year began the same as his previous three high school years. He found himself alone, without any friends, and still fighting his sexual addiction. He missed his friend Adrian, but he befriended a female classmate who gave him a glimpse of hope, helping him try to put his past behind him as well as strengthen his relationship with God.

Every day while eating lunch in the school cafeteria, John would sit watching the reactions of a girl named Angela Robison. One afternoon, Angela was sitting at a table all alone, eating lunch. One by one, all the other girls in the cafeteria would walk past her without inviting her to sit with them.

John watched as the girls would form clicks at their tables. He also noticed how fast Angela would eat her lunch and quickly leave, thinking that she might have wanted to quickly get out of the stuck-up atmosphere in the cafeteria, or maybe she was shy and felt uncomfortable eating in front of people. He would watch her practically come short of running out of the cafeteria and into the school library.

The next day during lunch, as John was observing Angela, something caught his attention that disturbed him. In between staring at Angela and eating his lunch, trying not to bring attention to himself, he noticed she would suddenly stop eating. When she would stop eating, a deep emotional sadness came upon her face, looking as though she was forcing herself into holding back her tears.

John turned his attention away from Angela to a table of girls where her eyes were focused. He noticed that everyone at the table was on the school gymnastics team, but nothing else out of the ordinary. When he looked at Angela again, she was crying, wiping tears from her eyes.

He was confused as to why she was crying until he looked again at the table where the girls were sitting. One of the girls who he knew as

Brenda, and who also appeared to be the ringleader of the group, was whispering to all the other girls while pointing at Angela. The girls continued to whisper among themselves, then let out a loud laugh. It didn't take John long to figure out that Brenda was saying negative things about Angela.

When the girls laughed out loud, that was enough to prompt Angela to get up without finishing her lunch and make her way out of the cafeteria. On the way out, she would have to pass by the table where the girls were sitting. As Angela passed by the table, Brenda dished out hurtful words to her. "That's right go ahead and get your worthless self out of here, who wants to be around you anyway? Do what you do and go to the library and cry like a baby you low-life."

John was heartbroken at what he had seen and the bitter words he heard directed toward Angela. Watching what the girls were doing to her brought back memories of his former friend Adrian. He was a victim of the same type of bullying. He didn't deserve it; neither did Angela.

Lunchtime was about over as John headed towards the cafeteria exit, tempted to say something to the girls who were making fun of Angela. He decided to hold back from saying anything, believing saying something might bring more harassment from the girls towards her. As he walked past the library on his way to his next class, he saw Angela sitting alone reading. He wanted to go in and console her but decided it wasn't the right time.

At lunchtime the following day, once again the girls on the gymnastics team were making fun of Angela as she ate her lunch. However, this time, John felt he needed to intervene on her behalf. He said to himself, "There's no way Angela should suffer through this humiliation every day."

While Angela was preparing to leave the cafeteria, John rushed over to her table and grabbed her by the hand, attempting to comfort her.

"No, you just stay put. You have as much right to be here as anyone else. You don't have to leave; they should leave. They have no right to do what they're doing to you; it's wrong and it's mean. I'm going to take you over there with me so we can put an end to this foolishness once and for all."

Angela was crying as she pulled away from John, determined to get out of the cafeteria. He grabbed her hand again, holding on to it tighter this time, and led her to the table where the girls were sitting. Still trying to pull away, Angela begged John to let her go. Brenda criticized him, "Why are you wasting your time with her? Why are you bringing that idiot over here? If she wants to leave, let her go. She's not worth the time of day."

John sat down with the girls, continuing to pull Angela by the arm and sitting her next to him. One of the girls sitting across from Angela backed away from her as if she was infected with a contagious disease. At the same time, John addressed Brenda's nasty attitude.

"Attempting to make someone feel as though they are beneath you or inferior to you does not make you special or superior to them. In front of these girls, you put on a mask, pretending to be someone you're not. You pretend to be strong and have it all together, but your mean words only show you to be weak, insensitive, and broken.

"You have surrounded yourself with a group of individuals who are obviously like you. One day, this group will break up, and you all will move on to live your separate lives, but the mean words you say to people right now are roots that will dig deep inside of them and hurt for a lifetime. The mean words you sow now are inflicting a wound that might not ever be healed, but one thing about it, you will find that your mean words will hurt you one day because we reap what we sow."

During the entire time John was speaking, Angela was sitting at the table with her head hanging down. When John finished talking, she looked up at him, then at the girls. All the girls at the table except Brenda said they were convicted by John's words and they were sorry for how they treated her. They asked her to forgive them for all the hurtful and mean words they ever said about her and to her. Angela's tender heart and Christian background gave her no choice but to forgive them.

Brenda became disgruntled, turning her nose up at the girls.

"You fakers and backstabbers make me sick at the stomach; I don't need friends like you. I don't know why I stooped so low to hang around you anyway."

She stood up from the table to leave, but while leaving, she dished out some insulting words to John and Angela.

"That lame speech doesn't change who both of you are, losers. I can say what I feel anytime I want, and no one but me can change that. You and miss holier-than-thou can take your self-righteous selves and leave me alone."

After lunchtime ended and everyone began heading to their classes, on the way out, the remaining gymnastics team girls apologized to Angela again. One of the team members whose name was Jennifer, stayed behind for a minute to have a brief talk with her.

"I wanted to come to you a long time ago, but I just got caught up in what I thought was fun, not thinking that I was hurting you. I'm sad to say that the more I did it, the more I liked it; it was like an addiction. I couldn't stop because I didn't know how to stop.

"I was afraid I'd be treated like we treated you. Don't worry about Brenda, she's the captain and star of the gymnastics team and loves being in control and getting all the attention. I know you and Brenda have a cloudy past, and that may be why she treats you the way she does, but hang in there. I believe your strength and perseverance are going to help a lot of people one day."

Before John left to go to his next class, Angela thanked him for looking out for her and standing up to Brenda. He explained what motivated him to stick up for her.

"This isn't the first time I've had to help a friend who was being bullied. I couldn't sit back then, and I couldn't sit back day after day and watch them attack you like they were doing. How about we meet after school and talk some more?"

Angela said, "I would like to, but I have a ton of homework to do, maybe next time."

John was looking forward to establishing a friendship with Angela but conceded he would have to wait a little bit longer to do so.

"That's okay; we'll get together some time. Just know that

whenever you need me to chase bullies away, I'm here for you. I guess that's been my way of making friends."

The next day during lunchtime, things were different, very different. Angela was sitting at her table. The girls on the gymnastics team were sitting eating lunch with her, except Brenda. John walked over to them with his lunch tray and asked if he could sit and eat lunch with them. One of the girls jokingly answered, "After that humbling speech yesterday, I don't know If we're worthy of your presence."

Angela welcomed John to their table.

"Of course, you can sit down, you can eat lunch with us anytime you want, and you don't have to ask."

John sat down next to Angela and asked the girls, "Where's Brenda?"

All the girls were hesitant to speak except Jennifer. She decided to boldly speak up on their behalf.

"Brenda's not here, and look at us; we're afraid to talk. I'm done with that."

Jennifer turned to John to fill him in on all the details.

"Brenda didn't want us to say anything, but the other day when she left the lunchroom angry and upset, she went down to the gymnasium to work on a routine all by herself, which she shouldn't have done; she knows the rules. We are not supposed to work out alone. She was so upset with us that she didn't want any of us around her anymore. I guess she considers us traitors.

"Anyway, she was working on perfecting her routine when she did something wrong and ended up slamming hard against the gymnasium wall. She's in the hospital now with broken ribs and a broken leg. She may not be able to do gymnastics anymore. I believe it's going to take months for her to heal."

Angela began crying, "It's all my fault. I made her so upset and caused this to happen."

Jennifer said, "There's no need to cry. Brenda chose her destiny by doing what she chose to do; we all do. We can't let someone choose our destiny by listening to the negative things they say about us."

Jennifer looked at John, reminding him of something he said that helped open her eyes to see the real Brenda.

"Yesterday you said we reap what we sow, you were right, but Brenda wouldn't embrace the truth; it made her more bitter. I think she was so bitter that she couldn't focus on her routine. Her bitterness and inability to focus were the reasons why she got hurt. Brenda may be the captain and star of the gymnastics team, but she has also been hurting on the inside for a long time. Sometimes pain accompanies popularity."

Jennifer looked at Angela once again and gave her some comforting words of encouragement.

"We bullied you from your freshman year up until now, no one taught us how to do that, we chose to do it. We chose to follow in the footsteps of someone who was considered popular because we wanted to be seen with someone with a name. We thought that was something great. Unfortunately, we were willing to do whatever it took to maintain that false status, even things we knew were wrong. We were not showing greatness but insecurity.

"For three years, we tried to drill in you that there was something wrong with you, and from seeing you cry in the cafeteria, we may have succeeded. We made you feel like an outcast and not worthy of being part of our group. For a long time, we wore masks that blinded us, and now that we have taken them off, we see you for who you were all along. We didn't see you as a unique individual, and that's what we feared seeing the most. You weren't what we were. You were different, but in a good way.

"One day, after we had talked about you and laughed at you, I followed you into the library. I heard you quietly praying for us. You never said a mean word back to us, but you prayed for us. I told Brenda about it, and that upset her even more.

"To hear you praying for us after all the meanness we directed towards you showed me how strong and unique you are just being Angela. And as I said yesterday, one day, your strength is going to help a lot of people overcome whatever they might be going through. It's already helped us."

All of the girls hugged Angela before leaving. While they were hugging each other, John began to think about his friend Adrian. He thought about the time when he bullied him into choosing to go into his dad's garage. He felt bad about trying to force him to look at sexually explicit magazines, and calling him a coward if he didn't do so.

John believed the day he convinced Adrian to go into the garage was the beginning of the end of a close friendship. When Adrian would not yield to his request to look at the sexually explicit magazines and be a partaker of his dirty deeds, John ultimately chose his addiction over a friend.

John and Angela became close friends. They were walking home from school when he asked,

"I'm not trying to hit on you or anything like that, but you are beautiful, smart, and a good Christian with a lot of Bible knowledge, does that chase the boys away? I have never seen you with a boy, other than myself, and I have never heard you talk about having a boyfriend, what's up with that?"

"First of all, the right person hasn't come around yet. And second, I had a few bad experiences during my freshman year. My best friend introduced me to a boy on whom at one time she had a crush. I admit that I had a secret crush on him as well.

"He was handsome, muscular, and the type of guy any girl would not hesitate to go out with, so I asked my friend why they never got together. She told me he never asked, and then she asked me if I wanted her to set up a date to go out with him. Although I wanted to, I told her that I was not ready to start a relationship with him or anyone else.

"As I said, I did have a secret crush on him. There were times when I would fantasize about going out with him, and both of us sharing personal things about one another. I also had this dream about him introducing me to some of his friends and all of us spending late nights together hanging out and watching movies.

"I even dreamed of meeting his parents, having dinner with them, and leaving them feeling that I was the best girlfriend their son ever brought home. I imagined that I was shy, going through a difficult time at home, but he had a particular way of getting me to open up and laugh, enjoying every moment I spent with him. But, that was all a fantasy.

"While sitting in the library doing my homework, my friend came and sat down with me, asking me if I changed my mind about going out with her friend. I told her that I still wasn't ready yet and to give me more time to think about it. She told me that she hoped that I would go out with him, and if I didn't, I would be passing up an excellent opportunity to enter into a good relationship.

"A few weeks had gone by since my friend first talked to me about hooking up with her friend. I kept thinking about how nice it would be to have a boyfriend. I also thought about how extra lonely I was feeling and that I could use another friend. I eventually made up my mind that I was going to go out with her friend. I was going to tell her during science class to set a date to go out with him.

"My fantasies and dreams of a romantic relationship with her friend ended with just being a fantasy and a dream. When the bell rang for classes to switch, I got a rude and hurtful awakening that going on a date with her friend was never going to happen. I was headed to my science class prepared to tell my friend to set up the date with her friend.

"As I was walking down the main hallway, past a small section of corridor that was strictly an emergency exit, I observed from the corner of my eye the image of two students kissing in the dimly-lit hallway. When they looked up at me, I was shocked to see that it was my best friend and her male friend who she practically begged me to go out with on a date. The first words out of my mouth to her were,

"Seriously! This is not what best friends do to one another!

"Her friend never said a word. But when my friend walked past me, tightly holding his hand, she gave him another long kiss, then stood an inch from my face mocking and insulting me.

'You think he was going to wait forever for you to make up your mind? I guess the saying is true, you snooze, you lose.'

"Needless to say, after that, our friendship ended."

John said to Angela, "That's cold, especially coming from your best friend."

If that wasn't enough, Angela told John of another bad experience she had, this time with a male friend.

"If you think that's bad, I had another hurtful experience with a boy who was not my boyfriend, and he is the reason why Brenda hates me to this day."

John asked, "What do you mean?"

"Brenda has disliked me ever since my freshman year. There was a boy who was deeply in love with me, but the feeling was not mutual. As far as I was concerned, we were only friends, but he kept sending me text messages, asking me to go out with him. I can't count the number of times I told him we were just friends.

"There was no way he was ever going to be my boyfriend because first, he wasn't my type, and second, he already had a girlfriend, and guess who his girlfriend was?"

John guessed, "Brenda?"

"Yes, you guessed it, his girlfriend was Brenda.

"I asked my friend why he was sending me text messages asking me to go out with him when he already had a girlfriend, but he never gave me an answer. I found out later that he was also sending text messages and going out with other girls behind Brenda's back. I had no choice but to tell him that we could no longer be friends, and that's when things took a turn for the worse. Someone told Brenda that I had gone out with him, but I hadn't.

"I was in the girl's locker room when all of a sudden, I felt someone pulling my hair; it was Brenda. She pulled me down to the floor; then we started fighting. Contrary to what Brenda was telling everyone about her winning the fight, the fight ended up in a draw. I was suspended from school for a week, but Brenda's rich parent's had connections with top school administrators. They managed to pull strings and keep her from getting suspended and kicked off the gymnastics team.

"Brenda told so many lies that I ended up being blamed for the fight. While I was out of school, her boyfriend began sending me text messages again. Even as he kept sending the messages, asking me to go out on a date with him, I found out that at the same time, he went out on a date with another girl, and unfortunately for me, her name was also Angela. Another unfortunate thing about this was that this other Angela was Brenda's best friend.

"After a night out with this other Angela, Brenda's boyfriend was secretly sending her text messages while sitting with Brenda, thanking her for a good time, including all the sick details of what they did. I guess Brenda got upset about him texting while they were supposed to be having a conversation. She grabbed his phone and read the text message and to whom he was sending it. When she saw the name Angela, she asked him why he was cheating on her with her best friend. For some reason, maybe he was trying to protect this other Angela, he said he was sending the message to me."

John asked, "So he lied, and Brenda believed him?

"Yes, she did. I believe Brenda wanted it to be me instead of her best friend. Needless to say, that was the end of their relationship. Ever since that day, although later on her boyfriend admitted he cheated on her with this other girl named Angela, Brenda didn't believe him. She always believed the text message was to me, and she has disliked me ever since.

"Sadly, I'm the innocent victim in all of this, but enough sad stuff about me. Let's change the atmosphere and talk about something different. I just shared with you a traumatic experience I'm still dealing with, but let's share something good and positive, something each of us has gone through and was able to survive and overcome."

John sat clueless as to what he could share with Angela that he had overcome, and he was not going to expose his sexual addiction. He said, "Alright, but I need some time to think about what to say."

"Okay, you think about it. I guess I'll go first. What I'm sharing with you is nothing the whole school does not already know. You may be the only one who doesn't know because it happened before you started attending our school.

"In my freshman year, I got hooked on drugs. I was angry all the time, especially with my mom, who was sick with cancer at the time. I was also angry with my sister, who was only trying to help me. Dad was in the military, preparing to be discharged so he could take care of mom. While I was hooked on drugs, I lost a good friend, and until this day, no one knows what happened to her except God and the person or persons who abducted her."

"You have never met my sister, who is five years older than me. I don't show her how much I appreciate her, but if it weren't for her, I probably would be dead or missing like my friend. Let me tell you what my sister did for me. Even though she knew I had a drug addiction, dad was unaware of it until later on.

"One evening, right after dad was discharged from the military, dad was in his study reading while my sister was in her room doing homework. I had finished my homework and was listening to music when my friend, who was the source of all my drugs, sent me a text message. She said she wanted me to go with her to this new place she had found where we could get drugs. I told her that there was no way my dad was going to let me go anywhere alone. She said a meeting had already been set up and that she didn't want to go alone because the meeting place was in an alley that even the adults in the neighborhood steered away from. I told her I would work something out.

"I went into my dad's study and made up a lie. I told him that my friend had missed school that day and the teacher had given me some homework to take to her that needed to be completed and turned in the next day. I asked him if I could ride my bicycle over to her house. He asked me why I waited so late to say something since I had been home from school for two hours. I told him that I had gotten so busy doing homework that I forgot. My dad called my sister into the room and told her to ride with me to my friend's house.

"My sister was suspicious, due to my drug addiction history, but hesitantly went with me as we got on our bicycles and headed towards my friend's house, with me leading the way. When we arrived at her house, my sister looked at me and said, 'Isn't that the house of the girl you got caught with smoking marijuana in the girl's bathroom at school, and the one who got you hooked on drugs? Something about this just doesn't feel right. Are her parent's home?'

"I told her that instance with the marijuana was a long time ago and that she was cool now. I told her that my friend's dad was at work, but her mom would be home soon. I managed to convince my sister to wait outside until I got back.

"I walked up to the door and rang the doorbell. When my friend opened the door, she hurried me inside, grabbed my arm and we both ran out the back door. While we were running she said, 'We need to hurry. We need to meet this guy. He will take us where we need to go to get the drugs. It's not far, it's down the alley.'

"We ran like crazy. My friend never said anything about meeting some guy to take us somewhere when we talked on the phone. I wasn't so desperate for drugs that I was willing to ride with a man who I didn't know, and to a place I had never been. I have seen some of my friend's drug connections, and most of them look shady to me.

"When we got to the meeting place in the alley, I couldn't believe how filthy it was. Needles were lying everywhere. It smelled so bad that I fell to the ground and threw up. While I was getting up, a car pulled up and I saw a strange-looking man talking to my friend. He was dressed like a pimp and looked like a drug dealer. My friend got into his car and waved for me to come with her saying, 'Come on, don't you want the drugs?'

"I was hesitant at first, but I only had drugs on my mind. My friend continued to rush me.

'Come on. Hurry. We don't have that much time.'

"As I was getting into the car, I felt someone grab my arm; it was my sister."

'Angela, what are you doing? Where do you think you're going? There's no way you are getting into that car. I knew you were up to something. Let's get out of this filthy place.'

"I left with my sister. I tried to get my friend to come with us, but she refused. When I looked back, I saw my friend looking out the back window of the car. That was the last I saw of her. No one has seen her since.

"To this day, my friend is still missing. I owe a lot to my sister for getting me out of that situation, but I'm always haunted by the image of my friend looking desperate out of that back window, knowing that

I could be missing today as well."

After finishing her story, Angela looked at John and said, "Now it's your turn, what about you? What's your story?"

While Angela was telling her story, John had plenty of time to make up a partially false one.

"I don't have much of a story, but the only thing I could think of is surviving my dad's pornography and sex addiction. Every night he would spend time in his garage with one of my mom's female friends he brought to the house while mom was at work. He also spent a lot of time in the garage looking at dirty magazines. He did all of this instead of spending time with me.

"I guess I can say I survived the loneliness that was the result of his rejection and isolation. I survived getting caught up in the same sexual addiction. I found out later that his dad lived his life the same way."

Unaware that John was not being truthful about surviving getting caught up in his dad's sexual addiction, Angela said,

"That's good you didn't get caught up in that addiction, following in your dad's, and even your grandfather's footsteps. I have learned through Bible study that some things that families go through are generational curses that can begin to be broken with spiritual deliverance and a genuine relationship with God."

CHAPTER 9
LOVE HAS NO SECRETS

Angela and John successfully graduated from high school. Angela had decided that after graduation, she was going to help her dad with his outreach ministry and shelter, and save whatever money she could from working at the local coffee shop to help pay for her tuition fees whenever she decided to go to college.

Working in the outreach ministry, Angela became an inspiration to John, even if she believed sometimes he didn't listen to her. Although his lifelong dream was to play baseball while in college and eventually play for a professional team, Angela had such a positive influence on him that he decided to attend a Christian college and possibly become a minister. He felt this would be a good step towards overcoming his sexual addiction.

Two days before John was to leave for college, Angela made a quick detour towards his home on her way to meet her dad. Beverly met her at the door and welcomed her in, inviting her to sit down and drink a cup of coffee with her at the kitchen table while they waited for John to come down.

"You must be Angela, John has told me so much about you. Come on in and sit down. Would you like a cup of coffee while you wait?"

"No thanks, but thanks for asking. I'll get my share of coffee today while working at the shop."

"Oh, I forgot, John did say you worked at a coffee shop. I understand you have had quite of bit of influence on John and his decision to go to a Christian college. Ever since he was a little boy and we stood outside throwing and hitting baseballs together, he dreamed of playing professional baseball, and that's what I would have liked him to do, but it's his life, not mine. I believe he's making the right choice, and he's going to do well."

Beverly asked Angela how she was dealing with John leaving for college. She asked her what she was going to do with all her time since she was no longer in high school, and John wasn't going to be around to keep her company.

Angela shared her post-graduation plans with Beverly.

"I'll miss John, but I'm fine with him leaving to get a college degree, especially at a Christian college. I figure I'll spend more time working at the coffee shop, trying to save up money for college. And when I'm not working there, I'll help my dad with his outreach ministry. He has a shelter downtown that provides a place for people who are homeless, people who have been abused, and also help people recover from addictions."

Unaware that she had lived with a sexually addicted husband and a son who was planning on going into the ministry, while still fighting his sexual addiction, Beverly said to Angela, "I think it's a good thing to have an outreach ministry such as your dad's in the city. It seems as though every friend and relative of an individual who is suffering from an addiction is affected, and some end up paying a high price as a result of trying to help that individual."

Working in the outreach ministry with her father, Angela had seen enough suffering, pain, and loss in the lives of individuals battling addictions. She said,

"I can't agree with you more. Some individuals who have reached out to help addicts have lost precious items they've worked hard to obtain because an addicted family member stole them and sold them to finance their addiction. Some moms and dads have dealt with an addicted son or daughter for years, draining their finances in the process of trying to help them, but the stress of it all ends up taking them to an early grave. Those are just some of the stories I have heard while working with my dad in his outreach ministry."

Beverly assumed Angela's mom was working in the ministry as well. "I'm sure your mom helps you and your dad in the outreach ministry."

Angela sat silent for a moment. As tears began to flow, she reached into her purse, taking out a bracelet. She handed the bracelet to Beverly, wiping the tears from her eyes.

"My stepmom works just as hard in the ministry as my dad, but my real mom passed away a few years ago. That bracelet reminds me of her and how much she loved me and my sister."

Beverly read the bracelet, and it read, "Love Has No Secrets."

She told Angela how beautiful the bracelet was, and how thoughtful it was for her mom to leave her something to remind her of her love.

"Right now, I have no doubts that our mom loved both of us, but there was a time when I didn't believe she loved me; that's why there's more to the story about that bracelet."

Beverly asked, "Love is a powerful and beautiful word. As long as you finally realize your mom loved you and your sister, what more can you ask for?"

Angela began to explain more about the history of the bracelet.

"It's not just about what was inscribed into my bracelet, but it's also about my bracelet and another one that goes with it. To make a long story short, in my freshman year of high school, I became friends with a girl who introduced me to drugs, and who was also my supplier. I got addicted to them. One day my sister, who is older than me, told me that the first step in getting off drugs was to get away from this girl.

"My response to her was that I was not doing drugs, and if I was, she needed to mind her own business. I didn't realize that my business ended up being her business. I found out later that even though my sister had graduated from high school, somehow she would hear about my classmates talking about me behind my back about my drug addiction.

"Even though my sister knew about my addiction, she would always stick up for me. Sometimes when she came to walk me home from school, she would ask me to point out who had been talking about me. Once I pointed them out, she walked up to them and dared them to say something negative about me again. She never got into a fight, but what she said and how she said it was enough to scare them into leaving me alone.

"The worse part about my addiction other than being addicted was how I treated my mom. I don't think she knew I was taking drugs; maybe she did. Mothers have a way of sensing things. Mom was dying of cancer, and at the time, I was only concerned about myself and feeding my addiction. I knew she was getting weaker by the day, but I was angry with her.

"I was angry because one day while lying in bed with her and my sister, we were all watching family videos together. We were also looking at pictures, some of her and my sister doing things together before she got sick, things she was too sick to do with me. They would go to the park together and play with dolls in the sand. She would hide what she called secret candy from my sister and play games with her to see if she could find it. But after I was born, she got sick.

"I didn't get to do the things with our mom that she did with my sister, and I was bitter and angry at her about it. Even though she was sick, I felt as though our mom loved my sister more than me. I wished so much for her to hide secret candy from me so that I might find it and celebrate with her. Today I realize how young and foolish I was.

"On the day mom died, everything changed. My dad, my sister, and I were in her hospital room when she died. Mom's hands were always gripping a Bible as she lay in her hospital bed; she didn't allow anyone to take it away from her.

"When she died, dad took the Bible from her hand. When he took it away, an envelope fell out and onto her bed covers. The outside of the envelope read, "For Angela and Rachel." Rachel is my sister's name.

"Dad opened the envelope; inside were two bracelets. One of them was the one you have in your hand that says, "Love Has No Secrets." The other bracelet was for my sister that says, "Honesty Only Sees Truth." I think we all cried more than we ever did that day because we knew that both these sayings reflected my mom's true character. I wouldn't listen to my mom when she was alive, but on her death bed, her final words to me on that bracelet, "Love Has No Secrets," helped me overcome my drug addiction.

"I realized that I was hiding a secret, looking at the drugs I bought and stole as if I had found hidden candy. Every fix I got was only temporary because I would end up searching for that prized drug candy once more. I didn't need mom to create a secret candy search for me; I created it on my own in search of drugs. Every time I found my drug or secret candy, the celebration came to a quick ending that left me unsatisfied. I wouldn't let anyone get into my inner personal circle except drug addicts like me, and drug dealers.

"I have learned that no matter how much I tried to hide my addiction, it was consuming me from the inside and the secret had to get out. I had to love myself and be honest and truthful, admitting to myself that I was an addict. I had to quit lying to myself and my family, and this required putting all my secret fears and guilt aside and asking for help, that's when my dad and my sister stepped in. My sister tried to help all along, but I chose to ignore her. My dad got me involved in an outreach ministry that helps other addicts, and that has helped me as well."

As Beverly rose from her chair to get a cup of coffee, she began sharing a part of her past with Brenda. She stood at the sink looking out the kitchen window.

"I'm glad to see you doing so well. You have a wonderful testimony, surviving your addiction and all. When you were talking about your mom, I began thinking about my mom and how she raised me in this house. We had a special bond. We had a lot of fun together. She practically treated me like a princess."

As Beverly was talking, she grabbed her chest, feeling a slight pain. Angela jumped out of her seat and ran to Beverly. "Are you alright? Why don't you come and sit back down? You don't look well. I'll go get John."

After sitting back down, Beverly begged Angela, "No! Don't get John. I don't want him to know about this, not yet."

"Know about what? Are you sick Beverly?"

"Yes, I believe so. I've had some problems going on with my heart for a long time, but I've survived. I refused to let any doctor mess with it. They probably would have wanted me to stop working and stay home. Over the years I have managed to set enough aside to pay for John's college tuition. If I had stayed home, John wouldn't be going to college. Who was going to pay for it? Certainly, his dad wasn't.

"I've been able to keep my heart condition a secret for a long time, but God's got me and whatever His will is for me, let it be so. My mom and her mom died of some type of heart failure, so I guess it runs in the family. Angela, promise you won't tell John about this. He's about to begin a new life. I've lived mine and I don't want my problems to get in his way. I'm begging you Angela, you are a Christin and you know what it means to have faith in God. Let me and God deal with this, promise you won't tell John."

Wiping tears from her eyes, Angela was hesitant to agree to Beverly's promise, but she yielded. "This is a difficult promise to make, but I won't interfere with your faith in God. I will pray for you and pray that somehow, God shows you how and when to tell John."

"Thank you Angela, I appreciate your secrecy."

Finishing her cup of coffee, weak and pale looking, and against Angela's wishes, Beverly managed to stand up again, walking towards the sink. "Angela, let's change the subject before John comes down."

Beverly turned her attention towards the kitchen window, focusing on the garage. At the same time, John was walking down the stairs.

He stopped halfway down without Angela noticing him when he heard Beverly say to Angela,

"You said something about not letting anyone inside your inner personal circle. My husband was the same way. He wouldn't let me nor John get close to him. For a long time, he said he was working in that garage out there on design plans to remodel the house and plans to restart his cosmetics business. He said he needed his private space to think, so I didn't bother him.

"Funny thing is, I never got to see those design plans. Carl spent more time in that garage than with his family; it was off-limits. I know what he said he was working on, but I felt that he was not telling me everything.

"You said your ministry helps people who are abused. I'm a victim of an abusive husband. I can't say he was addicted to drugs or anything like that, but I always felt he was hiding something in that garage.

"I was always busy working, sometimes double shifts. I've never been inside that garage since we moved here. Maybe it's time to one day take a look and see what Carl was really working on, or possibly hiding in there. It's not off-limits now because he abandoned us."

Listening to Beverly and hearing her say something about going into the garage caused John to get concerned. He thought to himself, "Dad's secret library of sexually explicit videos and magazines are still in that garage. I can't let mom go in there and find all that stuff."

John quickly finished walking down the stairs, interrupting the conversation, and distracting Beverly's attention away from the garage. Angela said to him, "Well, hello college boy and man of the hour. It's so nice to see you before you got on your way. The church is heading out of town early tomorrow morning on an outreach picnic. I was passing by to drop some things off to my dad. I know you won't be leaving until tomorrow, so after I meet with my dad, I'll swing back around to say goodbye before you leave."

"That sounds like a plan Angela. I pray that all goes well on the trip."

John turned his attention towards Beverly, who was struggling to hide the pain she was feeling. "Mom, you don't look so good, is something wrong?"

"I'm just tired and sad that my son will be leaving me, that's all. Don't worry about me, I'll be fine. Let Angela go so she can get back here and say goodbye."

John had a worried look on his face as he walked Angela out the door. Before she drove off, He asked her,

"What do you think about mom, didn't she look like she was in pain? I don't want to leave if she's not feeling well. If I need to, I can wait and start classes next semester. Mom and I have been through a lot together. If there is something wrong, I don't want her to go through it alone."

Angela struggled to hold back what she witnessed in the kitchen concerning Beverly grabbing her chest in pain and what she shared with her.

"John, don't be worried. After talking with your mom, she's been through a lot. Just stay focused on going to college and making your mom proud. When you leave, I'll make sure I look after your mom. Let me get going. I'll see you in a bit."

As Angela was driving to meet her dad, she felt torn between two decisions. Should she or shouldn't she tell John about Beverly's heart condition? Although out of love, she made a promise to Beverly not to tell, she felt as though she was being unfaithful to the words of her mom that were inscribed on the bracelet she had given her on her death bed, "Love has no secrets."

CHAPTER 10
DETERMINATION

Before John left for college, Angela stopped by his home to say goodbye. Beverly met her at the door and invited her in.

"Good afternoon Angela, I take it you're here to see John, he'll be down in a minute. Come on in and have a seat. "Before John came down, Angela quietly asked Beverly, "I know you're sad that John leaving, but How are you doing health-wise? Have you felt any more pain? Have you changed your mind about going to the doctor?"

"Angela, please don't be worried about me. You have a lot on your plate. I'll be fine."

"Beverly, I am concerned about you. But anyways, while John's away, I'll stop by every day to check up on you."

John came down the stairs to greet Angela. "Good afternoon Angela, I guess this is goodbye for a while." "Yes it is John. I didn't come by to just say goodbye, but I also want to tell you how proud I am of you. Before you leave, if you don't mind, can you show me something?"

John asked, "What is it that you want to see?"

Angela walked John to the front door. Looking outside, she pointed to the oak tree in the front yard.

"When I pulled up into your driveway, I noticed that big oak tree. I remember you telling me you would always find peace and comfort when looking at it from your bedroom window. I feel sad that you'll be leaving. I want to look at it from your window and see if it makes me feel a little better about you leaving, just like it made you feel better, if that's okay with your mom."

Beverly said to Angela, "Go ahead. I don't mind. And if you do find any peace and comfort, bring some down for me, I could use it right now."

John escorted Angela to his bedroom. They both sat on his bed, looking out the window at the oak tree. Angela told him how peaceful it was to sit and look at it. She asked him for a piece of paper and a pen to write something to leave with him before he went to college. He found a pen and piece of paper in his drawer and gave them to her so she could begin writing while he left the room to go to the bathroom.

While John was in the bathroom, Angela decided to get up and take a closer look at the oak tree. As she was getting up, she dropped the pen John had given to her. It landed on the floor, rolling under the bed. In her attempt to retrieve the pen, she accidentally pushed the mattress to the side, enough to expose what was hidden under it.

To her surprise, she saw a sexually explicit magazine that was hidden between the mattress and box spring. The magazine was the same magazine John took out of his dad's garage the night his friend Adrian got hurt. Her first thought was to leave the magazine under the mattress and cover it back up, keeping it a secret that she had stumbled across it.

After having second thoughts, Angela said to herself, "I can't keep this a secret. After I tried to keep my drug addiction a secret, I told myself I was tired of keeping secrets. 'Love Has No Secrets, Honesty Only Sees Truth.' Those were the last words my mom left me on her death bed. Honesty with myself was the first thing that helped me overcome my drug addiction. If John has an addiction, and from the looks of it he does, there is no way I can help him if I keep it a secret."

When John came back into the room, he noticed right away that Angela had found the magazine he had forgotten about under his mattress. She had laid it on his bed and was sitting on the bed looking at him, waiting for an explanation. John felt like crawling under a rock. He didn't know what to say to her.

After discovering the sexually explicit magazine, Angela had plenty to say.

"That day I shared with you some things about my drug addiction, I was transparent and honest; we both agreed that we would be. You were supposed to be honest with me. Obviously, you weren't totally honest. We're supposed to be friends.

"We committed ourselves to share something both of us have survived and overcome. I shared my former addiction with you, but you shared your dad's addiction, not yours. When I look at this magazine lying here, to me, it's no different than the drugs I use to crave. An addiction is an addiction, no matter what the source or root might be.

"There is no addiction worse than the other; they all lead to the same consequences. I have been where you are; that's why after finding this, I won't look at you differently than I always have. You are a friend, and as your friend, you need to know that I can help you with this. Open up to me about this. I love you as a friend, and love has no secrets.

"This magazine I see lying on this bed reminds me of my past drug addiction and why I'm involved in my dad's outreach ministry. It must have been in God's will for me to find out about your addiction before you went away to college. I'm willing to help you, but you have to open up and be honest with yourself first. As I said, I've been there."

John begged for Angela's silence.

"I'm sorry you found out about my addiction this way, please don't tell my mom. I never told her about my dad's sexual addiction and other secrets; it will break her heart to find out about mine. We have to keep this a secret. Please, Angela, please do that for me."

"John, you need to understand something. I was the same way when I was trying to hide my addiction from everyone, including my family. I realized that after I admitted that I was an addict, I needed some help. I had to expose that secret to myself first. After exposing my addiction secret to myself, even though my sister already knew about it, I had to expose it to my dad. Then they were able to help me see that I had a greater purpose in life than the life of an addict.

"Since you create stories and say you learn things from that oak tree outside your window, let me tell you a story my dad told me after he became a pastor. He told me that although there were many versions of this story, he was going to tell it his way so that I might get a full understanding of what he was trying to say relative to my situation.

"He told me the story of a thirty-year-old oak tree that sat in the middle of a vast forest. This oak tree was full of thousands of acorns. On this tree, there was one particular acorn who watched a large number of its fellow acorns get snatched off their branches by a violent storm that passed through.

"The wind was so strong and intense that it snatched these acorns off their branches and tossed them to the ground. As they fell in large numbers, the one acorn concluded that one day, its turn would come. The day would come when it would be snatched off its branch and tossed to the ground by a strong wind.

"One day, the acorn looked down from its comfortable branch and noticed that the fallen acorns that were tossed to the ground by the strong wind were being violently tossed, turned, and cracked open by squirrels. Their precious protein inside them was eaten or carried off to be used as a source of food for the winter by the squirrels. After the feast and fury of the hungry squirrels ended, all of the fallen acorn's protective shells were exposed and abandoned, the only memory of their existence that would eventually rot away.

"The acorn knew that its destiny dictated that one day, it would be dropped by strong winds, but it had no desire to go out the same way as its acorn friends. The acorn was determined to grow up to be as tall and strong as the oak tree that held it close to its branches. If the acorn could help it, there was no way its life was going to end violently. There was no way it was going to be tossed, turned, gutted, and left to rot as a grim memory of what was, could have been, but wasn't.

"After seeing the violent end of its acorn friends at the hand of the hungry squirrels, the acorn realized that it wasn't going to grow into a strong and mighty oak tree as long as it was attached to the branch. If it was going to be that great oak, the acorn knew that being dropped was the beginning of the process. What happened after it was dropped would determine whether or not it would be the oak tree it desired to be.

"The acorn would have to rely on some outside force, some help from the outside to bury it first. After it is buried, the moist and fertile soil would crack the acorn open. It wasn't the acorn's desire to lay on top of the exposed dry ground, allowing the squirrels, its enemies, to crack it open and eat it up from the inside, or carry it away for a winter feast.

"One cloudy day, while the acorn was resting on its designated branch, it thought about its fallen acorn friends. The clouds were getting darker, and a storm was approaching. The acorn looked down and noticed a squirrel digging holes into the ground searching for un-cracked acorns.

"The acorn made sure it kept an eye on every movement of the squirrel. As it sat on the branch, it became troubled as it continued to think about the violent demise of its acorn friends. The acorn pondered on the thought, then looked down and the squirrel was no longer in view, only the holes the squirrel had dug.

"Suddenly, the acorn heard a loud chirping sound. The storm clouds were rolling in fast as well. When the acorn looked across the branch, it noticed that the persistent and hungry squirrel was headed towards it. The squirrel's eyes were trained upon it as though it could care less whether or not a storm was quickly approaching. The squirrel was determined to get this last acorn before scurrying off to find a place of shelter.

"Because the acorn was unable to move; it was at the mercy of the squirrel and the storm. The acorn knew what its fate would be if the squirrel reached it. All hope of it becoming a strong oak tree would be lost. As the squirrel moved closer and closer, so did the storm.

"The storm became more violent as the winds picked up, accompanied by the crack of lightning and rolling thunder. The squirrel was one leap away from reaching the acorn when a strong gust of wind knocked it off balance and also detached the acorn from its branch. They both fell to the ground. The squirrel ran away into the woods for safe cover.

"While the storm was raging and the rains pouring, the acorn had fallen straight down and inside one of the deep holes the squirrel had previously dug looking for un-cracked acorns before the storm arrived. As the torrential rains poured and poured, the acorn was completely covered with mud. In the middle of the wind and rain, the acorn was completely hidden in a safe and prepared place; it was placed where it desired to be. The acorn was in a position to potentially grow into a mature oak tree.

"If it weren't for the aid of the storm and rain, the acorn would have been exposed to be gutted and eaten by squirrels, as was in the case of its fallen acorn friends. The acorn had to fall to the ground into a place of safety, the hole dug by the foraging squirrel.

While Angela was talking about the fallen acorn, John's mind reflected on his experience with the butterfly caught in the spider web spun among the groundcover at the base of the oak tree. He thought about how the butterfly, being caught in the spider's web, was supplying the spider with a source of food that would help preserve the spider so it could produce another generation of spiders; and that an unsuspecting insect getting caught in the spider's web was inevitable and the nature of things.

John continued to think how important the holes the squirrels were digging were to the acorn. The acorn falling into a hole, then being trapped and buried to produce another generation of oak trees was inevitable; it was the nature of things.

"John, it was vital that the acorn be buried by the storm's torrential rain. It would be cracked open, not by the squirrels, which were its enemy, but by the moist rainwaters and summer sun to receive the nourishment it needed from the soil to sprout, and over time, grow into what it was created to be, a strong and mighty oak tree."

Angela connected the story to John's situation.

"Out of the thousands of acorns that fall off the oak tree, it only takes one to keep the oak species alive. That's what Christ did for you and me. In his death, He is the One who fell to the ground and was buried in a prepared place. He is the One who was resurrected by the living water and nourishing life-giving Spirit and power of God to be glorified and transformed or cracked open to reveal his true greatness, divine glory, and divine nature. He is the One who brings spiritual life to those who believe and receive the true gospel of salvation.

"John, you are in a storm right now, and you have to allow God to work through me. You need to let me help you bury your addiction so that you might be nourished and cracked open to flourish into what God created you to be. You were created for a purpose, and that purpose was not to be an addict.

"You must have a desire and determination to be like the acorn in the story with a vision and destiny to become as strong as an oak tree. If you fail to have that vision and continue in your addiction, you will be tossed, turned, gutted, and left to rot. You will only be a grim memory of what was, could have been, but wasn't.

"The squirrel was desperate to get that one last acorn in the middle of the storm before fleeing. The devil will use your addiction, your storm, as a desperate attempt at all costs to get that final pull that will take you to a place of bondage, from which it will be difficult to find your way out. Once he gets you there, he will move on, seeking his next victim.

"Despite the fate of all the other acorns or addicts that have fallen, I'm just trying to save one because there is still room for one, a prepared place. Acorns produce oak trees. Every individual, or acorn, who turns to Christ keeps the gospel message moving forward as they grow into oak trees. As followers of Christ or oak trees, they will produce more acorns that will produce more oak trees. I think you get the analogy.

"Let me tell you something I learned after overcoming my addiction. We read in the Bible that after God created everything, including man, He declared that it was very good. There were no flaws nor imperfections in what He created. No suffering, disease, or death existed. Everything was looking good and working according to His perfect nature and plan.

"We often feel that Jesus healed individuals for their benefit only, but He did it for an even deeper reason. First of all, with every miracle that was performed, God was to be glorified and His power and authority were to be shown to the unbeliever; drawing him to salvation. Second, every healing should remind us of how things were in the beginning, how things should be, could be, and one day will be. One day, things will be good once again because disease and sin will be eradicated. As I said, God created everything good, but the introduction of sin due to man's disobedience altered the good in him.

"Mankind has moral issues, and according to the Bible, moral issues are sin issues that began with man's rebellion against God in the Garden of Eden. Some feel that they are not accountable to God, but the truth is, we are all accountable to Him because He said all souls belong to Him.

"Because Adam and Eve drifted off the spiritual path God created for them to walk, we are born with a sinful nature. No one sits down and teaches us how to lie, it's in our nature. No one takes us by the hand and teaches us how to disobey, it's in our nature. No one teaches us anger, bitterness, jealousy, or how to entertain lustful thoughts, it's in our nature.

"We have a desire to live right and above sin, but our sinful nature will not allow it. We are spiritually broken and no longer good morally, socially, biologically, or spiritually, without allowing God to work in us to do what is spiritually good. We must thirst after His righteousness and deliverance from sin.

"I was told that my drug addiction was a sickness or disease, but I began to wonder, if my addiction is a sickness or disease, in a physical or mental sense, why are millions upon millions of addicts in the world suffering from this same sickness or disease? More than twenty million people in the United States, from all demographics, suffer from some form of addiction. We can't simply brush this epidemic off as a physical or mental disease affecting millions upon millions. I thought to myself that the answer must be deeper than what science and medicine would like us to believe. What is the root of the problem?

"I learned that because of our sinful nature, the root of all addictions is spiritual. Sin is a spiritual disease that affects our physical desires and how we respond to them. The addiction I had was a sin disease that influenced me, controlled me, and held me captive. Overcoming my addiction only took God and His goodness to influence and captivate me."

John said, "Angela, I appreciate all that you have said. I know you are trying to help me, but I'm trying the best I can to break this addiction. I promise you, when I come back from college, I'm going to be a changed man. I hate to leave you because you have been a good friend to me. I beg you, don't tell mom about all of this."

Angela was disappointed in John's repeated efforts to keep his sexual addiction a secret.

"Based upon the fact that you keep begging me not to tell your mom confirms to me that you were not listening to anything I said. I talked to your mom downstairs, and she had suspicions about your dad, whether he had an addiction. Evidently, you didn't tell her about your dad's addiction when you knew about it all along.

"You keep hiding secrets, and that helps no one. Your mom needs to know. It's a shame that you don't trust your mom who has been there for you when your dad wasn't, and she is here for you now. It's a dishonor for you to leave, keeping this away from her.

"Since you are not listening to me and you won't let me help you, you have to talk to someone, and I suggest you start with her. You are walking in your dad's footsteps and what did he do to her; he destroyed her from the inside, leaving her lonely and depressed. Do you want her to live through that again? That's what you are about to do. You say you're going to come back a changed man, but you won't unless you get some help where you are going. You can't do this alone."

Angela broke out in tears as she headed downstairs and out the door. She stopped and turned to John saying, "John, please get some help. I'm going to miss you, but please, get some help. If not for yourself, do it for me."

 Beverly walked up to John and asked, "Is everything ok? It looked like Angela was crying."

"She'll be alright. She's just hurt because I'm leaving for college. She needs some time for everything to sink in."

Beverly walked out the door, leaving to pick up some things at the store, and then head to work. She said to John, "I won't come home from work after I get off. I need to sort a few things out, so I'll be staying with my friend Carmen for about a week. I'll meet you at the airport before you board your flight. Make sure everything is locked up and call me if you need me."

As she was leaving, she turned back towards John and pulled an envelope out of her purse, handing it to him saying, "I almost forgot to give this to you. It's something I want you to read. I know I'll see you again before you leave, but I just wanted to give you this now so I won't forget. You don't have to read it now. You can wait until you get all settled in on campus."

John watched Beverly pull out of the driveway and head up the road to work. He went to his bedroom and sat down on his bed, laying the envelope Beverly had given him next to him on the mattress. The only thing John felt like doing at the moment was lying down on his bed. While lying in bed, he began regretting what had just transpired between himself and Angela.

Disturbed due to Angela discovering his addiction, John thought about what she said and whether he would see her again, then he dozed off into a deep sleep. While he was sleeping, his arm accidentally shoved the envelope Beverly had given him onto the floor. When the envelope fell to the floor, it ended up sliding under his bed.

As Beverly continued up the road after leaving the house, she noticed a car speeding towards her in the distance so fast that it was partially shrouded by a cloud of dust from the road. "Whoever this is, why are they driving like a madman? There's never a reason to drive crazy like that. Just an irresponsible idiot putting other people's lives in danger."

Beverly reached the next intersection before the speeding car reached her. As she turned off the road, the speeding car, ignoring the posted stop sign, sped through the intersection only seconds before Beverly completely exited it.

She slowed down, attempting to get a glimpse of the driver and the car, but the dust and speed of the car as it turned a corner up ahead wouldn't allow it. She was clueless that the driver of the speeding car was her abusive husband Carl, who months ago deserted her and John. Beverly calmed herself down and continued on her way.

Carl had something more urgent on his mind. He was driving so fast and distracted that he didn't recognize Beverly's car. He was on a mission towards the house, hysterically talking to himself and increasing his speed to get to the house as quickly as possible.

"I don't know what I was thinking. I should have gotten every sexually explicit video and magazine out of that garage before I left. This has been nagging me ever since. I know I had no choice but to leave quickly because Bob would have killed me for having an affair with his wife, but I had to come back to take care of this. I don't think Beverly has been in that garage, she never goes in there, but I've got to get everything out of there before she does. She'll be devastated if she finds out what I was actually doing and storing in there."

Carl sounded as if he was losing his mind. Mentally unfocused, all of a sudden, he lost control of the car, spinning full circle in the middle of the road and flipping three times before landing against a utility pole. He was seriously injured and in need of medical care but managed to unbuckle his seat belt and stumble from the wreckage. Bleeding with a broken leg and internal injuries, instead of calling for help, he was determined to get to the garage, even if he had to crawl the remaining two miles.

Carl reached the garage, bleeding, barely breathing, and near death. He stumbled into the garage, not surprised to find that everything appeared untouched. Lacking the strength to do so, he realized that his intended plan to quietly and secretly load everything into his car and drive off was no longer viable.

Carl felt that his last resort was to burn every piece of sexually explicit material inside the garage. Even though he knew John was home after seeing his car in the driveway, at the moment, he didn't care. He was desperate and had one goal in mind, don't let Beverly discover what was in the garage.

In his attempt to find materials to start a fire, Carl collapsed due to his injuries, falling into unconsciousness and totally out of sight behind several tall stacks of wooden crates. He had returned to his sexually explicit private empire, at one time sitting on its throne in secrecy, but now, he was barely breathing, lying at death's doorstep.

John woke up a couple of hours later, thinking about how much he had lost because of his lies and secrets. He had lost his friend Adrian, a dad, and possibly Angela. He grabbed the sexually explicit magazine Angela had found under his mattress and ran outside to sit on the porch.

Looking at the garage, he said, "That's where all the trouble started, and that's where it's going to end. I can't allow mom to see all the filth that is in there when she gets back; that in itself will kill her."

John figured that with mom gone for a week, and before leaving for college, this was the opportune time to do what he thought he had to do. He took the magazine he had in his hand and threw it inside the garage. He grabbed a can of gasoline that was sitting on the side of the garage and doused the inside of the garage with gasoline.

As he exited the garage, he poured gasoline on the door and the sides of the garage. He went back into the garage to retrieve a box of matches that were on a nearby shelf. He hesitated for a moment, standing at the entrance of the garage.

Standing with his eyes closed, images of his dad, his friend Adrian, and the times he viewed the sexually explicit images in the magazines flashed before his eyes. When he opened them, he wanted revenge. The look in John's eyes made him look as though he was blaming the garage for all that he had lost, and the reason for his addiction.

Before striking a match and throwing it on the garage floor, John yelled, "No more! I'll destroy you before you destroy anyone else that is close to me or anyone I love."

Carl, now barely conscious, attempted to crawl from behind the wooden crates where he had collapsed. He tried to call out to John, but couldn't because of his internal and external injuries. After unsuccessfully using all his remaining energy to get John's attention, Carl collapsed and fell into unconsciousness once again.

Unable to hear or see Carl, John struck a match, threw it on the garage floor, and then quickly ran outside of the garage. In just a few minutes, the garage and everything inside of it, including Carl, was engulfed in flames. There were many times when Carl, for no reason at all, yelled at John, but at this desperate moment, he was unable to yell for his help, even if it was the last yell of his life.

Feeling the heat from the blistering flames, John stood, watching for a moment, then made his way across the driveway and sat down on the bench under the oak tree. He observed the burning garage, taking pleasure in seeing an object representing the dark side of his life go up in fire and smoke, illuminating the late afternoon sky. He became consumed and fixed on seeing this object that was utilized to hide so much evil, cause so much separation, and inflict so much pain, reduced to a pile of rubble. When his closest neighbors saw the flames and came driving down to investigate, he told them he was burning the old garage down to build a brand new one.

The next morning, John woke up to go to the airport. He finished packing his belongings and before leaving the house, took a walk around the inside of it. There was an eerie quietness against the rays of the rising sun that was shining through the kitchen window.

In his mind, he could hear his dad yelling at him for something he did wrong, and his mom crying from the abusive words his dad was dishing out to her. He said, "I've got to get out of here before this place drives me insane."

As he walked to his car, he passed by the burned-down garage that was still smoldering. Looking at it, he felt as though a violent chapter in his life had come to an end. Then, he thought about the night his dad left. As Carl was lying burned beyond recognition, buried under a pile of sexually explicit rubble and charred wood, John, unaware of it, said,

"Dad, when you abandoned us, things got tough. I'm sorry for burning your private space down, but I had to do what I had to do. I don't know where you went that night you left us, nor where you are right now. I was so angry that night you left. I did attempt to say goodbye, but it was too late. I hope you are somewhere getting the help you need."

John got into his car and backed out of the driveway, headed up the road, and disappeared into the sunrise. He met Beverly at the airport. While waiting for his plane to depart, she sat down with him and began saying goodbye.

"Son, no matter what your dad did to you or what he thought of you, I have always believed in you. Today is a special day. I know when you were growing up your dad forbid me to spend money on birthday parties and such, but as soon as you graduate from college and come home, we'll have one of the biggest graduation parties ever."

Confident that he would graduate and return home to celebrate,

John said, "That gives me something to look forward to."

Beverly asked, "Do you remember how we would pretend we were hitting home runs before a large crowd out on the road that goes past the house?"

"Yes, I remember, those were fun times. When you started working more double shifts, we stopped doing that."

"John, I do regret working all those hours and not being at home with you, but I'll be here to celebrate with you when you get your degree. I know your goal in life was to play professional baseball, but going into ministry work is good for you as well. Even though it's not baseball, remember what I told you. Life is waiting for you to hit a home run. Right now, the bases are loaded, and you are up to bat. Your loyal fans in the stadium, including myself, are waiting for you to hit a home run for the team."

John stood up out of his seat to board his plane. Beverly gave him a big hug, stepped back, and said, "Go hit that home run and make me proud. Make sure you don't strike out or else the entire team will lose. If you need to get in touch with me, remember, I'll be staying with Carmen for a week." Beverly was releasing John into a world of uncertainties, hoping that he will find his rightful place, and praying that he will hit a home run as he faces more of life's challenges.

John turned around to take one final look at Beverly before boarding his flight. As he watched her disappear into the dense airport crowd, he said to himself, "Even though you have been a strong and special woman in my life, there are things about dad and myself I want to tell you, but I can't. Mom, I know you have a lot of faith in me. I hope and pray that I don't disappoint you."

CHAPTER 11
THE SECRET ESCAPE PLACE

John began his first year of college looking forward to a new life, new goals, and even new friends. It was time to put negative things behind him and move forward. His goal was to step right into ministry, hoping that doing so would take his mind off of his ever-tormenting addiction.

His outreach ministry class gave him hope that he would meet that goal. He was required to visit clients in their homes who had overcome an addiction or any form of abuse, documenting their stories of survival and offering them further assistance if needed.

These clients would be assigned by the university, and a primary requirement of every visit was that the students were to go in two's, never alone. There was no exception to this rule. John would have to be dedicated and committed to this ministry as it made up eighty percent of his grade for the class. He had to pass this class if he were to graduate from college.

John was teamed up with a classmate named Victoria. Since they were going to be working together, they decided to meet at the local coffee shop to get to know one another. They were also going to devise a strategy for when they would meet clients.

Upon meeting Victoria, John was surprised at her quiet and shy demeanor, especially if she was going to be involved in outreach ministry, visiting clients in their homes. He told her some basic things about himself and almost everything about his mom. Victoria told him she was a shy and quiet girl, and she was hoping the outreach ministry would help her overcome it.

When Victoria told John where her hometown was located, he was surprised to learn that they were from the same town and the same neighborhood. Although they never met one another, they only lived two miles apart from each other. Victoria attended a private school in the city while John walked to a small school up the street from his home in a rural area of the city.

Victoria married after graduating from high school. Soon after, her husband was diagnosed with a severe case of lung cancer she believed he contacted at a chemical plant where he worked. She shared her predicament with John.

"Every day, my husband seems to get worse. The medical bills are becoming astronomical. They say he has a fifty percent chance of survival. I'm trying to do my best to hang in there. It gets tough sometimes, but I can't give up on him. I figured that if I go to college and get a degree, I will have a better chance of getting a good-paying job and making enough money to pay down the outrageous bills that are piling up. We are both determined to beat this." John encouraged her,

"After I left home for college, I had dreams of how lonely my mom might be. When I was growing up, she always felt lonely at home. We went through some tough times. I haven't talked to her lately, but I pray for her every day, and I will pray for your husband also. As newlyweds, you shouldn't have to face dealing with cancer or the financial strain that comes with it. As a team player, I'll do my best to work with you and help you get a good grade in this class so you can graduate and get one of the highest-paying jobs you can get. I won't let you down Victoria."

"Thanks for your words of encouragement John. I'm sorry to hear what your mom has gone through. What about your dad? Most dads love it when they have a son to nurture and love regardless of the choices and mistakes he makes. I imagine you take after him."

"Victoria, I don't mean to be rude, but that's far from the truth. I'm not in a place in my life where I want to share anything with anyone about my dad. All I'm going to say is that I never had a dad. He didn't nurture or love me. He emotionally abused whatever love I did have for him out of me."

A week after beginning their college studies, John and Victoria were given their first outreach ministry assignment. Their first client was a male client who had been physically abused. He was exposed to constant and undeserved spankings as a young boy. The assignment brought back memories John had of his dad's verbal and emotional abuse.

Later that night, John called his outreach ministry class professor on the phone.

"I can't do this client on my first run. I'm still dealing with hurt from my past that might interfere with me listening to this client and documenting his story. If he does need further help, I don't think I can offer that to him. Can you assign this client to another group?"

John's professor asked him, "Do you think you did anything wrong that warranted the abuse and the hurt you are feeling right now?"

John answered, "Absolutely not, I didn't deserve any of it."

"John, trust me when I say this, knowing and admitting you did nothing wrong makes you ready. Individuals who are abused did nothing to deserve it. If you believe that, then there are a lot of clients out there waiting for you to tell them that. Victoria will be there to help you. We do this together,"

The next day, John and Victoria drove to the address of their first outreach client, Mr. Lance Wilson. When they arrived at his home, Victoria was so nervous that her hands were shaking. John looked at her and said,

"You'll do fine. This is our ministry and what we must be committed to doing if we want to pass this class. I know this is our first client, but I believe it will get more comfortable for you with each visit. I have a friend back home named Angela Robison, who told me a story about an acorn and an oak tree.

"The story Angela told me helped me understand that we must have a determination to be like an acorn with a vision and destiny to become as strong as an oak tree. If we don't have that vision, life and our enemies will toss us around, gut us, and leave us to rot. Then we'll only be a grim memory of what was, could have been, but wasn't.

"So come on Victoria, get pumped up, and let's go in there with a vision to one day be good at what we love doing and what I believe we have been called by God to do."

John and Victoria were welcomed into Mr. Wilson's home with open arms as they sat down with him, excited to engage with their first client. As he began sharing his story of childhood abuse, he pulled out a book from his desk drawer explaining its origin and importance.

"This book right here was written and given to me by my brother. It has been a constant encouragement to me. One night, it helped me, my brother, and our mom escape something terrible that was about to take place."

John asked Mr. Wilson, "How was it able to help you all? Can you tell us what the terrible thing was the book helped you all escape?"

Mr. Wilson eagerly prepared to share his book with John and Victoria. "Make yourselves comfortable because this is going to be a very long and detailed, but true story, but I have a feeling it's going to help you as much as it helps me every time I read it. But first, let me give you a background of my family to help you understand why this book was written.

"I grew up down south with my mom, dad, and my twin brother, who as I said, wrote this book. We were eight years old at the time. My dad was a truck driver, so he spent very little time at home, especially during the week. My mom worked during the day at a laundromat while we were in school.

"In the evenings, although she was tired, she cooked for all of us, cleaned the house, and even had time to help us with our homework. She did this all by herself while dad was on the road. On Saturdays, she would spend time in the backyard with us throwing footballs and playing basketball. Even on weekends when he was not at work, dad would spend the entire weekend watching sports on television. Anytime my brother and I asked him to go outside with us; he would always say he was too tired.

"We lived in a three-bedroom house where my brother and I were privileged to sleep in separate bedrooms. At bedtime, our mom would always come into our rooms and read us a story until we fell asleep. As I said before, my brother and I are twins, identical twins.

"If you stood my brother and me side by side, it was almost impossible to tell us apart. We look exactly alike. Even after we had reached eight years of age, our mom dressed us in identical clothing. Mom and dad were the only ones who could tell us apart. Well, let me say this, when dad was drunk, he couldn't tell us apart at all. My brother and I made a promise to look out for one another, and that's the very thing that saved our lives one night.

"Things were always quiet and routine around the house. Everyone was content doing their own thing until one night, dad came home drunk as he had many times. He knew he drank alcohol too much, but he wouldn't admit that he had an alcohol addiction.

"After he came off the road from making his deliveries, he would hit the bars before coming home. But this night was different. Dad had never come home as drunk and belligerent as he had on this particular night, and he never yelled at mom the way he did. Any other time he would come home quietly, sit on the couch, then with the television on, fall asleep.

"For a long time, dad never came upstairs to check on mom after work or sleep with her. But for some reason on this night, he came upstairs and began yelling at her. Even with our bedroom doors closed, we could hear his deep and loud voice.

"My brother and I cracked our doors open to see what was going on. We heard dad through their closed bedroom door yelling at mom about how dirty the house was. We thought it was strange that he was yelling at her about this because even after coming home from work, we witnessed her working hard around the house, keeping it clean.

"Although dad was yelling at her, we never heard our mom yell back at him. He was yelling at her, saying so many bad things about her, but she never said a word. I guess she figured that while he was drunk, there was no use trying to reason with him or escalate the situation from verbal abuse to physical abuse.

"All of a sudden, we heard their bedroom door open. Dad stormed in the direction of my bedroom. We quickly closed our doors, jumped into our beds, and pulled the covers over our heads, pretending we were asleep.

"I heard a loud knock on my bedroom door and then dad's slurred, deep voice calling me to meet him in the kitchen. He said that there was something he needed to settle with me. As I rose from my bed, and as dad made his way downstairs, I could hear him yelling at mom about how lazy she was and that he was going to finally get things in order around the house, no matter what he had to do to get it done.

"Dad continued walking down the stairs and into the kitchen. As I walked out of my bedroom to go downstairs to meet him, I passed by my brother's bedroom. He was standing in his doorway telling me how scared he was. I whispered to him to go into our mom's bedroom and sit with her until I got back.

"Mom was sitting on her bed crying. She grabbed my brother and hugged him close. Then she looked at me and quietly kept saying she was sorry. I told her I was okay and that there was no need to be sorry. I tried to comfort her, telling her that none of what was going on was our fault while at the same time, reminding her that dad was under the influence of alcohol.

"Dad yelled at me from the kitchen to hurry up and come down. When I walked into the kitchen, he was standing there waiting for me with a belt in his hand. I was terrified at the look of rage he had on his face, a look I had never seen on him before.

"He told me that beginning that night, things were going to change around the house. To this day, I don't know why dad singled me out over my twin brother, maybe because I was born a few minutes before him, but he told me that whenever he was not around, it was my responsibility to help make sure things got done right. Although mom worked hard around the house, he said neither she nor I were keeping things up like we were supposed to and that he was going to teach me to do what he told me to do, exactly the way he wanted it done.

"Dad bent me over and spanked me with his belt until he was tired. The good thing about it was that although the spanking hurt, it didn't take long for him to get tired because he was under the influence of alcohol. After he told me to get back upstairs and go to bed, he turned the television on and fell asleep on the couch while watching the sports channel.

"In pain from the spanking, I went back upstairs and into my mom's room. She was curled up in her bed with my brother on one side of her. I crawled into her bed and laid next to her on the other side. Dad was still sleeping downstairs while we were snuggled up next to mom, all of us afraid and crying.

"Mom wiped the tears from her face, then reached over me and grabbed a book from her nightstand drawer, and began reading it to us; we fell asleep before she ended it. Mom woke us up early the next morning and told us to hurry back to our bedrooms before dad woke up and came upstairs to get dressed for work. It was too early to get dressed for school, so my brother and I laid back down and finished our sleep.

"For a long time, dad would come home drunk, repeating the same thing over and over again at least three or four nights a week. He would yell, verbally abuse mom, and then spank me with his belt, accusing me of disobeying and disrespecting him. These abusive nights would always end with him falling asleep on the couch while watching sports and mom reading us a story in her bedroom until we fell asleep.

"One morning, I woke up and sat on the edge of my bed and began to cry, asking myself why dad was so angry with my mom and me. My brother must have heard me crying in my room. He came in and sat next to me telling me how unfair it was that dad spanked me, but never spanked him. He said whenever I would get spanked, he would cover his ears to block out the sound.

"My brother also told me that he came up with an idea while dad was spanking me. He suggested that since we were identical twins, wearing identical pajamas, we could take turns getting spankings. He said dad wouldn't be able to tell us apart. As I said, we both knew he couldn't tell us apart when he was drunk.

"I told my brother how much dad's spankings hurt, and there was no way I was going to agree with his plan, but he insisted. He said we have always looked out for one another and that when we hurt, we hurt together, when we cry, we cry together. I cried as I conceded to his plan, but told him that the deal was off if he couldn't stand the spankings. My brother assured me that his plan would work and he could take the spankings because when he took the spankings, they were for both of us.

"A couple of nights later, dad came home his usual self, drunk and yelling at mom. When he called for me to come down into the kitchen, my brother signaled to me to stay inside my bedroom. He came out of his bedroom. As he proceeded to go downstairs, we both looked at mom; she was crying.

"Mom looked at me and then at my brother, noticing that it was not me that was going down the stairs. At first, she looked confused at what we were doing, but then she began crying even more after realizing that we had devised a plan to look out for one another, to share our tears and pain.

"Our plan worked flawlessly every time. When dad executed his alcohol-provoked spankings, he didn't know who he was spanking. Yes, I can say the spankings did hurt my brother and me, but for me, the spankings were half the hurt I would have experienced getting them alone. My brother and I refused to let the other suffer alone.

"One morning, a morning after a night I was spanked, my brother and I were getting dressed for school. He came into my room and said he woke up in the middle of the night after having a bad dream about dad hitting our mom and spanking both of us. He said everything was so loud in his dream that he woke up and wanted to get out of the house.

"He told me that he went somewhere while everyone else in the house was sleeping. He said that there was a secret escape place where he could go, and no one could find him. It was a place where he wouldn't hear dad yelling at mom, see him hitting her in his sleep, or hear him spanking me. He said he climbed out of his bedroom window and went to this secret escape place.

"I asked him what he meant when he said he went to a secret escape place and where this secret place was. I also asked him if he was in his right mind going outside in the middle of the night all by himself. He said that everyone was asleep and he knew that the place where he was going was safe.

"He said he had to go to a secret place that blocked out everything. A place where it wasn't dark anymore, but bright. He invited me to go to this secret place the next night while mom and dad were asleep. I went to bed wondering where in the world this secret escape place was.

"The next night, when dad came home, we could tell that he had been drinking, but he was not as drunk as he was the nights he would go off on mom and me. There was no yelling and no spankings. He fell asleep on the couch watching television as he had done every night. Mom and dad were sleeping when my brother came into my room, telling me it was time to go to his secret escape place.

"In the darkness of night, I got up and we proceeded to climb out of my bedroom window. I was curious as to where my brother was taking me. We walked a short distance. My brother removed a piece of plywood that was covering an opening under our front porch, waving for me to come inside with him. I kept asking myself what was so special under the porch.

"After my brother went inside the opening, although skeptical, I followed him in. It was dark and scary inside. I reminded him of when he said that in his secret place everything was blocked out, but I still heard crickets chirping and every other bug. He told me that just sitting wouldn't block things out. He said we were going to a place where everything we saw and heard on the outside was going to disappear.

"My brother invited me to lay down with him and look out the opening we had just come through. He reached over and grabbed a notebook he had hidden under the porch. It was a book he had written on the night's dad was spanking me. He told me to take a good look out of the opening and look at the clouds against the black sky and then, close my eyes.

"While my eyes were closed, he began quietly reading his book. As he read the book, still with my eyes closed, and obviously, it was dark, I felt a peace come over me; I felt like I was flying. I could still hear my brother reading the book. Then, all of a sudden, every sound I had heard before my brother began reading the book stopped. All I could hear was him reading the book. As he read, I wasn't afraid anymore because my imagination took me to a place where I felt safe.

"When I opened my eyes, there was no more darkness but sunlight. My brother and I had fallen asleep under the porch. The morning had come. We both quickly crawled from under the porch and climbed back through our bedroom windows and into bed before mom and dad woke up. The next day, I told my brother about the calmness and peace that came over me while he was reading his book under the porch. I told him that I felt as though I was at the edge of my imagination.

"I remembered how at first things were cloudy and dark, and I was afraid, then as my brother kept reading the book, things turned peaceful and quiet. I was in a place I didn't want to leave; I felt safe. Then the next thing I knew, I was waking up to the bright light of the sun; the darkness of night was gone. The spot under the porch became a routine secret escape place for my brother and me, and on one tense night, our mom.

"On this tense night, things between mom and dad made a turn for the worse. Dad came home super drunk, I mean he was violently drunk, yelling at our mom like never before. My brother and I looked out our bedroom doors to see what the commotion was about as we had done numerous times before. We were shocked and surprised to see dad strike mom. She fell on the floor next to their bed.

"We had never seen dad hit our mom, nor heard him say some of the awful and degrading things he was saying about her. He hit her again before going downstairs, sitting on the couch, and turning on the television. I figured he was catching his breath, but hoping he was remorseful about what he had just done to our mom. I knew that it was just a matter of time before he called me down to get my usual, and in his opinion, well-deserved spanking. My brother and I rushed out of our bedrooms to see about mom.

"As we passed by the stairs, we were relieved to hear dad snoring; he had fallen asleep on the couch, hopefully for a long time. My brother and I quietly ran into mom's bedroom to see if she was alright. He told her that there was somewhere we both wanted to take her where she would feel better.

"Mom looked at us with fear in her eyes and bruises on her face. She told us she couldn't go anywhere as long as dad was at home drunk. She was afraid that he would kill her if he found that she had left without letting him know. We told her dad was sleeping and that we all knew when he fell asleep, he would sleep for hours. Mom didn't know what to do, she was terrified, but we convinced her to come with us.

"Mom used to climb trees with us, so she climbed out of her bedroom window with us without a problem. My brother and I took her to the spot under the porch. She refused to go under until unexpectedly, we heard dad calling her name.

"Dad never woke up as soon as he did after falling asleep drunk. Mom was so afraid that her entire body trembled. My brother quickly and quietly removed the plywood covering from the opening under the porch. We helped our mom get inside, placing the plywood back over the opening to close us in.

"I peered through a fist-sized hole in the plywood my brother used to pull it over the opening. As I gazed through the hole at the clouds rolling through the blackness of the dark sky, I felt as though what I was seeing was telling me that this night was going to be the darkest night of our lives. We heard dad yelling from the couch for mom to come to him. Mom was so afraid that she started to crawl from under the porch and go to him, but changed her mind when she saw what he had in his hand when he came out of the house and off the porch.

"Standing directly in front of us as we were hiding undetected under the porch, dad yelled that he was going to give our mom something he should have given her a long time ago. When mom looked through the hole in the plywood covering the porch opening, she saw dad holding something in his hand. At first, she thought it was a beer bottle, but as he moved further into the moonlight, she told us he was holding a pistol. Mom began crying silently, but hysterically. I held my hand over her mouth so dad would not hear her. I kept it there until he went back inside, still yelling for her to come to him.

"After dad went back inside, and we could no longer hear him yelling for mom, we assumed he had fallen asleep again. I removed my hand from mom's mouth. My brother removed the plywood from the porch opening. Mom was well beyond afraid after seeing the pistol in dad's hand, so I took one of her hands, and my brother took the other; both of her hands were shaking. My brother encouraged her to calm down and let her imagination take her away from everything that was going on with dad.

"Pointing to the sky, my brother told mom to focus on the clouds that were rolling through the blackness of the night sky. He told her that we were going to ride on top of those clouds. Mom looked at the clouds, wiping tears from her eyes. My brother reminded her that every night before going to bed, especially those nights dad went off on her, the books she read to us put us to sleep, and we felt safe lying next to her.

"He told her we found an even safer escape place, and we wanted to invite her in. He instructed her to close her eyes and behold the darkness she was seeing. He told her to take a final listen to the noise she was hearing, assuring her that soon, it would all be gone. He told her to open up her imagination and fly away without wings on the clouds to a safe escape place, out of the darkness."

Mr. Wilson paused from telling his story, holding up the book he had taken out of his drawer saying, "This book right here is the book my brother wrote and would always read to me under that porch. It's also the one he read to our mom that helped her escape that night. We all experienced going to an imaginary escape place under that porch because of this book. It's not the original book, which was written in an eight-year-olds language, but my brother rewrote it after we turned eighteen years old. He gave it to me as a birthday present."

John asked Mr. Wilson, "It doesn't matter to me whether or not it's the original. I want to hear it. Do you mind reading it to us now? You said something about flying away to a secret escape place. I want to know how this book took you and your family to that secret place."

"Sure, I'll read it if you guys have time, but you'll have to be willing to take your imagination to the limit to understand how this book helped my brother, me, and our mom escape. You have to put yourself inside the book."

Victoria said, "For this, we'll make time. I'm good at letting my imagination run wild."

Mr. Wilson opened the book and began reading it exactly as his brother read it when they were under the porch with their mom.

"There was a family who was going through a financially difficult time in their lives. On a violently stormy night, they were on their way home from a meeting at which they were denied financial assistance. All of a sudden, they were trapped in their car by the storm. The storm picked up their car, spinning it and tossing it around and around until everyone inside of it was knocked unconscious.

"When they woke up, they noticed that they were high up in the sky, flying on top of a dark rain cloud. Darkness was all around them. When they looked down from on top of the cloud, they could see the rain pouring down out of the cloud and onto the ground below them. The dark cloud had taken them to safety above the rain and the storm. The darkness and rain reminded them of all the tears they had shed during the difficult times and dark stormy days in their lives.

"As they looked down from the cloud, they saw that the rain pouring from the dark cloud looked like teardrops. These imaginary teardrops were serving a purpose while they were falling. In the middle of all the darkness, the rain cloud the family was riding on above the storm was shedding good tears. They were tears of rain that had the smell of fresh rain that cools on hot summer days, waters the dry grass and thirsty flowers, and feeds the rivers and every living creature that drinks from them. They were valuable and necessary tears of rain.

"The dark cloud lifted them further away from the earth. The further they got away, the further they got away from the problems in the world and all the hardship in their lives. As they continued to move away, they realized that the cloud was carrying them to a safe place because they could see a glimpse of light deep on the other side of the dark sky, but they had to go through the rain and the darkness to get to the light. No wings were necessary to get there, nor was there anything holding them back; they could go as high as necessary to get to the light. If they got off or fell off the cloud, they would fall into the darkness surrounding them and never make it to the light.

"The dark cloud carried them closer and closer to the light until finally, the dark cloud was now white. There was no more darkness and no more rain or teardrops; the storm was over. The family was surrounded by nothing but sunshine. Looking behind them, they saw that the darkness had turned into a rainbow. They had just survived the greatest storm of their lives and came through it without a scratch. If it wasn't for the storm and rain in their lives, there wouldn't have been a cloud to take them above the storm into a place of safety. The storm, darkness, and the rain were the beginning of a new beginning."

After Mr. Wilson finished reading the book, closing it, he said to John and Victoria, "The same secret escape place where the family went in this book, and how they went, is the same escape place and the same way my brother, I, and my mom went on that night under the porch. For a long time, things were very dark around the house when dad was around. My mom, my brother, and I shed a lot of tears together. Under that porch, my brother led us into this book, and when we came out, we were safe."

John asked, "That's a very interesting book. What happened after you came out from under the porch?"

Mr. Wilson said, "I read the book to you as my brother read it from the beginning to the end, but what we discovered after we crawled out from under the porch and went into the house was the ending of a long history of abuse."

Mr. Wilson continued.

"When my brother finished reading the book under the porch, mom had fallen asleep with a smile on her face. We figured she was enjoying the imaginary flight and feeling free, so we left her alone. My brother and I ended up falling asleep under that porch as well. We all woke up the next morning to sunlight, no more darkness, nothing to fear.

"The sun was shining bright, but we were surprised to see dad's tractor-trailer still sitting where he usually parked it. We all thought that he should have gone to work already. I took mom's hand. It wasn't shaking like it was before her imagination flew her away to a safe escape place the night before. We crawled from under the porch and proceeded to go into the house, especially to see why dad was still home.

"Upon entering the house, I called dad's name, but he didn't answer. We searched the entire downstairs but saw no sign of him. We quietly went upstairs. I searched the bathroom which was across from the top of the stairs, but no dad. We went into mom and dad's bedroom and found dad, lying in bed, looking as though he was sleeping. We thought this was strange because he always slept on the couch. I figured that the only reason he could have been in bed was that he was waiting for mom.

"As we walked further into the room, mom loudly called his name, but he didn't respond. We all looked down, and the gun mom saw dad carrying while we were under the porch was lying on the floor on his side of the bed, so we immediately thought he committed suicide, but there was no blood.

"When we got closer to check dad out, we found that he was not breathing, he was deceased. Normally mom would have lost it, but I think that after all she had been through with him, especially after he had hit her the night before, she didn't know what to feel. But to me, she looked as though she was at peace. An autopsy was performed. It was determined that dad died of alcohol poisoning."

Victoria said, "Mr. Wilson, that's an incredible story." Mr. Wilson gave the book to John and said, "This book helped me, my brother, and my mom during the darkest moment of our lives. It helped us escape and fly away on a night we were facing danger and death, but, I don't need it anymore, I've replaced it with an even better book."

"Mr. Wilson, I can't take this book. It's sentimental to you, and means so much to you, are you sure about giving it away?"

"It's not about being sentimental anymore. It's about helping someone else escape. As I said, I have replaced that book with another book."

Mr. Wilson reached into his drawer and pulled out a Bible.

"Through every bad thing that happens in my life, this book right here has an answer and a way of escape, and it's not imaginary. When I open it up and search for what I need, I find a whole rainbow of truth that reminds me of God's justice in judging an abuser who never repents of it, and His mercy and grace in providing a way for the one being abused to be saved, free, and have the ability to look beyond every memory of abuse when those memories come to haunt him.

"In my opinion, on that night when my dad came looking for our mom with a gun, or maybe even my brother and I, that was a perfect and painful illustration of the dark cloud that overshadowed us for a long time. In that book my brother wrote, the cloud that lifted that family above the storm and took them to a safe place symbolized God taking us and protecting us under that porch. He extended His mercy and grace towards us on that dark and stormy night. In the end, dad's sin was judged. He paid a price for it, and justice was served.

"John, I know you are a Bible reading man, keep reading your Bible, but also make sure you read that book I gave you, I have a feeling they both will help you get to where you need to be. When you get done reading my brother's book, pass it on to someone else, just like I passed it on to you."

Mr. Wilson's story helped John see that when Carl walked out of his life, God was protecting him and Beverly from his abuse, just as he protected Mr. Wilson's family. God had His hand of grace and mercy on them. John thought it ironic that although his assignment was to listen to and document the story of Mr. Wilson, and help him if he needed it, Mr. Wilson helped him.

As John and Victoria were driving away from Mr. Wilson's home, John looked over at Victoria and noticed that tears were flowing down her face. He asked her, "I see Mr. Wilson's story had as much effect on you as it did on me."

"It did. His whole story and the book his brother wrote were very touching and an eye-opener of how it can be rainy and cloudy in our lives, but the rain is good and valuable because it sustains life even in the stormy dark times. God will always be there to sustain us and lift us above the storm and provide a way of escape.

"While Mr. Wilson was talking and reading, I was thinking about my husband and finding out the other day that he was going to need a few surgeries that are not covered by insurance. John, this surgery is going to cost thousands of dollars, and we don't have that kind of money. If he doesn't have this surgery within a year, he might not make it.

"Right now they're giving him medication until we can get the money together, but they can only do this for so long. Mr. Wilson's story gave me confidence that I will make it through this. It may be dark right now as I ride on this stormy cloud in this trying hour, but there's got to be a rainbow at the end of the storm. I'm going to do whatever it takes to get that money. There is no way I'm going to watch my husband die without a fight."

John reassured Victoria that everything would be alright and that he would do all he could do to work with her. He promised to help her get a good grade in their outreach ministry class, but that promise would be broken by some damaging hidden secrets.

CHAPTER 12
TRAPPED

While John was attending college, Angela learned more details about Beverly's heart problems. She learned that she had been diagnosed with coronary heart disease. Beverly continued to keep her diagnosis from John. From day one in college, John would call to check up on his mom and Angela at least once a week, but after a while, the calls stopped coming. Whenever he did call, Angela was tempted to tell him about Beverly's condition, but she would always remind herself of the promise she made to her to refrain from interfering with her faith in God.

Unfortunately, as Beverly's health was quickly fading, reluctantly, Angela felt she had an obligation to call John. Already concerned about Beverly, she was beginning to worry about John's well-being as she made numerous unsuccessful phone calls in her attempt to get in touch with him.

Frustrated, Angela said to herself, "I don't understand why he won't answer his phone or return my phone calls. Something must be wrong because this is not like John." Even after contacting the college administration and requesting that they give John a message to get in touch with her, she never received a return call from him.

Ever since Beverly returned home from staying with her friend Carmen, Angela faithfully checked on her every day on her way to work. On every visit, Beverly would always convince Angela to spend a little time with her sitting on the bench under the oak tree, sharing a cup of tea. Beverly loved sitting on the bench John placed there, surrounded by the groundcover she and he planted.

As they were sitting on the bench under the oak tree, Beverly asked Angela,

"What's going on with John? It's been a long time since I heard from him. It hurts that all of a sudden he's gotten so busy that he can't pick up the phone and check on his mom. That's something my son wouldn't do. I hope he's not beginning to follow in his father's footsteps who spent more time in that burned-down garage over there than with me. Every blackened piece of wood on that pile reminds me of all the dark and turbulent years I spent married to Carl."

On the night Carl left Beverly, she believed she would never see him again, but when she glanced at the burned-down garage, in her mind, Carl never left. She tried her best to avoid looking at the pile, but whenever she did, it was as though Carl was looking back at her with his intimidating eyes. To her, the garage was Carl. It was a representation of who he was, an expression of his wayward character, ideals, and controlling spirit.

Beverly said to Angela, "I keep forgetting to ask John if he knows anything about who burned that garage down. I never go near it and actually could care less about it because that was Carl's garage, his private man-cave. I never was allowed inside of it, but I am curious as to how it burned down."

Angela had a curious look on her face as well. "Whenever I do get in touch with John, I'll try to remember to ask him about the garage for you. I'm worried about him myself, I'm guessing he's busy with his college studies."

Even after Angela continued on her way to work, Beverly would spend hours on the bench, sipping her favorite blend of tea, talking to God, reminiscing about the good times she had spent with John, but also lamenting the humiliation and struggles she had suffered through with Carl.

One morning, as usual, Angela stopped by to check on Beverly. As she approached the house, she fought against the strong wind that was blowing, looking up, and noticing a butterfly struggling to stay in flight, then falling to the ground. Angela managed to make her way closer to the house and the oak tree in front of it, noticing many of the oak tree's leaves blowing off its branches and away into the wind. While all the other trees swayed against the fierce wind, she observed how the oak tree held its composure.

As she walked closer to the house, she was surprised to see Beverly, in the middle of the violent winds, sitting on the bench with her back facing her. Continuing to walk on the stepping stones leading to the bench where Beverly was sitting, she called out to her, "Beverly, Beverly, why are you out here in all of this?" Beverly didn't respond. "Beverly! Beverly!" Angela shouted.

When she arrived at where Beverly was sitting, she knew right away that something was wrong. Beverly sat lifeless and motionless, but with a smile on her face; she had passed away. Angela assumed it was due to her failing heart.

As Angela spent a final moment sitting down next to Beverly, the winds died down; there was complete calm and silence. Crying profusely, she lifted her head, looked over to Beverley, and observed how calm and at peace she looked. Angela managed to wipe the tears from her eyes, reaching over to the table to grab the empty teacup Beverly had sat out for her. After filling the cup with tea, she lifted it towards Beverly for a final toast, "After all you have been through, it's now time to rest."

On that bench sat Beverly, who left this life peacefully and content, unaware that directly across from her, entombed among ashes and blackened wood, was her husband Carl. He had abandoned her, and unlike her solemn departure, he violently left this life, unsatisfied.

After Angela made a final toast to Beverly, she noticed that the butterfly that had succumbed to the strong winds had fallen among the groundcover, but was now regaining its strength. After rising from the fresh green groundcover and then resting on Beverly's cold right hand, the butterfly flew over Angela's right shoulder and landed on the pile of charred garage rubble. It sat there for a moment, gracefully flapping its wings as if it was saying goodbye to Carl and his isolated and deceptive world on Beverly's behalf. The butterfly rose from on top of the blistered tomb and flew away into the sunlight.

Angela thought of how at one phase of its life as a caterpillar, the butterfly was trapped and isolated, yet protected until it gained enough strength to escape and lose its cocoon. The butterfly was trapped and isolated once again by the strong wind, but protected by the groundcover until it regained its strength to take flight again.

Angela had suffered a great loss with the death of Beverly. She learned a lot about Beverly's struggles and Carl's isolation from her. Watching the performance of the butterfly taught her a lesson about spiritual transformation, resurrection, endurance, and change.

Angela had a renewed hope that with God's protection, and a renewed mindset, she can endure and move on as did the butterfly when emerging from the shelter of its cocoon into adulthood, and now, from the groundcover that was in reality, its protection from the strong winds. To Angela, Beverly was like that butterfly, trapped and isolated in Carl's worldly cocoon; his prison. But while trapped and isolated, God was strengthening and protecting her for the moment of her passing on and resurrection to a newer and better life with Him.

Angela kept trying to contact John about Beverly's passing but was unsuccessful. She became so frustrated that she gave up trying to reach him.

John's college studies and the outreach ministry consumed so much of his time that he hadn't talked to his mom in weeks, and neither did he know about her passing. He was slowly keeping his sexual addiction under control. He was doing so well in his studies and the ministry that he was appointed associate pastor of the church on campus. Things were progressing fine until one failed client visit, one careless moment, things made a turn for the worse, and John would never recover from it.

John and Victoria were assigned a client named Tracy Torres, who had been abused by an alcoholic husband for years. Although she had been divorced for six months, she never talked to anyone about how he physically and emotionally abused her. Tracy was getting lonely and needed to talk to someone.

John and Victoria always followed campus rules, especially when it came to visiting a client. On some visits, Victoria would hitch a ride with John, and on other visits, she would give him a ride. They would always go on visits together as they were instructed to do.

John arrived at Victoria's apartment to pick her up to visit Tracy. He walked up to her door and rang the doorbell, but no one answered. He could hear her ill husband's weak voice calling for her to answer the doorbell, but was unsuccessful.

John was beginning to get worried because Victoria's car was still in the driveway. He figured that since it was about noon, she had to have gotten out of bed already. He said to himself, "Maybe she's busy taking care of her husband and can't come to the door, but then again, she could call to let me know she was home."

He decided to call her cell phone just in case she had it sitting next to her. As he was dialing her number, he received a phone call. His caller I.D. read, "Victoria."

John answered the phone. Before Victoria could get a word out, he said to her, "Victoria, where are you, what are you doing? We are due at a client's house in a half-hour, hurry up and come on out."

Victoria said, "I'm sorry, I was knocked out. We have to cancel this one. My husband is getting sicker, and I was up all night taking care of him, and I'm exhausted. On top of that, I must have eaten some spoiled food last night; I feel terrible. I took some medicine that knocked me out big time."

"Victoria, this is going to affect our grade. You have to find the strength to go."

"John, don't worry about our grade. It'll be alright. If I report that I was sick, that would be considered an excused absence. We can make it up. Sorry John, with my husband being sick and myself not feeling well, I need to take this day to rest and figure things out. I need to seriously think about where I'm going to get the money to pay for his surgery and medical bills. I don't feel like talking to anyone right now. Can you call our professor and explain everything to him."

"Okay Victoria, I'll call him. I think this client is one we need to see. Get some rest, and hopefully, you'll be up to visiting her tomorrow."

John slowly walked back to his car. When he got inside, he glanced at the profile folder of Tracy. After carefully looking at her file, he became desperate to talk with her because her situation reminded him of his mom. He thought that he needed to hear her story and possibly help her get over her loneliness.

He managed to convince himself that he was going to go ahead and visit her without Victoria, breaking a major outreach ministry rule that visitations must be made in groups of two's. John called their professor as Victoria requested, but instead of telling him Victoria had come down ill and they were canceling the visit, he told him that he and Victoria were on their way to visit Tracy.

The professor said, "I want you to know that you and Victoria are two of the best students I have had in my class in a long time. I wish you both well on your visit."

When John hung up the phone, a feeling of guilt came over him that he was about to do something wrong. He also had a gut feeling that something wrong was going to come out of this visit, but he ignored his convictions and gut feelings, letting his desperation take over.

As he drove into Tracy's driveway, he had to do a double-take as he observed a woman, maybe Tracy, looking out the curtains in the front room window in a revealing short robe. At that moment, his conscience was telling him to leave, but he had a strong desire to talk to her and possibly help her, maybe his sexual addiction was driving him to stay as well.

As he walked up the sidewalk and after reaching the front door, all of a sudden the door opened and the woman whom he had seen in the front window greeted him on the porch wearing the short robe. From looking out the window, she observed that John was alone. She gave him a hug that he thought was too close for comfort. She introduced herself as Tracy Torres while holding him tightly in her arms, but he managed to break free, and unfortunately, he continued to break away from the truth.

"Hello Tracy, my name is John Forester. I'm from the university outreach ministry. I'm here to document your story. Looks like you live in a quiet neighborhood."

"Well John, looks are deceiving. I don't know if you watch the news, but people are on edge around here. Some guy is breaking into homes, and the police have no clue as to who it might be. He broke into a couple's home up the street and they were at home at the time. He didn't leave without robbing them and pistol-whipping the husband. Well, anyway, sooner or later they'll catch him. Where's your partner? When they scheduled this visit they told me that there would be two of you coming?"

"Usually there are two of us, but my partner is sick and this visit is so important to us that they gave me permission to come alone. Tracy seductively replied, "Well, come on inside John, this should be an interesting visit for me and you."

Once again, something was tugging at John from the inside to turn around and leave, but because of a strong desire to hear Tracy's story, and being attracted to how seductive she was dressed, he ignored the warning signs and decided to stay. As they both sat next to each other on her couch, Tracy moved up closer to him, crying as she began telling her story of being abused and also how lonely she was. As she was talking, she abruptly stopped.

"I shouldn't be telling you this, I'm getting too personal. I made a mistake asking you to come here."

John took her by the hand and exposed some things about himself he would later wish he never did.

"Don't be ashamed. You didn't make a mistake. This visit is all about sharing your personal feelings. You may be hurting on the inside, but many women and men have experienced what you have experienced, including me. "I don't talk about my abuse often, but there aren't many people who know that I was isolated and emotionally abused by my dad when I was growing up. There are also many, including my partner Victoria, who are unaware of my sexual addiction I blame on my dad. Abuse comes in many forms.

"My dad isolated me, and that's a form of emotional abuse. He chose to isolate himself in his garage rather than do the things with me a dad usually does with his son, and that in itself created a curiosity inside of me. I wanted to know what my dad was doing in his garage that was more important than me.

"Even though I'm an associate pastor, I'm still having a problem dealing with my sexual addiction. Ever since that day I stumbled upon my dad's library of sexually explicit magazines and videos in his garage, I have been fighting a strong addiction to viewing explicit photos of women myself. To this day, I regret the day I walked into that garage. As a result of my isolation from my dad, I was curious as to what he was doing in that garage that fueled the isolation. Because of my curiosity, I came out of that garage with a major addiction. Between my dad isolating me, and in an indirect way, introducing me to pornography, you can say I got a double portion of his abuse."

John hadn't let go of Tracy's hand when she moved closer to him, then took her free hand and began rubbing his hand to comfort him because of what he had just shared with her. Considering how she was dressed and how close she had gotten to him, John was beginning to feel uneasy.

In an attempt to change the increasingly emotional and seductive atmosphere, John pulled his hand away from Tracy to remove two outreach cards out of his wallet. He laid them on a table that was in front of him and said, "Before I forget, here is my card and my partner's card, they have our contact information on them. If you want to call, send a text message, or email either one of us at any time, the information is on these cards."

The cards contained both John's and Victoria's emails, phone numbers, and addresses.

John was feeling very uncomfortable, so he asked Tracy, "Is there any way I could have a glass of water? I'm not feeling well right now."

Tracy said, "Sure, hold on. I'll get it for you."

As John sat waiting on his glass of water, he thought to himself, "I went too far telling a stranger all my secret issues and struggles. There was no reason for me to tell her about my sexual addiction. This visit was supposed to be about her abuse, not my addiction. What in the world was I thinking?"

When Tracy returned with the glass of water, John was shocked to see her sit down in front of him braless and with the top of her robe pulled down to her waist. At that moment, he discerned that he had sent her the wrong message after discussing his sexual addiction with her, or she had ulterior motives of a sexual nature all along.

He quickly rose to his feet and said, "I'm sorry if I sent you the wrong message, I'm not feeling well right now. I'm going to have to leave. I should not have come here alone. I really shouldn't be here."

Tracy became irate. Standing up to pull the top of her robe back over her shoulders, she angrily condemned John.

"You know exactly why you came here. You lied about being granted permission to come here alone. You have a sexual addiction that you wanted me to satisfy. How dare you come into my home and take advantage of my loneliness and vulnerability. You give me this sad story about enjoying looking at naked women while undressing me with your eyes, forcing me to expose myself, and now you want to get up and leave. To me, that's abuse, that's a type of emotional abuse that is just as bad as my former husband's physical abuse."

Tracy ran to the door, opened it, and said to John, "Get out of my house. You're the one who is sick and needs help, not me. There's no way I'm going to let you get away with this, you can count on that. You're going to pay a high price for what you did to me. Get out of my house right now and don't ever come back here again, you haven't heard the last from me."

John ran out of Tracy's house. He heard the door slam behind him and Tracy crying on the other side. He continued to run to his car, getting in and driving away. A block down the road he pulled over to the side of the road, stunned at what had just taken place.

Guilt and shame came over him as he sat parked and asked himself over and over again, "What has gotten into me? Why did I do this? I'm an associate pastor. Why did I lie to my professor? As soon as I saw Tracy dressed as she was in that front window, why didn't I turn around and leave? Why did I find myself inside her home? Did I want to hear Tracy's story or was this a trap my sexual addiction lured me into?"

John attempted to keep his visit with Tracy a secret, but Tracy had other plans.

CHAPTER 13
ONE MOMENT OF PLEASURE

After John left Tracy, she sat down on the couch, angry and wanting revenge for what she perceived as John trying to seduce her. Later that evening, she pulled out Victoria's card John had given her and called her. When Victoria answered, Tracy introduced herself.

"Hello, Victoria, my name is Tracy Torres. I'm the client your partner visited today. I hope you're feeling better, but I think you need to know about his sexual addiction."

Victoria was caught off guard. "I don't understand. You said you were visited by my partner, what was his name? How did you get my number?"

"He said his name was John Forester. Before he left or practically ran away, he gave me his contact card and your contact card."

"Ran away? What reason would he have to run away? And what is this about a sexual addiction? Why would he share something like that with you that he hasn't shared with me?"

"When he rang the doorbell, I had just gotten out of the shower and had my robe on. The visit started innocent enough. When we sat down, and I began talking about my abusive history, he changed the subject and began talking about how he was abused as a child."

Victoria was floored at what Tracy was revealing to her about John. "John talked to you about being abused?"

"Yes, He told me that he was abused by his dad who isolated him and because of that isolation, he became curious as to why his dad wasn't spending as much time with him as he was in his garage. He said his curiosity introduced him to his dad's sexually explicit magazines stored in the garage and from that day up until now, he still enjoys looking at sexually explicit images.

"While he was talking to me, he grabbed my hand and began saying seductive things to me that made me feel uncomfortable. I made up an excuse to get away from him by saying I needed a glass of water. As I was getting up, the top of my robe opened up accidentally, exposing me to him. I must have made him feel uneasy, so he quickly left. As he was leaving, I told him he was going to pay a high price for coming into my home, trying to seduce me."

Victoria was perplexed at what Tracy said John shared with her, yet troubled and angry. She lashed out at Tracy.

"Obviously, if you know I was sick, John did visit you. What I don't know is whether there is truth to your story. This just doesn't sound like the John I know. Women like you who falsely accuse men who are reaching out to help are the very reason why we visit in two's. John's not only a partner, but he's also a friend. If there is any truth to what you are saying, I'll get to the bottom of it."

Victoria hung up the phone and leaned back in her chair with all sorts of opinions about John bombarding her mind. She said to herself, "John knows the rules, why would he go into this woman's home alone? He knows better. What is all this stuff about a sexual addiction? He never shared anything like that with me, but tells it to a stranger. I don't know if this woman is lying or not, but if she is being truthful, this is a game-changer."

John arrived at his apartment and proceeded to check his email on his computer. He noticed that there was an email from Tracy. Assuming she was emailing him to apologize for what had taken place during his bazaar visit or to reschedule another less seductive visit, he opened up the email.

The email read, "John, I'm sorry for how I reacted during your visit. At first, I felt terrible about exposing myself to you, but the more I thought about it, the more I realized that you enjoyed looking at me as much as you enjoy looking at those women in those sexually explicit magazines. I wish we could have gotten to know each other, maybe we will. Please call me. And by the way, I've attached a link to a web page you will enjoy before our next meeting. Again, sorry."

John was curious about the sudden change in Tracy's attitude. As he was running from her home, the last words she said to him sounded like she was going to ruin his life. He had a strange feeling that she sent him something inappropriate to view. His eyes were fixed on the link to the webpage. He was tempted to click on it, but something inside of him said, "No, don't do it, don't click on it, you'll regret the day you ever did." He closed his email, then went to bed.

The next morning, John figured that before things got out of hand with Tracy, he was going to email her to tell her that if she didn't want another appointment, stop emailing him. When he opened up his email, there were at least ten more emails with links to web pages from Tracy. One of the emails said, "I can't show you everything, but let your imagination run wild about what you could have."

The temptation to click on the links became greater the longer John sat there indecisive as to whether or not he should click on them. He said to himself, "Maybe I'm exaggerating this whole thing. Maybe these links are not what I think they are. I'll click on one and see what it is that Tracy wants me to see."

John clicked on one of the links, and sure enough, as he has suspected, the web page contained a sexually explicit image of a woman, but the woman was not Tracy. He wanted to close the page, but his sexual addiction wouldn't allow him to do it. He sat staring at the image for a long time, just as he did when he found those sexually explicit magazines in his dad's garage. Before he knew it, he had opened up all the emails from Tracy and clicked on the webpage links viewing every one of the sexually explicit images; again, none of the images were of Tracy.

Up until now, John believed he was conquering his sexual addiction, but Tracy's emails and links proved he was far from it. After what little progress he had made climbing out of a pit that was drowning him in sexual temptation, all it took was one moment of disobedience, and one moment of pleasure to knock him off balance, causing him to fall back into a dark and lonely place of immorality.

John's addiction began to affect his effectiveness in his outreach ministry class and his work as an associate pastor. While visiting a client who was struggling with a drug addiction, Victoria became concerned about how he was addressing the client. There was something different. Something was missing. It seemed as though John was angry and bitter about something. She wondered if it had something to do with the phone call she received from Tracy about his visit.

After leaving their visitation with the client, John dropped Victoria off at her apartment. She sat down on her couch, still concerned about John and also how their meetings with clients were not as effective as they had been. She called him, asking him to meet her to talk. He said, "I have a few things to wrap up, and then I'll meet you at the coffee shop in fifteen minutes."

Victoria hung up the phone and said to herself, "There's just something different about him. He's changed, I can feel it."

Victoria was waiting for John at the coffee shop when he decided to check his emails before heading out to meet her. He figured it wouldn't take long, but he was shocked to find at least twenty new emails from Tracy. Once again, he couldn't resist opening them up, reading them, and clicking on the links to web pages full of sexually explicit images. He began wondering why none of the images were of Tracy. But that thought quickly went away as he became consumed in looking at all the images she had sent him; it didn't matter to him who the women were, he was enjoying what he was seeing.

About an hour later, John was shocked to see how much time had passed. He closed the sexually explicit web pages and said to himself, "I can't keep doing this. I need to fight this. What will people on campus and at the church think if they find out their associate pastor was viewing sexually explicit images?"

He sent Tracy an email, hoping to put an end to everything once and for all.

"Beginning tonight, all of this is over. Stop sending emails and links. This is harassment and it needs to stop. I won't allow you to take advantage of me anymore."

John rushed out of his apartment to meet Victoria at the coffee shop, hoping she was still there. He walked into the coffee shop, relieved that Victoria was still sitting at her table. He could see the frustration as well as a look of concern on her face as he sat down at the table where she was sitting. Angry, she said to him, "You said fifteen minutes, and it's been over an hour. Where were you? What were you doing?"

John made up a lie.

"I'm sorry. I was finishing documenting our last visit. It took longer than I thought it would take. I'm sorry for keeping you waiting."

Victoria didn't hold back on what she had to say to John. "Documentation never takes longer than fifteen or twenty minutes. Anyway, something is going on with you, and I have a feeling that it's not a good thing. I have always admired your gift of ministering to clients in such a way that they are not afraid to open up to you. You have a way of getting them to share their stories with us, and by the time we leave them, they feel inspired and encouraged.

"Lately, none of that has happened. During our last visit, I was confused. The client was upset at some of the things you were telling him. It was as if you were blaming him for his drug addiction, and that was not like you. Somewhere along the line, and for some reason, you have lost your effectiveness. You try to force it out, but it's just not the same."

Victoria also confronted John about the phone call she received from Tracy.

"There's something else I need to ask you. Who is Tracy Torres?"

Pretending he never heard the name he asked, "Tracy Torres, I have no idea who she is. Should I know who she is?"

"That's something I think you should know because this woman who calls herself Tracy Torres had my phone number. She called me and said she was a client you visited and you talked to her about a sexual addiction you have. She also said you tried to seduce her and when she resisted, you ran out of the house, got into your car, and drove off. John, is this woman telling the truth? Why did you go against campus rules and into this woman's home without me? I know you did go there because she knew I was sick that day."

"Alright Victoria, I did go to her house. There was a personal reason why I went, but the part about me telling her about a sexual addiction and seducing her is entirely false; the seducing came from her, not me."

"John, I don't know whether to believe you or not. You sat here and lied about even knowing this woman. Why would I believe you now?

Whatever the truth may be, you and I both know that you shouldn't have gone to Tracy's home alone. Based upon what she said took place between you and her, that's the very reason why we don't go alone."

"I know I did go against the rules, but I felt I needed to talk to Tracy because I wanted to hear her story. Since the meeting was about her being abused by her husband, I did share with her how I was physically abused as a child, which I know I should not have done; and that was it.

"I never shared anything about a sexual addiction. Things got out of hand after she said she was lonely. She exposed herself and tried to seduce me, that's when I pretended to be ill, and then I actually ran out of her house and drove away, and that's the truth."

Victoria, with a dilemma on her hands said, "I pray that you are telling the truth."

Even John himself knew he had been feeling out of touch with his clients lately. He also knew he wasn't candid with Victoria about Tracy. Only he knew why he exposed his addiction to Tracy but hadn't exposed it to Victoria. What should have been a confession from John ended up being a verbal attack on Victoria.

"I'm surprised at what you are accusing me of. Victoria, you're supposed to be my friend. Of all people, you waste my time with false perceptions. If we are going to work together, you need to get your act together."

After scolding Victoria in front of a room full of customers, John stormed out of the coffee shop, leaving Victoria embarrassed and less concerned about him than she was before the meeting. What he had just said to her confirmed her suspicions about him; he was falling apart from the inside out, he was not himself, and at that moment, she didn't care.

"I respected him as a friend and as an associate pastor. He sat there and lied about knowing Tracy. Then he has the nerve to criticize me and embarrass me, and then walk out the door saying I need to get my act together. For some reason, I don't believe he's being totally honest about himself and Tracy, and that may be the reason why he has lost his effectiveness in ministry.

"That's it. I've had enough. What just happened was more than enough for me to handle while trying to deal with a sick husband and all the other things that are going wrong in my life. Tomorrow, I'm going to ask to be teamed up with another outreach partner. This friendship with John is over. I can't risk failing the class because of his lies. I'm just too close to graduation to let that happen."

Later that night, John walked into his apartment, laid down on his bed, and began thinking about his meeting in the coffee shop with Victoria, trying to justify what he said to her. Did his lie calm her suspicions? Deep inside, he knew every harsh word he said to her was not right. John dozed off. When he woke up the next morning, he decided to check his email. There was only one new email, and it was from Tracy.

He had no desire to open up the email Tracy sent him. He had heard enough from her, and at that time, seen more than enough sexually explicit images, and he didn't want to see anymore. He proceeded to shut down his computer when he thought, "Maybe she's responding to the email I wrote yesterday demanding that she leave me alone. Maybe this is her last email."

John opened up the email, and when he did, there were no links to sexually explicit web pages. There was only one line in the email that read, "It's not over until I say it's over. I told you that you were going to pay a price, and you will." John immediately knew that this wasn't good at all.

When he arrived at the university that morning, the dean of the university, the senior pastor of the campus church, and his outreach ministry class professor were waiting for him in the entryway. The dean said to him, "John, we all want to have a meeting with you in my office about some serious accusations against you and Victoria."

As John followed them towards the dean's office, he tried to figure out what type of accusations there could be against him and Victoria. He kept wondering, but before arriving at the dean's office he concluded, "Tracy Torres, she's got to be behind all of this."

When they all entered the dean's office, John took a glance at Victoria sitting in a chair in front of the dean's desk, recalling that their last meeting didn't go well; then he looked away from her. Everyone sat down. John sat in a pre-arranged chair for him that was sitting next to Victoria. She looked at him with a confused, but angry look on her face. The last meeting she had with him confirmed her suspicions about him falling apart and not being himself. Was this meeting going to do so as well?

The dean proceeded to explain why John and Victoria were brought into the office together.

"John, we received word that you unofficially visited a female client named Tracy Torres. She visited my office yesterday. During this visit, she made an official complaint stating that during your visit to her home, you were very disrespectful to her. She said that when she tried to open up to you about her abusive husband, for some unknown reason, you refused to listen and made the conversation more about you than her. She wouldn't say what personal information you shared with her, but you are very aware that sharing your personal information with clients is against the rules. She said that during the small conversation she did have with you, she felt uncomfortable because you looked at her seductively.

"Victoria, Tracy also said that when she called you about what happened, you failed to address the issue with your professor. She has made it clear that she doesn't want anything to do with the campus church or its outreach ministry, and that she was going to discourage everyone she meets from having anyone on our outreach team enter into their homes."

Victoria broke down in tears as she gave John a death stare. She turned to the dean and professor crying, "I am in the dark about this whole thing. I don't know for sure what happened between John and Tracy, but on that particular day John visited her, I was sick. Professor, I asked John to call you and inform you that I could not visit Tracy because I didn't feel well. Evidently, for some reason, he went on his own. Whatever happened at that woman's home is on him, not me."

The professor asked John, "This disappoints me. I had so much faith in you and Victoria. Why did you break the rules and go to Mrs. Torres's home alone?"

John answered, "There was a reason why I decided to go alone, but how Tracy explained everything that happened in her home was not true."

John's senior pastor said, "John, whether Mrs. Torres lied or not is one issue, but being an associate pastor, knowing that there is no tolerance for a scandal is another. There are protocols set in place to prevent something like this from happening. You violated those protocols. The foolish and selfish decisions you've made have brought a black mark against the campus church and dampened the hopes of your classmate sitting in this room."

Victoria asked the pastor, "What do you mean?"

The pastor looked in the dean's direction and said, "I'll let the dean respond to that question."

Victoria asked the dean, "What does he mean dampened my hopes?"

The dean said, "First of all, it is important that this matter is dealt with swiftly so that no more condemnation can be brought against the school or the campus church. And second, Victoria, campus guidelines require that all absentees be reported by the absentee and no one else. Because you failed to do so, and the turmoil that has resulted because of your negligence, we are pulling you out of our outreach ministry program and placing you on a one-year suspension from the university. You are asked to gather all your belongings. You will not be allowed on campus during your one-year suspension."

"A year off! Are you seriously suspending me for a whole year? I'm so close to graduating, and you're suspending me for a year! This is not fair. How could you make me out to be the cause of all of this? Just forget it all. Because of your lack of sound judgment and stupid rules, I have no interest in coming back to this university."

Victoria directed her anger at John.

"And as for you, liar and fake friend, I knew something was not right with you. I know you are hiding something, and believe me, I know what it is. Everything I have accomplished, you have destroyed. You have set my ill husband and me back big time.

"I have done nothing wrong to deserve this. Well, I guess I was wrong for trusting you. I'm not going to let you get away with this. And to think I had faith in you. Just remember, you reap what you sow."

With that being said, Victoria walked out of the dean's office, slamming the door shut on her way out.

The dean looked at John and said, "What you have done is a serious offense that has greatly affected your goal in life as well as Victoria's. You have not upheld the standard of an associate pastor and model student. Your actions and apparent secrets have damaged this university and its pristine image. You were a great asset to this university, but now, you're a liability. As a result, you are no longer considered an associate pastor of this university, and you have been expelled, effective immediately. You will never be allowed to step foot on this campus again."

John addressed the dean, pastor, and professor.

"I'm sorry for what I have done out of poor judgment. I accept the decision you all have made and hold no bitterness inside towards you."

Standing up to leave and walking up to the professor, John said, "Thanks for the opportunity to help those who I have enjoyed helping. I abused the rules and guidelines of this university and the commands of God that I taught my clients to uphold. You have taught me a lot during the time I have studied under you."

Before leaving, John said to the dean, "Before I boarded my flight headed here, my mom asked me to make her proud. Only she would understand it when I say, "I failed to hit a home run for the team."

John exited the dean's office, packed his belongings, and for the last time, drove down the main college campus road lined with perfectly trimmed hedges on both sides. He was kicked off the college campus because he failed to kick his sexual addiction. The long drive away from the campus gave John plenty of time to think about how quickly life can take a turn for the worse.

CHAPTER 14
SECLUSION

John thought about his unsuccessful attempts to overcome his addiction, his unproductive college career, and most importantly, his failure as an associate pastor. Sadly, in his fabricated opinion, Tracy added fuel to the fire and was to blame for his downfall. He was fuming about her taking advantage of his addiction and her revengeful actions, and he wanted revenge. John had a feeling that Tracy would continue to haunt him like a plague, so he decided to use a radical and un-Christian method to deal with this plague.

It was getting dark when John stopped at a home improvement store to purchase items needed to carry out his devious plan. He continued towards his destination, rage building up inside of him with every mile driven. Like an enraged psychopath, he was unstable, preparing to do the unexpected.

John had brought his sexual addition to the college campus, but in his distorted and anger-filled perception, he was going to put an end to where he believed his downfall began; Tracy's house. The rage inside of him escalated to such an unbelievable and insane level that somewhere between leaving the college campus and getting close to Tracy's house, the real John was gone. A madman had taken the wheel, and he was on a devilish mission, trying to convince himself that he was doing the right thing.

"I need to do this. It's the only way to stop this mad woman from destroying my life. This is the right time to do what I have no other choice to do. I have to make this look like the man who has been terrorizing this neighborhood is the culprit. Yes, that's what they will believe, they'll never trace this to me. All I need to do is get the job done, clean and quick."

In the darkness of night, John turned off his headlights, stopping a block up the road from Tracy's residence. After getting out of the car and grabbing the items he had brought from the home improvement store, John carefully closed his car door, trying not to make a sound.

As he crept cautiously towards Tracy's house, he noticed a shadow against an old and shabby fence that separated her backyard from a wooded area that stretched at least a half-mile.

Dressed in all black, face covered with a black ski mask, John slid along the side of the house and towards the backyard. When he managed to get a closer view, he noticed that the shadow he had previously seen was from Tracy; she was taking out the garbage before going to bed. He planned to find some way to break into her house, but seeing her outside he said to himself, "This is going to be easier than I thought."

John, crouching like a desperate black cat on the prowl in the darkness of a peaceful night, turned the corner to walk towards Tracy. She didn't notice him approaching until his right foot snapped a large twig that was lying on the ground. Tracy turned around quickly, startled at the sight of a mysterious man concealed in black from head to toe, blocking the doorway into her house.

Tracy trembled at the sight of his hand holding a knife that revealed its sharpness against the moonlight. She immediately began to think that this might be the man who had broken into several homes in the neighborhood. She also asked herself why she went out at night, knowing this hardened criminal was committing his crimes on a nightly basis.

John saw terror in Tracy's eyes, a terror that reached down into the depths of her lungs that prevented her from saying anything or letting out a scream for help. As John ran towards her to execute his mission of assassination, Tracy turned towards the broken-down fence and ran barefoot into the dark woods; she didn't dare look back. John ran after her, but she was more familiar with the woods than he was, so she was able to put a fair amount of distance between them.

Fifteen minutes had passed, but to Tracy, it seemed like an hour as she continued her escape, trying to get to the other side of the woods. She periodically looked behind her, watching and listening out for any sign of her attacker. Her legs began to weaken and her feet began to bleed from stepping on the twigs and leaves that blanketed the floor of the woods. Then, all of a sudden, she lost her balance and fell to the ground.

Tracy managed to crawl and hide behind a large tree, silently crying as she prayed for God's help.

"Please God, why is this happening to me? I feel like a trapped animal, never imagining I would be out here all alone, hunted by a crazy maniac. I know I don't pray to you much because I feel I'm unworthy to talk to you. I know I have done so many bad things in my life that I deserve your condemnation. Please help me God. I'm begging for your help, even though I don't deserve it. If you get me out of this, I'll change; I promise I will."

Tracy peered from behind the tree where she was hiding to see if anyone was around. She put her hand over her mouth trying not to make a sound but was also afraid that the loud beat of fear from her heart would expose her hiding place. Seeing no one around, she proceeded to emerge from her place of safety until she heard the sound of footsteps pressing against the fallen twigs and leaves. She retreated into a large cluster of dense foliage, grabbing a thick piece of a fallen tree branch, just in case she needed it as a weapon.

John paused his pursuit only a few feet away from Tracy, exhausted and sweating from the ski mask that shrouded his face. He removed the mask to take advantage of the night's cool fresh air before continuing his hunt. In his mind, there was no going back, he had to find Tracy.

Tracy attempted to get a glimpse of her stalker's face but was unsuccessful because his back was turned away from her. With all the strength that was left inside of her, she threw the branch she had found away from where she was hiding in a desperate effort to throw John off course. The sound of the branch snapping twigs off other dead trees as it flew through the woods accomplished its purpose as John bolted towards the noise. When he was out of sight, Tracy stood and dashed as fast as she could towards her house, focused only on getting inside to call the police.

As she continued to run, she could see a faint glow of the backdoor light of her house signaling that she was getting close to a place of safety on what had become the darkest night of her life. Just as she did earlier in the night, Tracy threw herself through the opening of the run-down fence. When she reached her back door, with her hand trembling, she turned the knob on the door, discovering that she had locked herself out when taking the garbage out to her trash bin.

Although she didn't want to draw her assailant's attention to the house, Tracy had no other choice but to find something strong enough to break a window if she was going to get inside the house. After retrieving a fist-sized rock she had been using in her landscaping, Tracy used it to break a window. After entering, hands still trembling, she proceeded to lock all her doors and windows and grab her cell phone to call the police.

John was at the edge of the woods when he heard the sound of shattering glass echoing through the woods. Concluding that the sound had come from where Tracy's home was located, he figured she had doubled back towards the house. Rage and anger distorted his face as he felt that once again, Tracy had deceived him. He gave up the chase, running to where his car was parked, believing that if Tracy made it back to the house, she surely would have called the police.

John reluctantly left the potential crime scene, pulling over onto a country road two miles away, torn between two emotions.

"God, what has come over me? What in the world am I doing out here? This is not like me. Today has been the worst day of my life. In an attempt to keep my addiction a secret, I can't believe I have stooped so low as to not only have the thought of killing someone enter my mind, but also find myself carrying out that thought, and enjoying it at the time.

"I believed Tracy should die for making my life miserable, and I'm sorry, but I still do. I know you can help me escape all of this, but right now, I don't even know what to pray because I don't even know what I'm feeling right now." John pulled back onto the road, unsatisfied, mentally paralyzed, and emotionally drained.

Meanwhile, Tracy was terrified and also emotionally torn, waiting for the police to arrive. After walking up the stairs and into her bedroom to check the last window that needed to be secured, she stood, resting her head on the right side of the window frame, breathing a sigh of relief that she made it out of the woods alive. She trained her eyes on the fence and woods, praying that her stalker would not emerge.

Nervous and trying to figure out what she would do if her attacker made his way into her house, Tracy noticed flashes of light against the fence. She heard a loud knock on her front door; then the deep voice of a police officer announcing his arrival. The night of terror was finally over without Tracy knowing that it was John who had stalked her and brought her to the brink of death. She made a promise to God during her ordeal, a promise that would only prove to be desperate words, with no action.

A few months after terrorizing Tracy, John hit rock bottom. After being kicked out of the university and no longer receiving a salary as an associate pastor, John's funds quickly dried up. Behind in his rent, facing eviction, and still reeling from being banned from the university, and his failed assassination attempt on Tracy's life, he fell into a state of depression and unfortunately, deeper into his sexual addiction. His struggles and the emotional breakdown of living an addicted life were taking their toll on him, leaving him to resort to locking himself in his apartment and avoiding any contact with the outside world.

While in seclusion, the only satisfaction John found was in a stack of sexually explicit magazines that were hidden under his mattress. He would take breaks to eat and go to the restroom; then it was back to sitting on the bed, flipping through the magazines, and then falling asleep. He would wake up in the mornings and sit on the side of his bed depressed and lonely, thinking of all the mistakes he had made, the friends he lost, how disappointed his mom was going to be in him, and most importantly, how he failed God.

One morning, John woke up and pulled up a chair to sit at his window. His mind took him back to the days when he would sit at his bedroom window in his boyhood home, observing the oak tree outside.

He thought about how large the tree was and how it would always capture his imagination, taking him away from all the turmoil that surrounded his family. He often wondered how old the tree was, and how it was able to survive all kinds of adversity, towering as a symbol of strength and authority.

After getting up and stepping away from the window and out of his imagination, John felt a renewed strength as that of an oak tree, and a determination to take authority over his addiction. He decided that it was time to leave his cave of self-pity, spending the next two weeks planning and preparing to start an outreach ministry.

Stepping out to check his mail, John noticed an eviction notice had been posted on his door weeks ago. According to the notice, he had two days to move out. While John was sitting on his bed, trying to figure out his next move, his cell phone rang and his caller I.D. read, "Angela."

There was excitement in his voice when he answered the phone. "Angela! Angela! It's been so long since we talked. How are you doing?" "I'm fine John. It's so nice to hear your voice."

John asked, "How are things going back home? How is my mom doing? Things have been crazy down here. It's been a while since I've had a chance to talk to her."

"John, that's why I called you. Your mom and I got real close after you left. I've been trying to reach you, but you didn't return my calls. We were worried about you. Why did you stop calling your mom? Why didn't you call me back?"

"I know I should have returned your calls Angela, but things have really been crazy and moving fast down here. My studies and some personal problems have kept me busy."

"John, I'm sorry to hear that, but I have some sad news to tell you. I've been hurting on the inside for a couple of weeks."

"Hurting? Why? Angela, what's going on?"

"One morning when I went to check on your mom, I called out to her and she didn't respond. When I walked up to her, I discovered that she had passed away. The spot where I found her was the perfect place to spend the last moments of her life."

"Angela, what do you mean passed away? All of a sudden she passed away? From what? I didn't know she was sick. I've been so caught up in myself that I stopped calling to check up on her, and you. I feel so selfish and irresponsible. I should have been there. My heart is hurting right now. Where was she when you found her?"

"John, your mom had been sick with heart disease for a long time. She didn't want to tell you about it because she knew it would affect your decision to leave for college. I tried numerous times to call and tell you about her illness, but as I said, you didn't return my calls.

"Whenever I would visit your mom, I would always find her sitting on that bench you placed under the oak tree in front of your house. She found it to be a place to escape and find some peace. That's where I found her. We would sit on that bench drinking her favorite tea together.

"Your mom was sitting on that bench surrounded by her favorite groundcover the both of you planted around the tree, looking as though she died peacefully. I will miss her; she was in pain for a long time. You would think it makes it easier to deal with her passing away, knowing that she doesn't have to suffer any longer, but it doesn't. John, in my attempts to reach you, I called the university. After I called them for the second time, they said you were no longer enrolled. I'm sorry about your mom, but what's going on with you? What happened with school? You were so close to graduation. Did you drop out?"

There was a brief silence during which Angela heard John softly crying. After about a minute, he couldn't hold back any longer as he began crying loudly.

"Angela, I need some time alone for a moment. I'll call you back."

John hung up the phone and fell to the floor, violently pounding on it with both fists as a flood of grief and guilt engulfed him. He began thinking about his mom, the one person in his life who loved him unconditionally. His mom was always there to fill the void of an absent dad, but now, no one could fill an even greater void within him that the death of his mom hollowed out.

"I knew something was wrong with mom before I left. I shouldn't have left her. I feel so broken, empty, and torn apart because the most instrumental person who inspired me and kept me together has been snatched away. I'm in shock and afraid that I may never be the same because she was my first love."

John thought of the good old days when he would play baseball outside with his mom and help her around the house, but then the thought of him failing to stay in contact with her overwhelmed him with another flood of grief and guilt. John will forever be remorseful for neglecting to check on his mom's wellbeing. He will constantly face the fact that the things we don't do, that we know we should do, will leave the most lasting and painful scars.

Angela waited for about a half-hour, then called to check on John. "John, Are you alright? I'm sorry you had to find out about your mom this way. I can't imagine how devastated you must be. Are you going to be alright?" John somehow managed to hold on to his phone, despite swollen hands from beating on the floor.

"Angela, my life is shattered more than it's ever been. I've messed up so much. I've been through a lot down here and did something I never thought I would even think of doing. I have nearly lost everything I owned. I found a notice on my door saying I'm going to be evicted in two days. I have no transportation because my car has been repossessed. I have very little left to eat, and I'm seriously struggling right now. I thought about starting an outreach ministry, but that's hard to do with no place to stay and no transportation.

"Before you called, I was trying to figure out what to do next. Angela, there's no need for me to stay down here. I've decided to go back home and try to start all over again. It just seems as though every time a door opened down here, it's slammed closed as soon as it opened. I'm hurting on the inside after hearing about mom. I don't know how much of this I can take."

Angela was suspicious as to what John meant when he said he had done something he thought he would never think of doing, and whether John's addiction was the root of his downfall.

"John, when you left for college, you were so excited. I'm really worried about you. I know this might not be the right time to talk about it, but I need to ask you this. Before you left, we talked about how you were struggling with a sexual addiction. How are you doing with that? You said you got caught up with school, but you also said you had some personal problems. Were you referring to your addiction? Were you expelled because of it? What do you mean you did something you thought you never would think about doing?"

"Angela, there's something I can't share with you right now, and no, I wasn't expelled. I dropped out. I just have some other things I need to sort out. I do believe I'm getting more control over my addiction. Before you called, I was thinking about the oak tree back home. After thinking about the lessons observing that tree taught me, and feeling inspired to move ahead beyond my obstacles, I had the same feeling. I felt strong and determined to move forward and stand up and take authority over my addiction. Getting involved in the campus outreach ministry has helped me. Right now, I'm going to take things one day at a time, beginning with going back home."

Angela asked, "Are you sure that's what you want to do instead of going back to college? I hope you are doing the right thing and that you did get the help you needed. Whatever it is that you are not willing to share with me, I pray that you get it all worked out. Do you have enough money to take a bus and get here? If not, I can send you some."

Thanks for offering Angela, "I think I might have enough. When I get there, I'll look you up. I'll be so glad to see you. Thanks for calling and looking out for my mom. I feel so bad that I disappointed her in her final days. I'm going to miss her so much. If I hadn't been caught up in myself and what I was going through, I would have returned your calls and found out mom was ill. I may have been able to do something about it. Unfortunately, that's going to haunt me for the rest of my life. See you when I get there Angela."

After his conversation with Angela, John searched his wallet, every pants pocket, and every drawer, managing to scrape up enough money for a bus ticket. He caught the last bus that was leaving for the day, preparing himself for a long three-hour trip home, plenty of time to do some soul-searching.

CHAPTER 15
STRIKE THREE

While on the bus heading back to his hometown, John's mind once again went back to the last day he would ever see his mom, and that day was at the airport where she sent him off to college. He could still hear her final words, "Hit that home run, and make me proud."

He said to himself, "The only thing I hit was rock bottom. I feel like the prodigal son, running away, only concerned about pleasing myself, and in the process, finding dissatisfaction and disappointment. Look at me, broke, confused, and headed back to an empty home that has so many bad memories. At least the prodigal son had a dad to return home to; I never had one to leave."

As the bus proceeded down the highway, traffic began to get lighter and lighter. John could see a glimpse of the country road that ran alongside the house where he grew up. As the sun was setting, its rays illuminating the bus, the bus came to a full stop a mile up from John's home; that was as close to his home as it could take him. He began walking down the dusty country road.

As he walked, he felt as though he were a wounded soldier returning home from war, but without pride, honorable discharge, or even a victory parade. He walked a distance further. Through the blinding sunset, he could see a familiar sight, the old oak tree in his front yard. The memories forced a smile on his previously distraught face when all of a sudden out of nowhere, an old and beat-up pickup truck sped towards him, kicking up gravel and dust.

John held his head down and covered his eyes with a laptop he was carrying to avoid getting dust in his eyes. After the pickup passed by him, barely missing him, he lifted his head, looking back at the pickup. The excitement and smile that he had enjoyed just a moment ago, transformed into dusty tears, sorrow, and anger.

He stopped and stood in the middle of the road, watching the pickup disappear into the flying dust and sunset. The scene reminded him of the day he stood in the middle of the same road watching his dad exiting the lives of him and his mom, leaving them to fend for themselves. He remembered standing with mixed feelings. He didn't know whether he was sad that his dad was leaving or sad that he never really had a relationship with him.

John reached the house, stopped for a moment, and began taking in how the atmosphere surrounding the now-vacant house was so peaceful that it gave him a sense of purpose. For years, there was never any peace in the home, and with all the abuse, there was a feeling of an uncertain purpose. He thought to himself, "It's ironic that I left to find peace and purpose, but have now found it in an empty place where at one time, there was no peace and no purpose."

As John walked closer to the house, looking around, memories upon memories began to bombard his mind, some good and some bad. Everything looked the same as it did before he left. The groundcover he and Beverly planted, and the bench that held her up when she was down, even in her death, caught his attention. He sat on the bench, recalling Beverly telling him how much wisdom she absorbed while sitting on the bench reading, talking to God, or just thinking about life.

The sky was slowly getting dark when John looked over to where the garage once stood. To his surprise, the mountain of charred rubble was still there, along with the remains of his critically injured dad, whom he unknowingly and unintentionally incinerated when he torched the garage. While gazing at it, an uneasiness began to build up in him as he began to think about how his life changed the moment he went into the garage. He thought about all the sexually explicit materials he discovered inside, his friend Adrian getting hurt, and the sound of his dad's voice scolding him. He became so overwhelmed with emotion that he ran into the house and fell on his knees, trying to clear his mind of bad memories.

Nighttime had fallen. The house was dark and damp inside. John got up from his knees and walked into the kitchen to turn the light on, checking to see if it still had power. To his surprise, the light came on. When the light came on, it exposed more memories. John looked to his left and there stood the kitchen table at which his mom would sit with him during the week, helping him with his homework. He also remembered the many times his dad would sit at that same table at suppertime, insulting his mom until she ran upstairs crying, only to come home after working a double shift the next morning to cook him breakfast.

He walked up the stairs and into his bedroom, throwing his belongings onto his bed and sitting down. As soon as he sat down, he received a text message from Tracy. He said to himself, "I thought I was done hearing from this deranged woman; it's been months since I've heard anything from her. Why didn't I permanently take care of this woman when I had the chance?"

Despite his regrets, John opened up the text message and only read the first part of it which read, "You can try to run from me, but you cannot hide. I told you that it's not over until I say it's over."

John jumped up without reading the rest of the message and asked himself, "Is this woman stalking me? No, there's no way she could know that I'm here."

He looked out the window and ran outside, searching the perimeter of the house for some sign of Tracy. When he found no sign of her outside, he went back to his bedroom, sat down on his bed, and finished reading the text message from Tracy.

The remainder of the message read, "Don't worry, I'm not a stalker. I know more about you than you think. You owe me, and payday is coming. But just in case I scared you, I know what it takes to calm you down. Open the webpage link. And by the way, there's something I need you to do, and you'll regret it if you don't do it. I'll keep in touch."

John looked at the link that was attached to the text message, contemplating whether or not he should click on it. Evidently, the sexually explicit images he had been viewing for a month in his apartment before coming back home were old and not enough. Tracy was sending him some fresh images. After what he had told Angela about beating his addiction, he knew he had to live up to it, but he couldn't. He leaned back on his bed and opened up the link on his phone. There were so many sexually explicit images to view that he fell asleep viewing them.

When he woke up the next morning, although the bright and fresh sun lit up his room, he felt black and dirty on the inside because of what he had viewed the previous night. He fell to the floor alongside his bed, crying, "Why can't I beat this addiction? I know I should be able to beat this."

While he was on the floor next to his bed crying, he noticed an envelope lying under his bed. After he reached to retrieve it, he was elated to find that it was the envelope his now-deceased mom had given him before he boarded his flight headed for college. He knew he had lost it or misplaced it somewhere, but he didn't realize that it had fallen off his mattress and landed under his bed as he slept. His hands were shaking as he opened the envelope.

John removed the letter his mom wrote from the envelope. The letter read, "To my son John, this letter doesn't come close to expressing my love to you. I tried my best to provide a decent and loving home for you, but there were some things I had no control over. When I wanted to give up, you were a part of me and my life that brought me meaning and encouragement.

"We have an inseparable relationship. In that relationship, I know you care for me. As you leave for college, I will always cherish the moments we have had together. Life will not be the same while you are away. Take care son. See you at home plate. Love, mom."

The letter brought tears to John's eyes. He walked to his bedroom window, looked at the oak tree, and then at the groundcover he and his mom planted around it, and the bench on which she was found sitting when she died.

He thought of how he missed her funeral and what he would have said to her.

"Mom, that day I left you at the airport and said goodbye, I could feel your pain so much that I didn't want to leave. What you told Angela was right. If I knew you were sick, I would have stayed to take care of you. I knew I was leaving you alone, and I'm sorry. Although I left you to walk alone, I will never walk alone because you will always be on my mind.

"Mom, you put up a good fight to survive. I know you were looking forward to me returning home in a good way that would make you proud, but I would have only disappointed you. When I heard that you had passed away, I thought I was living in a dream, but now I face the reality that God has decided to put an end to your loneliness. Goodbye mom, I'll miss you."

After living in the house for two weeks, John had run out of food to eat. Also, the memories of his mom and the nightmares he had about his dad's abuse every night became overwhelming. He convinced himself that if he was going to maintain his sanity, he had to leave, he couldn't stay in the house any longer.

Late one night after waking up to a nightmare about his dad returning home and violently striking him and his mom, John gathered all his belongings and began walking to wherever his feet would take him. Trying to avoid seeing anything, whether good or bad that would trigger a memory in his mind, he swiftly walked away from the house with his head hanging down, even as he approached the oak tree that had given him so much wisdom and hope.

As he continued to walk away from the house, thinking of the letter his mom had written to him, he couldn't avoid taking one more look at the evenly spread carpet of ground cover under the oak tree. The ground cover spread as wide as the peaceful smile on his mom's face whenever she sat on the bench on top of it. He cringed and picked up his pace as he passed by the ominous remains of the burned-down garage, a monument of despair, deception, infidelity, and final resting place for his dad.

John, now homeless, headed down the dusty country road that was once a makeshift baseball diamond where there were only two players in the stadium, he and his mom, pretending to be the star players in a professional winner takes all championship baseball game. As he was walking down the road of uncertainty, in his opinion, there was no winning. His short run from home plate may have taken him to first and second base, but the cheering he wanted to hear from the crowd never came; only a loud voice speaking into his ear saying, "Strike three, you're out."

John walked and hitchhiked for hours until he found himself in the downtown area of the city. He was exhausted, physically, and emotionally. As he walked the streets, starving and degraded, he saw men and women begging for food; many of them living under makeshift shelters made of cardboard. He found himself foraging for food in trash bins but soon found out he had competition, sewer rats.

John was desperately hungry. He was on the brink of doing anything for a slice of bread. None of the other homeless individuals were willing to give up any of their food, probably because it was their only meal of the day. As he walked in search of food and shelter, he remembered that his friend Angela and her dad operated an outreach ministry shelter downtown for addicts and the homeless.

Since the city was a small city with a very small downtown, John knew he would have no problem finding the outreach shelter. He walked and walked until finally, he found the shelter, but it was closed for the night. He could have waited until the morning when Angela arrived at the shelter to get some food, but there was no way he was going to let her see him dirty and looking poverty-stricken.

John walked around to the back of the outreach shelter but found no way to get inside. He sat down in the dark alley, waiting for a miracle. While he was sitting and waiting, he received a text message from Tracy. The message read, "I'm in town now, and I'm ready to get paid. No matter how long it takes, we will hook up."

John was surprised that there were no links to sexually explicit web pages in the text message. For the first time since the ordeal with Tracy began, he was afraid of what she would do if and when they met again. Somehow, someway, she had found him and took a long and desperate drive to his hometown, bringing her cynical motives with her.

As soon as John closed the message from Tracy, a shelter worker came out of the shelter to dump a trash bin. He managed to get the worker's attention before he went back inside. He walked up to the worker and said, "Hello sir, my name is John Forester. I'm in desperate need of any help you can give me. I have no money, no food, and I need a place to stay. I know there's a woman who works here with her dad, her name is Angela. I need to see her, but I need a fresh set of clothes and somewhere to sleep. Please let me stay the night. I want to be here in the morning when Angela gets here. Please, I won't bother anyone."

The worker lowered his voice, looked around as if he didn't want anyone to see or hear him, and whispered to John, "If you drop me ten bucks, I'll let you in."

John was confused and irritated.

"I just told you sir, I don't have any money!"

The worker let out a big laugh and said, "Man, I'm just joking with you, any friend of Angela is a friend of mine. Come on in, I'll get you some clean clothes and something to eat."

The worker invited John inside, fed him, gave him some clean clothes, and laid a cot out for him to sit and sleep on. While John was eating, the worker asked him, "So, what's your story? And how do you know Angela?" John answered, "We both attended the same high school. We would get together and talk sometimes. She shared with me some things she was going through personally; she was being bullied at school. We helped one another out. She even talked about working here with her dad, who's a pastor."

John didn't want to share anything about himself. "I appreciate you giving me something to eat and letting me stay here tonight, but I am exhausted."

The worker decided to give John his space.

"With that being said, Mr. Forester, I won't keep you up. Get some rest. I'm glad I was able to help you out. We'll talk more in the morning when Angela gets here." After eating, John laid down to get some sleep. While lying down, he began thinking about how dangerously close Tracy was getting to him, and asking himself what she meant when she said that there was something she wanted him to do. But the main question he was asking himself about her was, "How did she find me?"

CHAPTER 16
AN ADDICTION TO HELP

John woke up the next morning at the outreach shelter feeling as though he had gotten the best sleep in days; no nightmares, no bad memories, no text messages from Tracy. Breakfast was being served. All the residents of the shelter were lining up to get their portion of pancakes, bacon, and eggs. The smell of breakfast cooking took John back to the many Saturdays his mom would cook breakfast. The smell of bacon cooking would travel up the stairs and into his bedroom; the aroma was his Saturday morning alarm clock.

As he stood up off his cot to get in line for breakfast, someone grabbed his shoulder; it was the worker who let him into the shelter through the back door. He said to John, "No, wait a minute, you can't go up there yet, no one knows I let you in last night. They keep daily records of everyone at the shelter. They'll take a count in about an hour. By that time, Angela will be here to sign you in as a resident. Just sit down and lay low until she gets here, I'll get you something to eat."

John said to the worker, "I said it last night, and I'm going to say it again, I appreciate what you are doing for me, when I get back on my feet, I'll repay you for sticking your neck out for me."

The worker left saying, don't worry about it, "I just have an addiction to help."

After the worker left to get John a plate, John was stunned at what he had just said to him before leaving. When the worker returned with John's breakfast, they both sat down on John's cot. John said to him, "When you left, you said something that just left me reeling. I've never heard it said like that before."

The worker said, "And what was that, if I may ask?"

"Right before you left to get me a plate, you said, "I just have an addiction to help." Why would you say it in that context? I have heard many confess that they have an addiction, but not an addiction to help."

The worker said. "Let me tell you a story. Several years ago, there was a man who enlisted in the military with a friend he had grown up with; they were best friends. If you saw one, you saw the other. Even on the battlefield, they fought alongside one another, watching out for one another.

"When these two soldiers and friends were discharged from the military, they were awarded all kinds of medals for bravery on the battlefield; they were war heroes. After all the accolades and celebrations were over, they went on to start living normal lives; then life took a turn for the worse.

"Six months after being honorably discharged from the military, one of the soldiers was sitting on his porch with his nine-year-old son, proudly showing him a photo album of all his military friends. Although he was considered a hero, he considered everyone pictured in the album a hero. While he was reminiscing with his son, all of a sudden they heard the squealing tires of two cars coming out of nowhere around the corner, then gunshots.

"Within seconds, the soldier was lying critically wounded on his porch. The two cars sped away, bullets still flying from both driver-side windows. The son was clutching the sentimental photo album that was now spattered with his father's blood. The soldier breathed his last breath in the country for which he proudly served.

"The son of the soldier who had been shot dropped to his knees next to his deceased father in shock and yelled for help while clutching the bloody photo album. When the son's mom ran out of the house, distraught and hysterical, it took all her strength to pry the open photo album from her son's hand. She looked down at the bloody page that was open, then broke down, devastated to see that it was a photo of her husband in military uniform, decorated with all his medals, but now covered in his blood. It was later discovered that the drivers of the two cars were shooting at each other due to a drug deal going bad.

"When the deceased soldier's best friend found out what had happened to his friend, he fell into a state of depression. He had a difficult time dealing with the fact that a soldier can survive eight years of bullets flying at him on the battlefield among foreign enemies, but six months later, he's lying dead in front of his home in his homeland. He was shot right in front of his nine-year-old son, both victims of collateral damage. His friend was so angry and confused that he turned to alcohol for comfort, unfortunately becoming an alcoholic. He almost lost everything he owned, until his two daughters refused to see his alcohol addiction slowly kill him from the inside out.

"His daughters refused to let another soldier survive walking through the streets of an enemy overseas with a vengeance to inflict pain and death, only to return to the land of the free to be killed by gun violence fueled by addiction. They viewed their dad's alcoholism as an enemy with the same vengeance as an overseas enemy, but only this time, the enemy was in the same country he fought for and served. The phrase, "I have an addiction to help." originated from his youngest daughter.

"His youngest daughter coined the phrase on the night their alcoholic dad disappeared from home. His daughters searched and searched for him, finally finding him behind an empty building, this building you are sitting in right now, drunk and lying in a filthy puddle of water. They picked him up and held him as he staggered away with them. The youngest daughter said to their dad, 'It's going to be alright dad. You are not going to fight this addiction alone because...'

In the middle of the worker's sentence, he and John heard a female voice coming from behind them saying, "I have an addiction to help." John and the worker turned around, and to John's surprise, the female voice came from his longtime friend, Angela. He stood up, and they both embraced in the hug of a lifetime. Angela said to John, "How long have you been in town? You were supposed to call me. How did you end up here talking with my dad?"

Pointing to Angela's dad, John asked, "This is your dad? I remember you telling me a lot about your dad, but I never got a chance to meet him. I've been sitting here talking to your dad all this time and didn't know it."

John asked Angela's dad, "So the story was about you and your friend?" Angela said, "I heard a little bit of what my dad was telling you as I walked up, and yes, the story he told you was about him, his best friend he served alongside in the military, me, and my sister."

Angela's dad stood up and put his arms around her shoulders and said, "If it wasn't for my oldest daughter, and her sister right here in front of us, and her addiction to help her dad, or in other words, her craving to help, I and this facility would not be here today. Because of her, we have helped hundreds of individuals break their addiction, as well as provided a home for the homeless. We have coined our motto off what Angela said to me that night she and her sister found me in the alley, I have an addiction to help."

Angela's dad continued to say to John, "From now on, just call me Pastor Robison."

He then said to Angela, "I'm sure you guys have a lot to talk about and a lot of catching up to do. I'll go help take the daily resident count and sign John in."

As he began to leave, John asked him. "Pastor Robison, when I saw you taking out the trash, I never would have thought you were a pastor. You weren't dressed like a pastor, and pastors don't take out the trash when they have someone else who can do it. Also, why didn't you say you were Angela's dad from the start?"

Pastor Robison explained, "Let me put it this way. I'm very protective of my daughters. If a stranger, especially a man, tells me he knows my daughter and is looking for her, I'm going to go out of my way to find out from her how much she knows him. If she does know him, before letting her know he is looking for her, I want to know from her if she wants anything to do with him. In this day and time when stalking and abducting women are on the rise, dads and husbands need to be around to protect their daughters and wives. You have to be careful these days.

"Now as to the way I was dressed, I have learned that it is not wearing a fine suit and carrying around a briefcase and title that makes an individual a pastor, but it's his sacrificial actions that make him worthy of the title. I can dress the part on the outside. The question is, on the inside, am I dressed with a burden and compassion for the lost, and faith that God will help me?

"Do I possess all that is required of me to go, without hesitation, on the battlefield where there is spiritual warfare going on? Will I take action to help individuals claim victory over the temptations of the world or anything else that is holding them back, whether it be homelessness or an addiction? That's what this outreach ministry and shelter is all about, having an addiction to help."

As he began walking away, Pastor Robison turned to John and said, "Now you know who I am, but I want to say this to you before I leave to take count. Last night, I asked you two questions, how do you know Angela, and you answered that question. But I also asked you, 'What's your story?' And you didn't answer that question. You don't have to say anything now, but I feel you have something you need to get off your chest and talk to God about."

After Pastor Robison walked away, John interrogated Angela.

"Your dad has been through a lot. He said he knows that there is something I need to talk to God about, then he just walked away. You have known about my sexual addiction for a long time. Did you tell him anything about my addiction?"

"No, I didn't, but ever since my dad became a pastor, he can discern when someone needs help or is hurting on the inside. The last time I talked to you on the phone you told me that you had beaten your addiction, were you telling the truth, the whole truth? You know we've been down that road before. That time, you weren't honest with me."

John found himself defending himself once again with a lie.

"Angela, don't worry, it's not a problem anymore. I admit I do get cravings sometimes, but I try to stay busy doing things, and that helps me overcome those cravings."

Angela cautiously accepted John's answer.

"Ok John, if you say you are over your addiction, I'll accept that, but please, don't disappoint me with lies again. I know most addicts need help getting over their addiction; they can't do it alone. That's what we do at this shelter. We help individuals realize that right here, in this shelter, they are not fighting their addiction alone. Well, enough about that, let's go talk to my dad and see if there is something we can do about getting you a permanent place to stay and maybe even a job."

John asked, "Do you and your dad enjoy what you do here?"

"Yes we do, the most rewarding part is seeing individuals get back on their feet, finding a job, a home, and overcoming their addiction, living normal lives. My dad told you I was there to help him when he was going through his alcohol addiction, but what he didn't tell you was how much he helped me when I was addicted.

"He was on his last tour in the military and due to come home soon. Mom was sick, and as I told you before, I gave her a hard time. When my dad returned home, it wasn't long before he found out I had a drug addiction. When he did find out, he went crazy at first, but his experience in the military helped save my life. Some of his friends had gotten hurt and were still serving, addicted to painkillers. Dad studied and learned how to help them overcome their addiction. As I said, his experience helped me overcome my drug addiction, and now, he has helped a lot of people since starting this outreach ministry and opening this shelter.

"Everything my dad told you about his military friend is true. I saw my dad wasting away, and I could not bear to see that happening, so I had to do something. I said that if he helped me overcome my drug addiction, I have a responsibility to help him overcome his alcohol addiction. After I found him lying in filth behind this building, I did everything that I could to help him get back on his feet, and you see where he is now. He's cleaned himself up and founded this outreach ministry, and then became senior pastor of a church. My dad has come a long way."

After falsely telling Angela he was addiction-free, John was determined to prove to Angela that he had beat his addiction. Angela and her dad found him an apartment and hired him to help clean and serve food at the shelter. He was slowly getting his life together as he was soon able to buy new furniture and a used car. During his free time, John would assist Angela and her dad when they counseled residents, helping them overcome their addictions.

After about two months, things were moving fast and in John's favor. He seemed to have his addiction under control until he received a long text message from Tracy. He opened up the text message, and it read, "Hello again. Miss me? Are you enjoying your life? Unfortunately, mine is miserable because of you. I said you were going to pay and now it's time to pay up. I've been busy taking care of a few things that have drained my finances. I need some money to get back on track.

"What would all those people who have put their faith in you say when they find out about the secret you have been hiding? If you don't want them to know, it's going to cost you ten thousand dollars cash. I'm not stupid, thinking you have all of that right now, but before I'm done with you, I will get it all.

"This is what you need to do. I need two thousand dollars of the ten thousand tomorrow. I'm going to tell you where to leave it. If it's not there by eleven tomorrow morning, I will expose you.

"If you don't have it, find somewhere to get it. Maybe you can get it from your girlfriend, Angela. Either way, get the money. You won't have trouble finding where I want you to leave it. I want you to go to that old abandoned house you grew up in and place it under that bench that sits under the old oak tree in the front yard.

"Just so you know, I've been watching you ever since you came back home, and I have someone else watching every step you make; they also want to get paid, so don't try to be a hero. Just leave the money where I said and walk away."

John stood devastated and staring at his phone, trying to figure out if what he just read was real. He barely had two thousand dollars in his bank account. He wondered how Tracy knew Angela. And of all places, why did she want him to leave the money at his boyhood home, the last place he wanted to return?

How could she demand that he put this extortion money in the only place where his mom went to escape, find peace, and breathed her last breath; a place he considered sacred? John had to make a decision and make one quick. Was it time to come forward with the truth, telling Angela everything, or was it time to get the police involved? Should he pay the money, hoping that when it's all paid, Tracy would disappear and walk out of his life?

After all he had accomplished, John decided that there was no way he was going to let Tracy expose him. He was getting back on his feet, and if Tracy exposed him, he would be ruined. He decided to give

Tracy the money she requested. He made the solemn journey back to his former home and left the money under his mom's bench, regretting the next text message he would get someday from Tracy requesting the rest of the ten thousand dollars.

Although he was concerned about how the issue with Tracy would play out, he walked into the shelter after dropping the money off, serving lunch as if nothing ever happened. While he was serving the resident's chili for lunch, he turned around to take a dipper full to fill the bowl of a woman who was next in line.

John didn't see the woman's face before dipping the dipper into the pot of chili, but when he turned around to deposit the chili into her bowl, he looked at her and noticed that her face looked familiar. He took a closer look at her and said, "You look very familiar. What's your name?"

The woman said, "I know it's been a long time, but I'm Brenda, we went to the same high school together."

With excitement in his voice, John said, "Oh, Wow! Brenda! I remember you now. You were on the gymnastics team. I remember you got severely hurt and all. Hold on, let me get someone to cover for me and I'll call Angela to let her know that you're here. Just grab a seat over there at that table, I'll be right over."

After getting someone to cover for him and calling Angela, John sat down with Brenda asking her, "How have you been, you must be going through a tough time, else you wouldn't be here."

Brenda sadly answered, "Things have been going downhill ever since high school. I heard about this place, and that's why I'm here to get some help."

John said, "Brenda, you came to the right place. If you want help, you will get all the help you need right here."

At that moment, Angela came out of her office. When Brenda saw her coming towards her, she stood up to go toward her, meeting her halfway and falling into her arms crying, "I know it was a long time ago, but I'm so sorry Angela. I'm sorry for every mean thing I said and did to you."

Angela tried her best to hold back her tears but failed.

"Brenda, you're right, that was a long time ago. I forgave you a long time ago. Come on, let's sit down and do something we were never able to do in high school, talk to one another."

After they both sat down with John, Angela said to Brenda, "I have always wondered what happened to you. I don't want to bring up bad memories, but after you left the cafeteria, we never heard any more from you or about you. It was as though you vanished."

Brenda explained how the injury she received in the high school gymnasium was the beginning of a long journey downhill.

"Ever since that injury in the gymnasium that day I went off on you and John, and my friends in the school cafeteria, things have gotten worse and worse. After I found out that I wouldn't be able to do gymnastics anymore because of my injuries, I lost it. I fell into a deep state of depression. Although I was only a few months away from graduation, I dropped out of school.

"My mom and dad kicked me out of the house because I started stealing from them and selling some of their things to buy drugs. I've been living in the streets for a long time. I'm just tired. I didn't know what else to do or where else to go until I found out about this place."

Brenda gave Angela another hug, crying and saying, "I know I've said this already, but I'm sorry for how I treated you."

"That's okay Brenda. I've been where you are. I had a drug addiction also, but I had my dad and my sister there to help me, you didn't have that. And that's what we are going to do for you; we are going to help you. Don't feel sorry for what you did in the past. If I don't have a compassionate and forgiving spirit, then I shouldn't be working here."

While Angela was holding on to Brenda, John asked Angela, "Although I'm officially just a server, and you normally assign ministers to counsel residents, you know that I have worked with you and Pastor while you were counseling residents at this shelter. When I was attending college, I was an associate pastor and also worked in their outreach ministry program. I have experience counseling abused and addicted individuals. Let me help Brenda. I know I can help her." Angela welcomed John's help.

"I've been watching you work with residents, and so has dad. You are good at what you do. You said you are just a server, well, in this shelter, to serve is to minister. Go ahead, Brenda needs your help."

John, with excitement in his voice, said to Brenda, "Hold on, I have something to give you." He ran to his sleeping cot to retrieve the book Mr. Wilson had given him during his client visit while working in the outreach ministry on the college campus. He gave the book to Brenda.

"While working in the outreach ministry on campus, a client by the name of Mr. Wilson gave me this book. His brother wrote it. One night, this book helped him, his brother, and his mom, escape a tragic situation. It has also helped me get through some dark days in my life. I believe it will help you as well. Take it, read it, and just as Mr. Wilson instructed me to do when you're done reading it, and have the opportunity, pass it on to someone else."

Brenda was overwhelmed by John's willingness to help.

"John, why are you so willing to help me after how I treated you in high school? I'm confused, but also overwhelmed by your offer to help me."

"Brenda, all of that is in the past. Let's say the motto of this shelter, I have an addiction to help, has greatly affected and overwhelmed me."

"Okay John, I'll read it. I've always seen some good in you and Angela, even though in high school I refused to acknowledge it. If you say this book has helped you, what do I have to lose by reading it?"

John was thrilled that his help and the book he gave Brenda turned her life around. Within a few weeks, she was beating her drug addiction, came off the streets, and began helping at the shelter. Because of his faithful work, John was facing promotion, but a hard fall was down the road.

CHAPTER 17
THE SINS OF THE FATHER

Pastor Robison and his daughter Angela were holding their annual appreciation night for all of the ministers and helpers at the outreach shelter. Past and present individuals who had been helped by the ministry were also invited to attend. Because the ministry and shelter were well known and considered a vital asset to the community, the ceremony was scheduled to be broadcast live on one of the local television stations.

The ceremony began with an introduction of all the outreach ministers and helpers. After the appreciation awards were given, the floor was open to anyone in the audience who wanted to say words of appreciation to any of the ministers who had helped them overcome their addiction battles or helped them find a permanent home. Although he was not a minister, a majority of the individuals who spoke appreciated John for his help.

While he was receiving an appreciation award for his service, he received a rousing standing ovation. He looked up to heaven and whispered, "God, all glory goes to You. Mom, I believe I just hit a home run."

As if things were not moving fast already, after the ceremony, John grabbed Angela by the hand and said, "I know a place where we can go celebrate the night. I've only been there once, but I love the food and the atmosphere." He rushed Angela out of the building and drove her to an exclusive restaurant that specialized in great seafood and serenading its guests during special occasions. Angela had already had a place in mind to celebrate his award with him, but yielded to his wish since he was an award recipient; it was his night.

While Angela and John were eating dinner, a group of musicians came over, stopped at their table, and began playing soft music. Angela smiled at John, believing the musicians were playing solely for him in celebration of his award until he got on his knees, pulled out a ring, and asked her to marry him. Angela sat stunned and crying as

John held her hand, waiting for an answer. After about thirty seconds of crying, Angela looked into John's eyes and said, "Yes John, I will gladly marry you."

After John placed the ring on her finger, Angela cried, "John, you surprised me tonight. Although I had a feeling this day would come, I had no idea that it would be tonight. I've been waiting for you to ask me to marry you for a long time, and right now, I'm glad I waited. But still, tonight is also about you, and I have something just as special for you."

John asked, "Something special, what can you do tonight that will top getting engaged to be married?"

Angela gave him some inside information. "I told you a while ago that dad and I were watching you counsel residents at the shelter. I'm giving you a heads up so you won't be surprised. Dad's thinking about retiring about a year from now, and he wants to start grooming you to be the senior pastor of the church when he steps down. For about a year, he wants to take you under his wing. He has gained a lot of respect for you. Every staff member in the ministry and resident at the shelter looks up to you."

John was elated at the opportunity to become a senior pastor.

"Are you serious? I want the position, but I don't know if I can do it. I was an associate pastor when I was on campus, but right now, I'm not even a minister, I'm a server. I don't know what to say; this is a lot coming at me all at once."

Angela wasn't finished telling John the good news.

"John, I told you once before, to serve people is to minister to them. Anyways, things are going to be made official, your title is going to change to match your work. And that's not all, hold on to your seat. I'm so excited for you. Along with title changes and everything, my dad also wants you to take over the outreach ministry and run the shelter, beginning immediately. He will make himself available anytime you need him. I'll also be at your side to help you."

At that moment, John's phone rang. Pastor Robison was calling him to schedule a meeting with him in his office the next day at noon.

The next day, John walked into the meeting with Pastor Robison.

As soon as John sat down, Pastor Robison asked him a question to get the meeting started. "Did you and my daughter go out to celebrate your award last night?"

John carefully answered, "Yes, we did; it turned out to be a wonderful celebration and dinner. Is there something wrong?"

Pastor Robison said, "No, there's nothing wrong. Angela did call me to tell me that you asked her to marry you. I guess there's not much else to say, knowing Angela and how much she loves you. I would have liked for you to come to me first and ask for her hand in marriage, but you're a good man and that's water under the bridge. I'm sure during your meeting she filled you in about me grooming you to be the next senior pastor within the year, am I right?"

"Yes Pastor Robison, she did mention it."

"I thought she would, I know my Angela. I know she did more than mention it, she was just excited about it as you were. Anyways, there's no one else among our church leaders who I feel is better capable, or has worked diligently in the outreach ministry more than you. As a server, you have ministered to and helped numerous individuals get back on their feet. You have the spirit of a pastor.

"Son, I want you to know that you have my blessing. In the short time that I've known you, I've seen great potential in you; I see leadership. I still feel as though you have some things that need to be worked out, but before I retire, I'm going to do my best to help you get to where you need to get as the pastor of the church and my future son-in-law.

"Since you are now head of the outreach ministry and shelter, you will also be my assistant pastor. I am in the process of writing a grant proposal for twenty thousand dollars in funds to help with some needed improvements to our shelter and church. I want you to help me with that grant. Although the deadline is further down the road, I want to get started early. When it is done, we'll both sit down to review it. I'll sign it, send it off, and the church will have a week of consecration, asking God to send a miracle."

John thanked Pastor Robison for having faith and confidence in him to run the outreach ministry, and one day take his position as senior pastor. After John left the meeting, low and behold, the dreaded text message from Tracy came. The text message read, "The remaining eight thousand dollars and you're in the clear. Leave it in the same place as before."

John didn't have nearly that amount of money to give her. Although he did not want to send her a text message, he sent one back saying, "I have a lot going on right now. I don't have the money and besides, you're not fair. I need some time to get that amount of money together." He waited to get a response, but there was none. He waited for days, and weeks that turned into months, but there was no response from Tracy.

John was bewildered at what was going on with Tracy. He said to himself, "One moment she demands money as though she needed it right then and there. Then, I don't hear from her in months. I don't know if she's trying to make me suffer or what she is doing, but this is getting old. I regret the day I failed to end this all."

After months of waiting on a response from Tracy, John decided that he had too much on his plate to be paranoid about what she threatened to do to him. He had a wedding, the outreach ministry and shelter, and one day, pastoring a church on his mind.

Step by step, everything was coming together for John. The outreach ministry was adding more ministers to counsel the addicted, and the shelter was helping a record number of homeless individuals get off the homeless list. Every day, John would meet with Pastor Robison, who would instruct and teach him the details of being a pastor.

John and Angela's wedding was a spectacular and memorable event. Pastor Robison was proud to have John as his son-in-law. Angela even used Brenda, her high school adversary turned friend, as one of her bridesmaids.

Almost a year had passed since the wedding, but then they began having marriage problems. John and Angela welcomed a baby boy into the world, but soon after that, even a newborn baby couldn't bring sunshine into their marriage, especially since he was born with a respiratory ailment that demanded special care and treatment.

John was disappointed in not having a healthy son. He did little to help Angela care for him, and at times, she felt he regretted having him as a son. Every evening, John was spending most of his time locked up in his home office, and Angela fumed about it.

"John, for a year I have single-handedly taken care of our son. Your son doesn't know who you are because you have rejected him and neglected to address his condition. You spend so much time in that office, rather than spending it with your family.

"You say you're in there doing church work and working on sermons, but I question whether God is involved in what you are doing. God is not a God who promotes division, hatred for His creation, and isolation in the family. Our son is a blessing no matter what condition he came into the world. You need to step back and take a serious look at what you are doing to your family and marriage. And by the way, why is it necessary for you to keep your office door locked?"

"You may not like hearing this, and I'm not trying to judge anyone, but this needs to be said. I hope you're not blind to the fact that you're following in your dad's footsteps. You don't like to talk about him much, but I remember you saying that he isolated himself from you and your mom, and his dad did the same thing to him.

"There are scriptures in the Bible that warn us about the sins of the father or in other words, sins that are passed down from one generation to another. Step back and take a look at what you are doing, and not doing with your family. There's no doubt in my mind that those scriptures are relevant to what's going on with you right now. Am I standing here looking at another Carl? I believe you know what I mean."

Although John knew Angela was addressing his sexual addiction he constantly told her he had overcome, he became highly vocal and irritated, avoiding her question.

"Don't stand there and say you're not judging me. Don't dare compare me to my dad, you didn't know him at all. You don't have a clue as to how I feel about having a son who probably won't amount to anything, and we'll just leave it at that. Whenever I'm doing spiritual work for God and the church, I don't need anyone, including you, interfering with God working through me. I answer to Him and

Him alone. My office is always locked because it's off-limits. You need to be clear on that, and that's all you need to know."

Ever since becoming a pastor's daughter, Angela never recalled her dad using the reason John had just given for locking his office door as an excuse to seclude himself from his family. Her dad's home office door was always open to welcome anyone. Angela left John alone and in God's hands concerning his opinion about his son and what he said was "spiritual work," but she had suspicions.

John became so distant and cold that there was no romance nor intimacy in their marriage. Angela noticed this coldness began right after he began locking himself in his office alone for hours. He was different from the man who went down on his knees in an elegant restaurant, putting a ring on her finger, promising to stand by her side and love her.

John was following the same pattern as his dad, Carl, isolating himself from his family. Angela had so many questions about John and the future of their marriage going through her mind. Their marriage problems escalated one Saturday afternoon when Angela was out shopping and John was working in his office at home.

After months of hearing nothing from Tracy, John received a text message from her that read, "It's been a long time. I see you have been busy. I guess congratulations are in order on your wedding, your new addition to the family, and your new position at the outreach ministry. I hear one day that you're going to be assigned the position of senior pastor of a church. I have watched and waited, and now I have you where I want you.

"Now you're a big man on campus, but the bigger they are, the harder they fall. When I expose you, you're going down harder than you could have ever imagined, and that's what I've been patiently waiting to see. I have you cornered in a spot where you'll pay whatever it takes to keep your dirty little secret hidden. I've been hiding in the shadows just for this moment to see you rise and fall unless you give me what I want. And by the way, plans have changed, I left something at your front door."

John opened his front door, finding a large envelope on his porch.

He was hoping it was Tracy's request for the last eight thousand dollars she demanded. He had saved all of the money and wanted to get this all behind him. After this, he assumed it was all going to be over. He took the envelope into his office, closing and locking the door behind him.

When he opened the envelope, there was a note demanding that he leave the eight thousand dollars in the same place as before. The note also read, "I have been thinking about the pain and suffering you have caused me. Because of what you have done to me, I deserve a lot more. When you become a senior pastor, I want another ten thousand dollars. I'm not going to sit back and watch you rise to success without giving me my fair share. And just so we don't lose focus on the most important part of our relationship, I've included a video, and it's in your best interest that you watch it."

John figured that since Tracy stated that the video was essential for him to watch, he inserted it into his computer and began viewing it. The video turned out to be the most sexually explicit video he had ever seen. Therefore, his addiction would not prevent him from watching it to the end.

After watching the video, John sat back in his chair and said to himself, "I need to think of a way to end all of this, the sexually explicit material and the extortion. Where am I going to get another ten thousand dollars above the eight thousand she wants? All of this must come to an end, but how?"

John withdrew the remaining eight thousand dollars of the first ten thousand dollars Tracy demanded from his bank account. He rushed to leave it at his old house under the bench. This time, he included a note which read, "This has gone on for too long. You have gone from sexually explicit images to extortion. You have taken advantage of my addiction, but I won't allow it anymore. I don't know the real reason why you need the extra money, but I kept my end of the deal. However I have offended you, I'm sorry. Let's part and go our separate ways and end this extortion. You will not get another ten thousand dollars out of me."

John left the note with the eight thousand dollars, hoping he had heard the last from Tracy and that the money was the final payment to correct mistakes he made in his dad's garage and Tracy's home, but he would find out later that it wasn't that easy.

Even after leaving the note demanding that Tracy end her exploitation, John enjoyed watching the video she sent him so much that he frequently viewed it in his locked office. His sexual addiction became more and more uncontrollable. After a while, he wasn't satisfied with the one video. He searched online, having no problem at all finding more sexually explicit videos to view. Every night he would lock himself in his office downloading sexually explicit videos to his computer.

John was so dangerously caught up in his addiction that he never considered that every video he downloaded was contributing to his downfall. While his marriage was suffering, he managed to conceal his sexual addiction from his wife and pastor. He continued as head of the outreach ministry and shelter. Under his leadership, many of the homeless and addicted individuals that the shelter helped were able to leave with a clean slate and a fresh start.

They were also able to lead positive lives free from their brokenness, but John was failing to see that he was leaving a trail of broken lives and loss of life. Unfortunately, the devastating trail would get longer.

CHAPTER 18
EXTRAORDINARY LOSS

On a stormy and rainy night, Angela was sitting in her bed reading while their infant son was lying next to her. As usual, John was locked in his office, engrossed in his growing library of sexually explicit videos. Also, as usual, Angela assumed he was working on church business or sermons. As the videos John became obsessed with became more gratifying to him, Angela became less and less physically appealing.

While the storm on the outside of the house was getting more violent by the minute, there was a storm brewing on the inside between John and Angela that would leave a greater path of destruction and devastation. As the lightning illuminated the bedroom, and at the loud sound of thunder, their son began crying. When Angela reached over to take him into her arms and comfort him, she became concerned about how hot he felt. She quickly rushed him into the bathroom where she kept her thermometer. When she took his temperature, it read quite a bit higher than normal.

Angela was frantically carrying their son when she ran to John's locked office and banged on the door screaming,

"John! John! Unlock the door! I think our son has a fever!"

John rushed to shut his computer down in an attempt to quickly conceal any incriminating sexually explicit evidence of what he was doing behind closed doors. Agitated, he said, "Hold on a minute. I'll be right there. Is all that screaming necessary?"

Angela waited and waited longer than it should have taken for John to open the door. She yelled through the closed door while their son's cry began to get louder and louder.

"I don't know why it's taking you so long, but it can't be more important than our ill son, open this door right now!"

John violently pulled his office door open, going off on Angela.

"I don't know what your problem is, but you need to chill. Don't ever disrespect me like that again in front of my son."

Angela didn't come close to chilling as her anger hit a boiling point. "Your son, are you serious? You despise your son, and it's obvious. You never spend time with your son. You've spent more time locked up in that office than you ever have with him or me. Right now, our son, and I stress, our son is sick.

"I know you don't believe in giving your son medicine or care about whether or not he gets any, but I need to give him something. We don't have anything here to give him. You need to go to the drugstore to get him something that will get his fever down."

All of a sudden, there was a loud clap of lightning, knocking the power out.

John went into the garage to get a couple of flashlights. When he came back into the house, he looked at Angela grumbling,

"I told you before, you don't have a clue as to how I feel. All that medicine they're giving kids is like poison, and I'm not into poisoning my son, and that's how I feel about that."

Angela retaliated, unconcerned about how John felt. As a loving mother, her thought was on her son, whose health was deteriorating by the minute.

"You know how I feel about our son. I love him, and I'm not going to sit here and watch him suffer. He's sick, and that's all I need to deal with right now, not how you feel and your bad attitude."

John walked to the window, concerned more about the conditions outside than what was going on in his home at the moment.

"Looks like the power is out all over, it's probably out at the drugstore as well."

Angela corrected him.

"The drugstore has two powerful backup generators, they'll be open, but they will be closing in an hour and a half. I know it's a half-hour drive, but you have time to make it."

John continued his attempt to get out of going out in the rain to the drugstore.

"Are you aware of the fact that it's pouring down out there? Do you seriously want me to go out in the middle of a storm and get some medicine I don't want to give my son? Can it wait until the storm is over and you go get the medicine?"

Angela became highly frustrated at John's lack of compassion for their son.

"What are you talking about wait until the storm is over, and I go get the medicine? Our son is sick. I think his temperature is getting higher and higher, and besides that, it's been storming for a couple of hours, who knows when it will let up.

"Whether you want to be or not, you are his dad. You need to go to the drugstore right now. I told you it will be closed in an hour and a half. Quit wasting time fussing about taking care of our son and leave now, and pick up some extra batteries for the flashlights while you're there, we might need them."

John was on the verge of blowing up as he swiftly walked towards his office, upset and checking to make sure the office door was locked. He got into his car, speeding down the road on his way to the drugstore while the rain was heavily pouring down. While he was driving, he received a text message from Tracy.

Unaware that his cell phone battery was low and he had no way of charging it, he opened up the text message. This time, instead of links to sexually explicit web pages, Tracy sent him something she had never sent him before. There were no images, but seductive written messages, one seductive message after the other. John pulled over to the side of the road, enjoying what he was reading. While he was on the side of the road sending text messages to Tracy and vice versa, Angela was left alone as always, to decide what to do with their son whose health was failing rapidly.

Tracy continued sending John text messages and he responded to every one of them until his battery died and his phone went dead. Unable to reach John on his cell phone, Angela had no choice but to venture out into the pouring down rain on foot, hoping to find help for her son. She walked a half-mile down the road in the dark, and on the muddy country road to a neighbor's house.

When she arrived at her neighbor's door, she was drenched, and her son was having seizures off and on. As the torrential rain blended with the tears streaming down her face, Angela pleaded with her neighbor,

"Connie, please help! I need to get my son to the hospital right away. He has a fever, and he's having seizures off and on. I think something's seriously wrong with him and he's getting worse. John drove the car to the drugstore to get some medicine and some batteries, but I haven't been able to reach him. I don't think I have time to wait for him to get back."

With all the lights in the area out due to the storm, Connie managed to maneuver around her house, finding a few blankets to place over Angela and her son. Breaking all speed limits, Connie rushed Angela and her son to the hospital. By the time they arrived at the hospital, he was unresponsive with a weak pulse. The emergency room personnel rushed her son away for treatment while she waited in the waiting room. After about a half-hour, Angela had an eerie feeling that her son was no longer among the living.

As she was mentally preparing for the worse, the emergency room doctor came out with a downcast and grim look on her face with news no parent wants to hear. As she approached Angela with the news, heartbroken tears began to flow from Angela's eyes.

The doctor sat down next to her, struggling to hold back her tears and looking just as distraught as Angela. She delivered the gut-wrenching news.

"I'm sorry, we did all we could do. If you had gotten him here sooner, it might have made a difference."

Devastated as any parent would be, Angela dropped to her knees wailing,

"God, what have I done so wrong that you have taken away my son? This hospital is where you led me to bring him into this world, and I was full of so much joy. But now, there is nothing but sadness as you have led me to the same place once again, only to see him depart, and I don't' understand why."

Connie knelt next to Angela, attempting to console her, but there was not a single word she could say to her that would comfort her in her devastating time of sorrow. She could almost feel Angela's grief because it was so thick in the room.

"Angela I'm so sorry, you and John don't deserve this. I don't know what to say. There are no right words that I could say. Whatever you need, I'm here for you, but right now, let's go say goodbye to your son."

Angela was so grief-stricken that she needed the assistance of Connie to walk her into the room where her infant son was lying in bed lifeless. After Connie helped her sit down in a chair, the nurse carefully lifted Angela's son from the bed and laid him in her arms. Holding her son and looking down at him, he looked as if he was smiling back at her.

Connie whispered to her, "I'm going to give you some time to be alone with your son. I'll try to call John, and if I can't reach him, I'll swing by your house and see if he's there. My prayers are with both of you."

After Connie left the room, Angela clutched her soft and still warm son's body tight and close and whispered in his ear, while at the same time crying,

"Mommy misses you already because you are a special part of her. I am falling apart on the inside because my heart is broken. I am crying so much now because I have to say goodbye. When you came into this world, you changed my life. I enjoyed every moment I was able to spend with you. You helped make my life worth living, and for that, I will always love you. Goodnight, mommy's going to tuck you in now."

Angela pulled the blanket over her deceased son's face and placed him back in the bed. She sat down and leaned back in the hospital room chair, still in shock as to how quickly someone she so dearly loved was snatched away from her.

Connie called John before leaving the hospital, but there was no answer. She decided to head towards his home, praying that he was there. On her way, she received a phone call from her husband informing her that he was at the drugstore.

"I'm at the drugstore picking up a few things, how are Angela and the baby?"

Connie thought the power was out at the drugstore in their area. "How could you be at the drugstore when all the power in the area is out?" Her husband answered. "It's a blessing that the drugstore has one or two powerful backup generators running. They were able to stay open throughout the storm, but they are about to close as we speak."

Connie was getting closer to John and Angela's home when she gave her husband the bad news and asked him about John.

"Unfortunately, we didn't get their son to the hospital in time. He passed away. I believe it had something to do with his respiratory problems. Angela's hurting right now. I haven't been where she is right now because I have never lost a child, but it has to be heart-wrenching."

"I'm close to their house right now looking for John. He doesn't know their son has passed away. Did you see any sign of him at the drugstore? Angela said he had gone there to pick up some medicine for their son and some batteries."

As he was rushing to get into his car and out of the rain, Connie's husband replied, "I didn't see his car when I drove into the parking lot. I'm getting ready to leave right now."

When Connie arrived at Angela and John's house, there was no sign of John. She called Angela.

"Angela, I tried to reach John on the phone before I left the hospital but got no answer. My husband called me from the drugstore while he was picking up some items. I asked if he happened to see John and he said no, and at that time, the drugstore was getting ready to close. I'm sitting outside your house waiting to see if John pulls up."

Angela, who had just lost a son, was now concerned about her husband.

"I pray that nothing bad has happened to him. He left the house two hours ago, upset and speeding down the road. Connie, I don't know how much of this I can take. I'm trying to lean on God, but I feel like my heart is being ripped out of me."

Connie tried to ease her concerns.

"Spend all the time you need with your son. John probably got held up by the weather or something. As soon as I see him drive up, I'll send him your way."

In the meantime, with his cell phone dead, John looked at his car clock and realized that an hour and a half had passed during the time he and Tracy were sending text messages back and forth to one another. In his haste to get back onto the road and to the drugstore before it closed, he was blinded by headlights coming directly at him.

John was unaware that he had pulled into the other lane and headed straight towards an oncoming car until it was too late. He swerved back into his lane, but the oncoming car skidded off the road and into a deep ditch. John jumped out of his car and ran to the area where the car slid off the road. He looked down into the ditch, seeing that the car had flipped and rested on its top.

Shaking and afraid, John fell to his knees, crying in the drenching rain. He raised his hand to his neck, snatching off a gold cross necklace from around his neck that Pastor Robison and his wife had personally given to him as a wedding gift. He threw the necklace into some nearby bushes, blaming God for why he had been unable to break his addiction, and for everything else that was going wrong in his life.

When he looked down into the ditch again, he noticed that a man's hand was reaching out of the driver's side window, waving for help. When the hand seemed to have become lifeless, no longer waving for help, John panicked, ran to his car, then left the scene.

While he was speeding away from the scene of the accident, he couldn't get the image of the flipped-over car and the hand reaching out for help out of his mind. He pulled over to the side of the road, overcome with guilt. He thought of the time when he was out in the cold and rain, homeless and on the street begging for bread. Then, on a day when he felt like giving up, Pastor Robison took him in, a stranger, and rescued him, and helped him get on his feet. But now, he had a title behind his name; assistant pastor and head of the outreach ministry.

He was reminded of the talk he had with Pastor Robison in the shelter about carrying a title. He remembered him saying that it's not a suit, a briefcase, and a title that makes a pastor, but it's his sacrificial actions that make him worthy of the title. He also recalled the slogan of the ministry, "An addiction to help." Helping individuals in distress was what he was supposed to do and had a responsibility to do, but right now, he was running away from that responsibility.

After a strong conviction came over him, John turned his car around and headed back to the scene of the accident. When he arrived, he got out of his car to check if there were any survivors inside the wreckage. From the top of the ditch where the overturned car rested, he immediately saw a small spark, then all of a sudden the car exploded and burst into a ball of bright orange flames with black smoke billowing into the dark sky. He was knocked to the ground from the force of the explosion.

Struggling to get back on his feet, dazed and terrified, John managed to get back into his car, speeding away. After driving a short distance from the scene of the accident, he pulled over to the side of the road, sweating and feeling sick, but also trying to justify his role in the crash.

He said to himself, "This is not my fault. That car came speeding out of nowhere. I couldn't avoid the collision. Although I pray for the family of the individual or individuals who perished, if it gets out that I left the scene of an accident, there goes my career and my hopes of being the senior pastor of the church. I can't go to jail for this, I've been through so much already and worked so hard to get to where I am right now.

"I did go back to help, I was just too late, but at least I did go back. God, I think that should count for something. No one saw what happened; there are no witnesses. I know it's tragic, but I have to keep this to myself, I have to."

John pulled back onto the road and headed towards the drugstore, but when he arrived, the drugstore was closed, so he headed back home. Connie, who was sitting in her car outside his home waiting for him, got out of her car and ran up to him after he pulled into his driveway. Before he had a chance to get out of his car, she tapped on his window.

Already shaken and still sweating after the accident, John lowered his window and asked, "Connie, what are you doing out here, you scared the daylights out of me?"

Connie asked him, "Why are you sweating so much? Are you

alright? It looks like you just committed murder." Connie was not aware of how close she was to the truth.

John looked shocked at what Connie had just said to him. He became tenser saying, "It's just that you startled me, that's all. Is something wrong?"

Without giving him details, Connie replied, "We've been trying to reach you. It's been crazier than you know. I rushed your wife and son to the hospital, and it's not good. You need to get there right now. I'll call you later."

Before backing out of the driveway and racing to the hospital, John said to Connie, "My phone is dead, call Angela and tell her I'm alright and on the way. Just like you said, it's been a crazy night. Thanks for waiting for me and all your help."

As soon as John entered the hospital's emergency room doors, he was approached by about a dozen members of the church, including a deacon.

John asked, "What's going on? Where's my wife and son?"

One of the church members told him she would get the nurse to take him to his wife and son, while the deacon said to him, "We are here to give you and your wife support and also support for Pastor Robison's wife."

John asked, "Pastor's wife? Why? What's happened?" The deacon sadly gave him the news.

"I don't want to put a lot on you right now, but Pastor Robison and his wife were in a fatal accident tonight. Sadly, he didn't survive the crash. His wife was in the car with him, she's in intensive care as we speak."

John felt as though he had run full force into a brick wall.

"Deacon, how could this tragedy happen so fast? Pastor, my father-in-law, gone? He shouldn't have gone out like this. Not like this!"

"John, it's hard for all of us to believe he's gone, but right now you may not have heard as yet, but your wife is with your son, he developed a severe respiratory infection and passed away a couple of hours ago. From what I gather, no one could reach you."

John became distraught and hysterical as the deacon grabbed him, giving him a comforting hug. John began blaming himself for his son's death.

"I should have been here with them. I have forsaken my wife and my son. I really should have been here for them. I can't believe my son is gone. I need to see my wife and son. Where are they? I should have been here."

The nurse came over to take John to his wife and son. As he walked into the hospital room where his wife and deceased son were, John looked at his son lying on the hospital bed. He fell on the edge of the bed, crying. When he raised his head and looked at Angela, her eyes swollen and drenched with tears, he could see the anger on her face. Before he could get out a word, she stood up from her chair, walked up to him, and said,

"You fall on your knees before our son acting as if you care. You have never been a dad to your son, even in his death. Two hours! For two hours we tried to reach you! Where were you?

"We lost our son tonight, my dad, and a good pastor. My stepmom is in intensive care fighting for her life. But where was their assistant pastor? Where was their son-in-law? God only knows. You better have a good explanation as to why you weren't here for your son. You don't have the right to kneel before him. Get up and explain to me where you were."

John stood up with a look of sadness and anger saying to Angela, "Now is not the time to find fault. I don't have to stand here and explain anything to you. I'm the head of the house, and I don't answer to you, so stay in your lane. Obviously, you have a problem doing that. I'm hurting from all of this just like you are; it's like a nightmare. Back off and give me some time with our son."

Angela headed out of the room so angry and distraught that she could barely walk, saying to John, "You take whatever time you need pretending to be the dad you never were. I'm not going anywhere but to find out more about my dad and stepmom. When you are done doing what you do, we need to talk, head of the house, or whatever. You will tell me where you were, whether you want to or not."

John walked up to his son, looking at him lying as if he were sleeping. He grabbed him by the hand, which was now cold to the touch, and said his final goodbye.

"Son, forgive me for being absent in your life. It's just that I have weaknesses; some are greater than others to overcome. Even though I failed to show it, I have loved you from day one. I know that as you would have grown up, you would have been disappointed in me as I was with your grandpa who abandoned me, of whom I have unfortunately become. Forgive me. I'm sorry for not being there when you needed me the most. Goodbye son."

John walked out into the waiting room where his wife was sitting with the church members, inquiring about the accident. The deacon of the church gave John what little details he knew about it.

"Going by what the police told us, the accident was a hit-and-run. Pastor Robison had called me earlier this evening and said he and his wife were on their way to your house to discuss the details of the grant.

"All we know is that the police said that when they came on the scene, the car was in a ditch, burned out. Pastor Robison was burned beyond recognition. The only way they determined it was Pastor Robison was because there were papers strewn across the scene from his briefcase that was thrown from the car when it flipped over.

"As they investigated the scene, they heard the faint voice of his wife crying for help. They found her lying in some thick bushes a few feet away from the accident. She had been thrown from the car before it went into the ditch."

After the deacon explained more details of the accident, where and about what time the accident occurred, John came to the agonizing realization that based on what the deacon told him, he was the hit-and-run driver that killed his father-in-law and injured his mother-in-law. The thought came to him that one day his father-in-law, who pulled him out of a ditch of despair, hopelessness, and loneliness, needed him to pull him out of a dirty and rain-filled ditch facing death, but he turned away from him, leaving him to die alone.

John, asking to be excused, ran into the men's restroom and fell on the floor.

"How could I have done this evil act? In one moment of pleasure, I have changed the lives of my family, my pastor's family, and the church family forever. My sexual addiction caused this. I can't continue destroying people's lives."

John regained his composure and walked out of the restroom, never saying a word about his role in the accident. He and Angela walked down to another wing of the hospital to check on her stepmother, but she was sedated and still in intensive care. After a long and devastating night, John and Angela headed home, absent and with only memories of a beloved infant son, a dad, and a pastor.

CHAPTER 19
TREES OF RIGHTEOUSNESS

The ride home from the hospital for John and Angela was somber and quiet until about halfway into the ride, John pulled over to the side of the road. He attempted to explain to Angela where he was for two hours, but his explanation was far from the truth.

"You said we needed to talk, so let's talk. I know you are upset with me right now. Whether you want to hear it or not, this is what went down tonight. When I left to go to the drugstore, you know as well as I do that all the power in the area was out. It was dark and stormy, and the rain was pouring down hard.

"When I got to the drugstore, all of the store lights were out; the store was completely dark. I know you said they had generators, I don't know what happened to them, maybe they weren't working, but as I said, the lights were out and the store was closed. They had no power.

"When I turned around to head back home, I came across the utility company working on power lines that were down, blocking the road not too far from our house. I had to take a back road that took me way out of the way. I must have been driving around for an hour. When I finally got back home and into the driveway, our neighbor Connie came up to me as I was getting out of the car and told me you were at the hospital with our son. I immediately headed towards the hospital, and you know the rest."

Angela sat silent for a moment, trying to figure out how or if she should respond to the lie John had just told. After about two minutes of silence and anger building up, she exploded.

"What's burning me up inside other than the way you spoke to me in the hospital is the fact that I have been forever wounded due to the sudden stripping away of a child and a dad I so deeply loved, and regardless of how I feel right now, you sit there and pour lying salt on my wounds. How dare you!

"Our neighbor Connie was out looking for you. She called me at the hospital and said her husband was at the drugstore. He was there at a time significantly later than when you would have gotten there. He told her that the drugstore generators were working and the store was open all day until closing time.

"Also, on the way to the hospital, the same road we took on the way out from our house is the same road you would have taken to the drugstore, there were no power lines down and no utility crew. Why would you sit there and lie to me? What are you trying to hide?"

John refused to confess to his lie.

"I explained to you what happened. Whether you believe me or not, that's up to you. It's been a tragic and life-altering night; we both are tired and need to take some time to heal. Unfortunately, we have two funerals to plan. After that, we need to move on."

"John, you are so right. And for the first time in a long time, you are being honest. We do need to take time to heal, and we do need to move on. After our son and my dad's funerals, I'm going to stay with my sister for a while. This has all been too much for me. I have some decisions to make, and I need someone to talk to who I know can help."

After all of his dishonesty, John was offended.

"Someone to talk to, that's what you have a husband for."

"That's exactly right John. You are exactly right. A husband should be there for his wife to talk to anytime, but you have not been that husband. You isolated yourself from our son and me as if we didn't exist. I'm sitting here trying so hard to hold myself together after what I have instantly lost, and it hurts. I need to sort things out. Right now, I can't see you helping me with that at all. So let's get home. As you said, we have funerals to plan."

Angela's dad's funeral occurred while her stepmom was still in intensive care. A couple of days later, on the day of John and Angela's son's funeral, it was cloudy and gloomy. Although the day was overcast, what was said at their son's eulogy put a spotlight on everyone in attendance, in particular, John.

The eulogy began with the eulogist saying, "Whatever a tree is planted to be, that will it be from life to death. In the sixty-first chapter of Isaiah, King James Version, God calls His people trees of righteousness."

What the eulogist said next seemed to be a message directed unintentionally at John, challenging him to take inventory of himself and the choices he was making in life.

"The passage of scripture I just read to you refers to God's people as trees of righteousness. Let's use an oak tree to symbolize a tree of righteousness. If we are to get an understanding from this scripture, we must first understand that when an oak seedling is sown into fertile ground, there's only one result that can come out of that seed, an oak tree. That seed can't produce an apple tree, peach tree, walnut tree, etc.

"When the oak tree sprouts from the seed, it remains an oak tree, nothing more, nothing less. From the moment the seed sprouts until the oak tree's demise, the tree will remain an oak tree. In the lifespan of the oak tree, it will become deeply rooted and grounded in one designated spot. Once rooted and grounded, it will be difficult for anyone or anything to move it from that spot. If we step back, looking to find evidence and proof that it is a full-grown oak tree, we will find that evidence and proof displayed in no other way than in a visual display of its vast and wide-spreading branches in a display of strength and authority.

"This young son of John and Angela Forester we eulogize today was sown and sprouted to choose to become a tree of righteousness as all of us have been. Unfortunately, he was cut down before he had an opportunity to spread his branches in a display of strength and authority. But, we who are alive and remain, have a choice as to what type of seed we sow, where we sow that seed, and what we become.

"A drug addict is the result of an individual who chooses to sow into drugs. We see evidence and proof of his choice to be a drug addict displayed in no other way than as a drug addiction or the individual's inability to control his use of legal or illegal drugs, or medication, which also includes alcohol.

"An individual who is addicted to pornography is the result of an individual who chooses to sow into pornography. We see evidence and proof of his choice to be a pornography addict displayed in no other way than as a pornography addiction, the individual's compulsive need to view sexually alluring and tempting images, most often to the point of damaging any natural human interaction.

"A righteous individual is the result of an individual who chooses to sow into God's righteousness. We see evidence and proof of his choice to be a tree of righteousness displayed in no other way than as a tree of righteousness, the individual's ability to stand and stretch out on God's Word, refusing to walk in the counsel of the wicked, stand in the path of sinners, or sit in the seat of scoffers.

"His roots are fully grounded in the Lord, and nothing can remove him from that place. The divine influence of God is upon him, not the influence of the world that would only pull him down into a pit of bondage. Let your life bring glory to God. You must shake off what is preventing you from being a rooted and grounded tree of righteousness, laying down any selfish agenda, and lifting your branches high so that others might be partakers of the same strength and authority you enjoy."

The eulogist's message hit John so hard that on the way home from his son's funeral, he was silent. Angela looked over at him, definitely noticing that the eulogist's message had him under conviction. She also thought this conviction might have come upon him because of what he was hiding and the lie he told her when they were driving home from the hospital on the night their son passed away.

As they pulled into their driveway, Angela received a phone call from a church member that her stepmom had regained consciousness, but she was slowly drifting away. On their way to the hospital to check on her, John was afraid that she might have seen him at the scene of the accident after she had been ejected from the vehicle and thrown into the bushes. She might have even seen his car at the scene.

When John and Angela arrived at the hospital, nearly all the church members were present in support of the family. Angela proceeded to go into her stepmom's hospital room with John slowly and nervously walking behind her. To John's satisfaction, she was sleeping.

As they moved closer to her, she woke up and slightly raised her head. Her face lit up at the sight of Angela, but when she trained her eyes on John, she backed away with a look of fear in her eyes. Angela looked perplexed at her reaction toward John. Feeling as though it was in his best interest to find an excuse to leave the room, John whispered to Angela,

"It's tough for me to see my mother-in-law lying there, especially since the image of our deceased son lying in his hospital bed is still fresh in my mind. I'll meet you in the lobby." John left the room without saying a word to his mother-in-law.

About five minutes after John left the room, Angela's stepmom, unable to speak, lifted her head and pointed with a weak hand towards a table that was sitting next to her bed as if she wanted Angela to give her something. Angela asked her if she wanted a sip from a glass of water that was sitting on the table. She shook her head, signaling "No." Angela's stepmom, getting weaker, pointed towards the table again. The only other item on the table was a Bible.

When Angela lifted the Bible off the table, asking her stepmom if she wanted her to read something from it, her stepmom shook her head, signaling "No." Her stepmom pointed directly towards the table drawer. Angela placed the Bible back on top of the table, confused as to what her stepmom wanted until she opened the desk drawer. When she opened the drawer, the only item in the drawer was a necklace that looked very familiar; she was sure it was John's necklace.

Now more confused than ever, Angela was wondering why her stepmom had John's gold necklace in her possession, especially since it was the necklace she and her dad had given to John as a wedding gift.

At the scene of the accident, John was unaware that his mother-in-law was lying fighting for her life in the bushes where he threw his necklace. After landing directly in front of her, she grabbed the necklace and clutched it tightly in her right hand. As she lay in her hospital bed, she observed her nurse placing the necklace in the drawer.

When Angela removed the necklace from the drawer, holding it up in front of her stepmom, her stepmom shook her head to say, "Yes, that's what I wanted you to see."

While Angela was holding up the necklace, her stepmom's facial features changed drastically into a look of fear. Angela noticed that it was the same look she had on her face when she looked at John earlier.

Angela was already curious as to why her stepmom looked at John in the way that she did when he entered the room. Seeing her react the same way at the sight of his gold necklace didn't make her any less curious.

She thought to herself, "Maybe John lost his necklace somewhere, and she found it. I'll make sure I ask him about it. Something's strange about this."

Angela sat and watched her stepmom slowly drifting away; there was nothing else the doctors could do for her to keep her alive. She grabbed the Bible off the table, searched for her stepmom's favorite scripture, and began reading it to her. As she was ending her reading, the life of a devoted pastor's wife and stepmom came to an end as well.

Angela left the hospital to prepare for another funeral. She was saddened by the loss of her stepmom but also troubled about John's necklace being in her possession. Unfortunately, adding to the pain of losing a son, father, and stepmother, Angela had a mystery to solve.

CHAPTER 20
SEPARATION

After the sudden and tragic death of a son and losing a father and stepmother, Angela was at a point where she felt as though things were not getting any better. She had seen enough strange things from John and heard enough of his lies. As promised, she began packing her belongings, preparing to leave to stay with her sister for a while.

John walked into the room, concerned about his image and nothing else.

"You don't have to do this. What will the church say about the assistant pastor being separated from his wife? Maybe you're not concerned about it, but I don't want people talking behind my back."

Angela wasn't going to take the blame for their separation.

"If they do talk, just know that it was you that gave them a reason to talk, not me. You are more concerned about how you look to the church rather than how you look to God."

Before walking out the door, Angela turned around and asked John, "With all the other things I'm confused about, there is one more thing that is blowing my mind right now. Why did my stepmom have your gold necklace at the hospital? When I held it up in front of her, she was terrified at the sight of it. I saw the same terrified look on her face when you walked into her room. Maybe I'm being too suspicious, but I think she wanted to say something about you. Without lying to me, what's your take on that? Don't you think it strange for her to react in the way she reacted?"

John, with a mortified look said, "Just like you said, you are being too suspicious. All I know is that she was injured, in pain, and heavily medicated. Maybe that's the reason for the reaction. Concerning the necklace, I did lose it somewhere, maybe she found it. That's the only thing that comes to my mind."

Angela struggled to believe John's explanation. "I know you have secrets you haven't shared with me and I believe that is the root of all of our problems. I'm praying that one day you will come out of the shadows and confess what you need to confess; it's up to you."

While staying with her sister, Angela avoided any contact with John. She stopped attending church services and gave up working in the outreach shelter. There were just too many memories of her dad and his work that she needed some time away.

Two weeks after John and Angela separated, the church board chairman arranged an emergency meeting with John and the rest of the board members. At this meeting, the chairman informed John that there was a personal issue involving his marriage that needed to be addressed before the church could move forward.

"John, thanks for meeting with us. We know you have been busy taking care of things with your family, the funerals and all, but we have been deliberating during the past few weeks about appointing you as our new senior pastor. You have worked as head of the outreach ministry, and you were a great supporter of Pastor Robison, your father-in-law. We understand that he was grooming you to be the next senior pastor, but there is one thing that needs to be cleared up before making our determination. We have heard that you and your wife are separated. Is that correct?"

John answered, "Yes, that's correct. As of now, we are temporarily separated."

The board chairman pressed John for a more detailed explanation. "With all due respect and following board policy, can you elaborate as to why you both have separated from each other?"

"Chairman, It's not what you might be thinking. I assure you that there's no infidelity or anything like that. As you all know, we suffered a great loss, and Angela is having a hard time emotionally dealing with it. I tried my best to comfort her, but she felt the need to spend some time with her sister. I accepted her decision. I knew separation would raise some eyebrows, but I had no problem with her getting help from whoever she thought could help her the most, even if it wasn't me."

The chairman delivered some good news, at least for the moment, it was good news for John, considering all that had transpired.

"We didn't call this meeting to pass judgment. We just wanted to get some clarification before making a decision. That being said, on behalf of the board, we applaud you for humbling yourself and letting your wife go where she needed to go to get help. Our prayers will be with you both. As of this moment, consider yourself our new senior pastor. Congratulations senior Pastor, John Forester.

"And by the way, before Pastor Robison passed away, I'm sure you are aware that he was working on a grant proposal that would bring in needed funds for building improvements for the church and outreach shelter. The original copy of the grant proposal he was bringing to you for you to read was destroyed in the accident, but if you look around his office, I imagine you will find a copy. Pastor Robison always made a copy of important documents. We need to submit that proposal as soon as possible.

"Also, after Pastor Robison passed away, we have had several members who were loyal to him leave to attend other congregations. Some more will leave before you take over as senior pastor. Our treasurer and secretary, Brother Hill and his wife have already stepped down from their respective positions. We asked them to stick around until we had someone trained to take over, but they declined to do so. Unfortunately, this happens when a congregation loses a pastor who has been their leader for years.

"At this point, we don't have anyone left who is qualified to fill the Hill's positions. We have an acting secretary until you appoint one, but for now, while the church is going through this transition, you will have to do all the treasury work."

John accepted his new position and all the other responsibilities he inherited, unlike accepting the responsibilities he had as a husband and father.

"I gladly accept the senior pastor position. I'll be sure to fill those positions that may need to be filled as soon as possible. I'll meet with the acting secretary, and I have no problem making sure the church finances are in order until a treasurer is appointed. I'll also make sure the grant proposal gets submitted."

John settled into his position as senior pastor while at the same time, handling the church finances. The church was struggling to financially keep its head above water because it was losing members.

There was also someone else missing, Angela. John thought that when he was appointed senior pastor, she would return and support him, leaving everything in the past. But Angela only saw the same old John, pretending to be a new pastor, but acting out the same old John script.

As John was boxing up Pastor Robison's office belongings, he came across the copy of the grant proposal the chairman of the board said he might find. The deadline for submitting the proposal was only a few days away, so John decided to take it home to review it, sign it, and mail it off.

When he arrived home, he stood inside the door, and for the first time in a long time, he was feeling lonely. He missed his wife's smiles, even amid the turmoil and adversity that surrounded their marriage. He missed watching her cuddled up in bed with their son every night when he chose to isolate himself in his office. He was feeling empty inside. Unfortunately, his seductive adversary was waiting in the wings to take advantage of that emptiness.

John walked into his office. Although he was alone, out of habit, he closed and locked his office door behind him. In an attempt to take his mind off how much he missed his wife and deceased son, and his in-laws, he pulled the grant out and began working on reviewing it before signing it.

While he was reviewing the grant, He received a text message from Tracy, whom he hadn't heard from since before the accident that killed his father and mother-in-law, and the night he lost his son. Frustrated, he said to himself,

"I can't believe this. I told this woman she wasn't getting any more money from me. I thought I heard the last from this deranged extortionist." As far as John was concerned, he had given Tracy the last of what he was going to give her; their relationship was over. He placed the grant into his desk drawer to review later.

After opening the text message Tracy sent him, he was annoyed at the disturbing message that read, "I enjoy watching every move you make; it makes good drama. I gather a lot has been going on with you after being appointed senior pastor and everything. I know that's what you always wanted, but you already know that I don't have a problem patiently waiting for the right moment to get what I want as well.

"I hear the church is not doing so well, and you are losing members. Are you having problems with your wife? I hear you two are separated. I'm not surprised considering how perverted you are. Did she find out about me? If she doesn't know about me now, she will, and your entire congregation will unless I have the ten thousand dollars I requested in my possession by ten o'clock tomorrow morning. I know so much about you that I can end your career with just one phone call. You know where to take the money, that old abandoned house where you grew up. Place the money under the bench as usual, then walk away.

"And by the way, I know you must be lonely right now, at home alone and missing your wife, and no one to cuddle up with at night. As always, you can count on me to give you just what you want and need to feed that loneliness."

At the end of the text message, there was a link to a webpage. John has been in this position many times before. Yes, he was fighting loneliness, but he was also fighting a sexual addiction as well as a persistent enemy, Tracy Torres, who was winning the battle every time.

John knew he only had eight thousand dollars in his account, and although financially struggling to pay its bills and operate the outreach ministry, the church had at least two thousand dollars in its general account. He said to himself,

"It has never failed. Everything I have built up and worked for is once again in jeopardy of being snatched away. This is such bad timing. I have lost a lot and gained a lot. I can't afford to lose any more than I already have. My life is on the line here. I'll withdraw the rest of the ten thousand dollars from the church account. I'll make it look as though the money was used as an emergency withdrawal to fund our outreach ministry; no one will question it."

After deciding to withdraw the remaining two thousand dollars from the church account, John sat in his seat, staring at the webpage link that was included in Tracy's text message. He typed the web address in the browser on his computer, opening up a pornographic website. Once again, sexually explicit images filled John's computer screen. He was in a place where he thought he would never go again, but was enjoying being there.

Late into the night, John was captivated by what his eyes were viewing online. He even viewed a few of the hundreds of sexually explicit videos he had stored in his office, similar to the mass library of explicit videos and magazines his dad had secretly hidden in his garage that fueled him and his dad's sexual addiction. He sat in his office chair, indulging and sinking deeper into a pit of lust; and he could not control it.

While viewing the explicit images on his computer screen, John's cell phone rang. He was so caught up viewing what was on his computer screen that he ignored the first call. He usually would turn his cell phone off when he was viewing sexually explicit material on his computer.

His phone rang at least two more times. Thinking that if the caller attempted to reach him three times, the call must be important. With sexually explicit images still on his computer screen, John picked up the phone to answer. The voice on the other end was a member of the church. Her voice was scratchy and she was coughing off and on. It turns out the member was stricken with strep throat and was calling for John to pray for her over the phone.

Without shutting down his computer, John walked away from the computer into a corner, attempting to pray for the church member, but there was something wrong. The prayer which should have been simple was the weakest prayer he had ever prayed.

John attempted to force his prayer into an effective prayer, but God's presence was not in it, and the church member noticed it. She asked, "Pastor Forester, are you alright, you just don't sound the same?"

John tried to justify his ineffectiveness.

"You called for me to pray for you, but I need you to pray for me instead. All the deaths in the family get the best of me at times, and this is one of those times. I know my prayer wasn't what you expected, but I'll be over tomorrow to check on you as well as pray for you."

After John hung up the phone, he walked around his office, acting as though he had just lost his mind. He was yelling, crying, frustrated, and concerned at how ineffective he was in praying a simple prayer. He was affected by it so much that after bolting out of his office, he unknowingly forgot to turn off his computer and lock his office door. He went to bed depressed, ashamed of himself, and also still lonely and unsatisfied by what he had just viewed on his computer.

He found himself waking up at two o'clock in the morning thinking about Angela. Very rarely did John cry, but considering Tracy's threats, his inability to be effective in ministry, and missing his wife and son brought tears to his eyes.

Restless, John grabbed his cell phone, and for the first time since Angela left to stay with her sister, he sent her a text message. The message read, "I know I have not loved you the way I should have, and I was not there for our son. I am lying here breathing but suffocating in guilt and shame. I'm lonely and miss you and our son. I gave you so many reasons to leave, and I am sorry for that. I don't know how much longer I can live without you. I wish you were here."

Later that morning, Angela woke up, noticing the text message John had sent her. After opening and reading the message, she ran downstairs to show it to her sister.

"Rachel, read this text message John sent me early this morning. I've always felt he was hiding something from me, but this doesn't sound like him. It almost sounds like he's suicidal. I need to check on him. I feel as though something is seriously wrong; I feel it. Maybe I shouldn't have left him. Maybe I should have waited until he was ready to sit down and talk things out. There's just been too much coming at me that I just haven't been thinking right. I should not have left."

After reading the text message, Angela's sister grabbed her and held her close in her arms. Angela began to pray.

"God, you know how much loss I have suffered and the pain I feel right now. Please forgive me for my bitterness towards John and for giving up on him. Right now I'm asking you to do this one thing for me.

197

If any secrets need to be uncovered, please reveal them to me so that I might be at peace with you and my husband."

While Angela was on her way to check on John, he woke up, realizing that he had overslept. He only had an hour to get dressed and meet his ten o'clock deadline to go to his boyhood home and leave the ten thousand dollars in the spot as requested. In the process of him rushing to leave, he failed to do something he always did before leaving the house, close and lock his office door.

John was unaware that every sexually explicit magazine and video, and every visit to a pornographic website was open for the whole world to see. Other than getting addicted to pornography, when John left his computer on the previous night and his office door unlocked, he had made one of the biggest mistakes of his life that would bring everything to a terrible and unexpected climax.

CHAPTER 21
TRUTH REVEALED

When Angela arrived at the house to check on John, she noticed that he was not home because his car was not in the driveway. At first, she was going to leave, but she decided to go inside the house anyway to make sure that nothing was going on out of the ordinary. After entering, she didn't see anything unusual or out of place. She walked around, stopping at John's office door. Although she knew he kept his office door locked, she decided to check whether or not it was locked anyway.

Upon slightly turning the handle, to her surprise, she discovered that the door was unlocked. Since John was not home, and his office door was unlocked, she stood at the door, contemplating whether or not she should investigate if there was something inside that he was hiding from her.

She said to herself, "If he was in there busy working on church stuff, as was always his excuse, there should be nothing in there to hide. But if he is hiding something, I'm tired of secrets. It's time out for this. And besides, this is still my house. I deserve to go into any room I please. I was foolish to let him put restrictions on me in my own home."

Angela opened John's office door and walked inside. For the first time, she trespassed into a restricted area in her home. She looked around, surprised at how neat and organized John kept his office. Everything seemed to be okay until she stumbled on a rug John had placed under his office chair. After bumping into his desk, his computer, which he had left on all night, came out of sleep mode, revealing a pornographic web page full of sexually explicit images he had failed to close. Angela was stunned at what she saw on John's computer screen.

Upon further investigation, looking inside his desk drawers, she discovered his library of sexually explicit videos. She walked around, checking every shelf and closed cabinet, finding hundreds of sexually explicit magazines. Angela was so sickened at the sight of what John was hiding in his office that she lost control.

She grabbed John's computer off his desk and threw it against the wall. Then she grabbed the sexually explicit videos and magazines off the shelves, pulling out as many as she could, throwing them on the floor. She created a heaping pile of the pornographic material on the floor until she was exhausted. With evidence of her suspicions right in front of her and surrounding her, Angela fell to her knees emotionally devastated.

"This filth destroyed my marriage. John, how could you have lied to me for so long? How could you let this happen when all you had to do is ask me to help you, but instead, you isolated me?"

Angela struggled to get off her knees, feeling sick and in pain as if she had been beaten with a baseball bat. Before she walked out of John's office, she left a note on his desk that read, "I told you your secrets were the root of our problems, and all this pornographic stuff proves that I was right. Do you honestly think your addiction has made you a victim? Unfortunately, I have become a victim of your deception."

Angela left the house determined to find John, but on her way out, she forgot to close his office door. After getting inside her car, she sat for a moment before driving off.

"All this time he kept this from me. I knew something was going on with him. There were signs, but I ignored them. I can't believe all that junk in his office was more important to him than his son and me. I need to find out where he is; he needs to get some help. How can he call himself a pastor and keep this a secret."

While Angela was calling church members searching for John, she received a phone call from the chairman of the church board.

"Angela, I just called to pass along some vital information. By the way, we miss having you around. I hear you are looking for John."

"Yes, I am chairman. As you well know, we are temporarily separated. I received a strange text message from him that's got me worried."

"Angela, I'm worried as well. It seems as though you're not the only one looking for John."

"What do you mean? Who else would be looking for him?"

"Angela, it took longer than they expected, but the police completed viewing all the evidence and video's from some of the cameras in the area of the crash that killed Pastor Robison and his wife. They wouldn't go into detail, but they want John to stop by the station to answer some questions."

A chill went through Angela's spine as she sat in silence. She began to put things together. She thought about the terrified look on her stepmom's face when she held John's gold necklace after finding it in her hospital room desk drawer. She also thought of the look on her stepmom's face when John walked into the room.

Angela screamed, "Please God! Please God! Don't let it be true! Please God, this is too much! I don't know how much of this I can take!" The board chairman was confused at Angela's reaction. "Angela, are you alright? What's going on?"

Angela tearfully responded, "Just have your board members and congregation pray for John. You said the police are looking for him to question him, but I need to find him first. I'll get in touch with you when I do."

John had just left the bank after withdrawing two thousand dollars from the church account. He drove to his boyhood home to the spot where he was to leave the money, under the bench that sat under the old oak tree. John was placing the money under the bench when all of a sudden, he paused to look up at the oak tree, thinking about what he had gotten himself into and the condition of his life.

He looked at the oak tree as he had done many times from his bedroom window while he was growing up. He thought about how full the tree had been throughout the spring, summer, and fall. But today, in the dead of winter, it looked as if it was resting. As the soft pillows of light snow rested upon it, the time had come for the oak tree to go to sleep.

The butterfly had performed its final dance at center stage against the backdrop of a sunny blue sky, orchestrated by the out-stretched branches of the oak tree. But now, the curtain had closed, and the butterfly and the oak tree had taken their final bow for the season.

Until next time, there will be no summer storm winds to slam against the oak tree, forcing it to drop its acorns, and no leaves to depend upon its branches to sustain them. As the oak tree takes its rest, the stripped leaves exposed its true form that was hidden for three seasons.

As always, observing the oak tree taught John a valuable lesson. Although the lesson he learned this day was the most valuable of them all, it was identical to the warning he was given during the eulogy at his son's funeral. Observing the stripped leaves on the oak tree that revealed the tree's true form, John realized that it was time for him to come clean, strip himself from all the lies, secrets, and most of all, expose his sexual addiction. He had endured many seasons of pain, heartache, and loss that hid his true form as a tree of righteousness. He was weary, tired, and messed up. Now it was time to rest from it all, and the first step in getting that rest was to confess and then expose Tracy's manipulation and extortion.

Tracy had been a thorn in his side for too long. He could care less about her threats. No matter the consequences, John was prepared to confront Tracy once again; this time face to face without hiding behind a ski mask. It was time to end it all, once and for all, something he believed he should have done a long time ago. She had invaded his life, and he was determined to let her know how much damage she had caused him and his family.

John left the money in a bag under the bench, then drove off. After driving about a half-mile down the road, he stopped, then looked into his rearview mirror to see if anyone was around; he saw no one. Because he had grown up in the neighborhood, he knew a quick way to get back to the house. He pulled his car over into an area where it wouldn't be seen from the road and ran as fast as he could towards the house. Coming upon a ditch that ran along the back of the house, John, nervous, yet determined to confront Tracy, hid in the ditch behind a row of tall brush, waiting for her to show up.

After about five minutes, he heard a car coming down the road. As the car approached and came closer to the house, he noticed that the car looked familiar. He had never seen Tracy's car, but he thought that maybe it was a coincidence that Tracy's car looked like the one a former friend owned.

After the car pulled into the driveway, from his view, he was able to determine that there were four individuals in the car, two women in the front seats, but he couldn't see their faces. He decided to move closer without being detected. He managed to make it to the pile of wood from the garage he had burnt down without being seen. As he was lying next to the pile, he observed two muscular men getting out of the backseat of the car, both standing on each side of it, checking the perimeter around the house. When the passenger side door opened, he was not surprised to see Tracy get out of the car. But he asked himself, "If Tracy wasn't driving, who was the woman driving the car?"

As he gazed upon Tracy checking out the perimeter, in the winter cold, John became heated with rage. Only a few feet away was the woman who threatened him, devastated him, took advantage of his addiction, and could taint his reputation. She had set him up for a fall the day he came to her home, and he fell big time because he failed God and his family.

Tracy walked up to remove the money from under the bench as the two men stood as lookouts. When she returned to the car, she placed the bag on the hood of the car, inspecting its contents. At the very moment John was prepared to come out of hiding and confront Tracy, the woman who was driving exited the car. He couldn't see who the woman was until she walked to the side of the car where Tracy was standing. At that point, John got the shock of his life. He couldn't believe his eyes were seeing who he was seeing.

John was looking at the same woman he had spent so much time working with in the outreach ministry. She had confided in him, and he had befriended her. In return, as one of the many forgotten victims of his sexual addiction, he deceived her and left her broken. The last time he saw her was when she stormed out of the dean's office on the college campus, slamming the door behind her. John was bewildered to see that this woman was his former college friend and outreach partner, Victoria. He said to himself, "What is going on here? How on

God's earth is Victoria involved in this scheme with Tracy? This doesn't make sense, but I'm not afraid to go out there and find out what's going on."

When John emerged from the pile of burned-out wood, Tracy quickly closed the bag containing the money and the two muscular men stood in front of her and Victoria to protect them. John approached the group, staying at a distance, and addressing Victoria.

"Victoria, what are you doing with this evil and deranged woman? What is your involvement in all of this? This is ridiculous. I have a right to know."

Tears flowed from Victoria's eyes as she angrily responded, "Ridiculous? You have a right to know? How can you have the nerve to stand there and say that? The only thing you have a right to know is that I had a future, but you destroyed it with your lies and secrets. I know you haven't forgotten what happened in the dean's office on the college campus. When I stormed out of his office, I told you that you were going to pay for ruining my life. When Tracy called me, telling me about what happened when you visited her home alone, I felt something did happen between you and her. At that time, I wanted to believe you were telling the truth, but I did have my suspicions.

"After personally meeting with Tracy, she promised to expose your secret, therefore the reason for all of the sexually explicit videos and messages. Your perverted secret sexual addiction led you straight into her trap. At first, I felt sorry for you until Tracy called me again and told me that her trap was working and how she swindled ten thousand dollars out of you. After my husband died, I decided that it was payday for me also; I was going to get my share. I told her to do whatever it took to get another ten thousand dollars out of you. I wanted you to pay because my husband died because of you and your attempt to keep your addiction a secret. Funny thing is, every individual who was affected by your secret, exposed your secret."

John scorned Victoria. "All along, I wondered how Tracy knew how to find me. This is your hometown. You knew exactly how to find me. You say you are a victim in all of this. How could you be so insensitive, causing so much pain to me and my family? All of this blackmailing you both have done is evil at its core."

Tracy, laughing said to John, "Evil? Evil? You call us evil? You are evil in disguise, you two-faced pervert. The hurt and pain doesn't feel so good when someone else is inflicting it, does it?"

John's rage escalated to a higher level when he said to Tracy, "You stand there and laugh! This is no joke! You both have destroyed my life. I have lost a lot, and there's nothing funny about that. I realize I did you wrong, but what you have done to me is beyond revenge. You should be locked up for this. I should have taken care of you that night out in the woods"

Tracy exploded.

"Are you serious? That was you who came to my house that night? You have lost your mind! I knew you were a low-life, but I would have never thought you would sink so low as to try to kill me in an attempt to cover up how evil you are! It just blows my mind that you would even think about hunting me down and killing me! This is not over, but consider life as you know it over!"

Victoria gave John a final dose of her rage and anger before leaving. "You're sick in the mind, and you need to get some help. Your secret has been exposed and you still say we have destroyed your life. What about Tracy's life? What about my life? I was close to graduation when I was expelled because of your negligence and hypocritical ways. You say you have lost a lot. I am a victim, even a victim of your arrogance right now. You don't have any idea what I went through after that meeting in the dean's office.

"I nearly lost my mind. I couldn't go back to school. I couldn't get a job making enough money to pay for my husband's surgeries, medications, and medical bills. I could care less about bringing you down and what you suffered in the process. Whatever has happened to you is your fault, not ours."

Victoria, Tracy, and the two men quickly got back into their car with the ten thousand dollars. As they pulled out of the driveway, Tracy rolled down the passenger side window of the car and said to John,

"You see, this scene right now, you coming at us as you did wasn't supposed to happen. You were supposed to leave the money and walk away. After this deal today, I was going to walk away and end it all, never saying another word to you or exposing your wicked ways. But now, because you had the boldness to confront me, attempt to assassinate me, and expose Victoria, I'm bold enough to make some phone calls. Now let's see who gets exposed."

Victoria, who was driving the car, sped down the road, kicking up the fresh layer of fluffy snow that had fallen. John went crazy as he began grabbing parched wood and rubble from the burned-down garage and throwing everything he possibly could at the car as it sped up the road.

The car quickly disappeared into the wintery horizon. Tired, crying, and exhausted, John fell and sank among the pile of rubble he had made from throwing it at the speeding car. He got up and jumped into his car, speeding down the road like a madman towards his home. His only concern was to destroy every piece of evidence in his office that would expose his sexual addiction.

As he was driving, he was overwhelmed with so many thoughts, so many condemnations, saying to himself,

"It's over! My life is over! They're both going to make public everything about me, everything. No, maybe not. It's going to be their word against mine. As long as I destroy and delete everything associated with them and my addiction; the videos, magazines, text messages, everything; it will be their word against mine.

"Everyone will believe me because I'm a trustworthy and outstanding pastor in the community. I can't confess that I have an addiction, not right now. No one can know about this, especially Angela. I have helped a lot of people who were down and out get back on their feet. They need me. I can handle Tracy and Victoria, they are disgruntled nobodies.

"Yes, that's it, they are clients I once counseled who have become disgruntled because I told them the truth about themselves. That's what I'll tell everyone, and that's what everyone will believe. I need to get home quick to delete and destroy every piece of incriminating evidence."

CHAPTER 22
COLLATERAL DAMAGE

After John pulled into his driveway, while preparing to exit his car, he felt a sharp pain in his chest. He sat in his seat for a moment before running into the house, leaving his car door open. Upon entering the house, he noticed that his office door was open. Feeling a tightness in his chest, he took a quick look around to make sure no one had broken in before entering his office.

Once inside, he saw the pile of sexually explicit tapes and videos Angela had thrown on the floor and his computer that she had thrown against the wall. He sat down in his chair in pain, with his head bowed low, knowing that from the looks of things, it only could have been Angela who had violated his space and desecrated his private collection; she must know his secret. His suspicion was confirmed when he found and read the note Angela left on his desk.

When John thought about Tracey's threat to make phone calls to expose him, and Angela discovering his sexually explicit library, he began acting like a wild man. He grabbed the remaining magazines and videos off the shelves, throwing them into the pile of sexually explicit tapes and videos that were already on the floor. As he was violently throwing items into the pile, all of a sudden, he grabbed his chest. The pain was sharp and excruciating.

John began staggering around the room, eventually falling directly on top of the pile. While he was near death on top of the pile, holding his chest, experiencing a heart attack, his mind took him back to the day he set his dad's garage on fire, including the sexually explicit magazines and videos that were inside. Getting weaker by the second, he had a final thought of how ironic it was that in his private office, his own pornographic and illicit empire, just as the garage was his dad's private empire, he found himself brought down to lie on a pile of pornographic laced rubble, reaping what he had sown.

As John breathed his last breath, Angela arrived at the house. After seeing that John's car door had been left open, she ran into his office fearing the worse. Finding him lying on top of the pile on the floor, she immediately fell to her knees to help him but soon realized that it was too late. She took him into her arms, expressing how she felt at that moment of his passing.

"Right now, I can't find a single word to explain how much it was a blow to me to find out you may have killed my father and stepmother. I felt like someone was ripping my heart out when the chairman of the church board called me and told me the police wanted to question you. To this day, I don't know what you were doing that night, but if you are responsible, you physically erased my parents from the face of this earth due to your negligence.

"I am searching for a reason to disprove the mounting evidence against you, especially the necklace in my stepmom's possession. Despite what you refused to admit you did, I still have mixed emotions. I could be angry and bitter, but that won't bring my parents back. I have to look beyond what you may have done and look to God, who has always been there to take me through the toughest of times.

"I can't focus on the how and why; my parents, especially my dad, wouldn't want me to. If it turns out that you are guilty, I will never forget the lives you have destroyed, but I have to forgive you. Forgiving you honors my dad's legacy of compassion and forgiveness, and all the good he stood for and represented.

"I have never forgotten that day back in high school when I was being bullied, and you came to my rescue. I failed to see how your addiction bullied you. You became my best friend, and then my husband who was crying out for help, never realizing how near your help was to you. You were there for me to dry my tears and lend me your shoulder to hold me up whenever I was falling. I'm sorry for failing to come to your rescue when you needed me."

Nearly mimicking the fate of his dad, who was incinerated among a heap of pornographic videos and magazines, John passed away in his office on top of a pile of sexually explicit filth and rubble. He had an addiction, but in the process of keeping that addiction a secret, there was collateral damage. Innocent people were hurt, and some lives were changed, destroyed, and even lost.

Angela cleaned John's office, throwing out and burning every piece of sexually explicit material before his body was taken away. She felt that since he was gone, there was no reason for anyone else to know about his addiction other than those who may have already known.

The church never discovered the missing funds John had withdrawn from its account. After discovering the withdrawal receipt, Angela assumed John had withdrawn it for personal reasons. She replaced it with funds from her bank account and money she borrowed from her sister.

Angela never found out about Tracy or Victoria because Tracy never followed through on her threat. Maybe learning about John's death gave her and Victoria closure. Also, without the police being able to question John about the fatal car accident he caused, the case was closed.

About a week after John's funeral, Angela drove to his boyhood home with her sister to show her the old oak tree John always talked to her about and where she found his mother deceased. As they sat on his bed, looking out the window, and as the wind started blowing, Angela expressed her regrets.

"Rachel, I failed John. I left when I should have stayed to help him. I should have known he had an addiction. Before I left the church and quit working at the outreach shelter, I worked with people every day who were suffering from addictions. How did I miss it in John? When he needed me, I gave up on him."

Rachel grabbed Angela's hand and began to console her, sounding like their dad whenever he had an encouraging word for them.

"Sometimes after we have helped addicts, they may be strong for a little while, but as the storms of life get stronger and the need to hold on tighter gets tougher, they will give in to their addiction, break and fall. People suffer from addictions for various reasons, but the problem with some of us is that we won't settle for being who we are or what we have; we always want more. We are influenced by other people, trying to be someone else so that we may fit in.

"The vast majority of individuals who have an addiction have not been that way all their lives. There was a time in their life when they were not addicted. They were as strong as you and me.

"Some people become addicts because somewhere along the line, something or someone influenced their thought process. It may have been peer pressure, abuse, curiosity, stress, hardship, rejection, environment, etc. They needed help and guidance, but sought it in something they allowed to negatively take control of them and their lives. An addiction is birthed out of a bad or negative experience rather than a good or positive one. Everyone has a responsibility to be one of those trees of righteousness the eulogist talked about at your son's funeral."

"Rachel, as you know, I had a drug addiction at one time and you and dad helped me get through it. I had given in to peer pressure, and as you know, I wasn't as close to our mom and our stepmom as you were, but after I got cleaned up, allowed God to influence me rather than my addiction, I was dad's shadow. I was always there for him and he was there for me. He truly was one of those trees of righteousness when I was a weak branch, destined to snap off.

"After my son passed away, then dad, and then our stepmom, I didn't know what to feel. Some expected me to lose my sanity, but God had me. The Bible says He will give you a peace that no one else will understand; He gave me that peace. I will say that on the first night I stayed with you after leaving John, I cried so much that my pillow was soaked. I got up early in the morning and wrote a goodbye letter to dad from me and you. Let me read it to you."

Angela reached into her purse and pulled out the letter. She began to read.

"Dad, Rachel and I miss you so much. We remember the day you sat down with us and we had a conversation about what we should do in case of your death, but even that conversation couldn't prepare us for the pain we feel right now. We wish we were at the scene of that car crash to hold your hand. We wish we were there to hear your final goodbye when you took your last breath. We wish we were there to come to your rescue, just as you were there for us.

"Working in the ministry together, you and I saw our share of grief, but you never truly can understand how those grieving individuals were feeling on the inside until grief lands on your doorstep. If you were here right now, I know you would talk Rachel and me through our grief, just as you did with numerous church members. Although we are in pain and grieving right now, you taught us that grieving pain originates from having an individual to love, and that same individual loving you. We all had a loving bond that couldn't be broken.

"Dad, you were an extraordinary father, grandfather, husband, and pastor. Whenever we were down, you had a sense of humor to make us laugh, even after becoming the church pastor. Whenever I was broken, especially during the time I was hooked on drugs, your faith in God and boundless compassion helped fix me. You sacrificed so much for us; we wish we had time to do more for you.

"Dad, at the funeral, your casket was closed. Before they took your body to the cemetery, Rachel and I placed a hand on top of it for one last touch. We pretended to be touching your face, and at the same time, trying to remember every detail of it, knowing we would never touch your perfectly shaved beard again. We pretended to be holding your hand tight, knowing it was for the last time. Although your hand was cold, strangely it reminded me of how warm your strong hand felt when you would take us by the hand and walk us to the park when we were little girls.

"Dad, we're proud to have had you as our father and pastor. We cannot express how we miss you. We have so many memories of you, and that's why saying goodbye hurts. Although you are absent right now, one day we will be together again. Until then, we will forever cherish and treasure the time God gave us while you were present. Goodbye dad."

Rachel grabbed Angela and hugged her tight. They both struggled to hold back a river of tears. Within the reflection of each teardrop was a memory of the good times they had with their dad.

Rachel struggled to regain her composure but managed to compliment Angela on the letter she wrote.

"Angela, that's a beautiful letter, spoken from the heart. Dad would be proud; he loved us both. He groomed you to help addicts look beyond their days of addiction, the times in their life before they broke. You have encouraged them to focus on that time in their life when they were not broken, not addicted, and use that focus to regain their strength and confidence that they can get back to that place where they once were, and that place where God has purposed for them to be.

"I want you to look at that oak tree out there. As I look at it, I can see why John greatly admired it and learned so much from just observing it season after season. There is a spiritual lesson to learn. That large oak tree that is barely moving as the wind rocks the other trees back and forth is showing those trees how to stand firm when the storm winds blow or in the face of opposition. It's very amazing how that oak tree's roots have dug deep into the ground, as deep as its height and wide as its large branches.

"That oak tree has survived many storms. When you look at it, you can't begin to imagine its resolve to be bigger than any storm that rises against it. It adapts so that it might bend and twist with the wind of the storm. It seems as if all the other trees see its resilience and draw strength from it.

"That oak tree will fight hard in an attempt to keep itself from snapping under pressure. The wind will do its job on it. After the wind has done its job, you will see branches from the oak tree that have held on for years become casualties lying on the ground next to the tree. Those fallen branches tried to prevail, but couldn't stand against the pressure of the storm, despite how much the oak tree tried to save them.

"What that oak tree is teaching me and you right now is that the casualties or the branches that fell off during the storm were not its fault. The oak tree does its job of nourishing even the weakest branch. If that weak branch refuses that nourishment or allows disease or insects to continue weakening it, that branch will snap off and fall under the pressure of the fierce stormy winds. When you were working in the outreach ministry, as you have always said, you had an addiction to help individuals prevail and find rest from their fierce stormy winds or in other words, their addiction.

"That oak tree out there is an example and pillar of strength to the other trees because it does what it does. It will not change what it has been created to do, but it will adapt to change or whatever comes against it; that's where its strength lies.

"Sometimes when the storms of difficulty rage in our lives and we take a hit here and there, we bend in fear, refusing to adapt to whatever comes against us, then we break. Our doubt fails to turn into confidence, our sorrow fails to turn into joy, and our weakness fails to turn into resilience. We fail to fulfill our purpose. We must remain standing during the storm. Even if the bending and breaking leave open wounds, we cannot let a few open wounds infect the whole body.

"Angela, I want you to listen to what I am saying; I can't stress this enough. A rainy and stormy day, and a broken and fallen branch here and there will not change what that oak tree is. That oak tree does its best to protect and nourish the remaining branches. Although the fallen branches have changed the physical appearance of the oak tree, they have not changed it from remaining an oak tree. The oak tree adapts to the change and moves on to maintain its purpose.

"Angela, you are that oak tree, and every addict you have an opportunity to help are the branches. You cannot save every branch; there will be casualties. There will be times when during the storm, a weak and infected branch will fall on other branches in its pathway downward, causing them to fall as well; that's collateral damage.

"As John was falling deeper into his addiction, innocent people fell with him; that's collateral damage. You are an oak tree of righteousness that has been wounded, but those wounds are a testimony of your strength and faith in God. Adapt to the change that has taken place in your life and continue doing the good that you were created to do. God has changed your drug addiction into an addiction to help; that's where your strength lies. For every addicted individual you do help, you are preventing a whole lot more innocent people from being a victim of collateral damage.

FROM THE AUTHOR

Thank you for choosing this book. My prayer is that Christian families and even businesses who have individuals, employees, and leaders struggling with sexual addiction will glean from this book, learn from it, and use it as a discussion tool for engagement, interaction, and healing.

Although the characters in this book are fictional, the sensitive issue it deals with is real and growing in the church body. This book addresses the less talked about issue of sexual addiction that is occurring within congregations, and the collateral damage caused, especially by failing to bring it to the surface.

Some addictions don't end as success stories. Some addicts are never rehabilitated. Some take their addition with them to a lonely grave and unfortunately, indirectly they take the innocent along with them. Whether or not an addict recovers, every addiction creates collateral damage. There is no addict, especially those who refuse to admit they are an addict, who has not left an imprint on an innocent victim in the form of stress, financial loss, family separation, church disruption, and even death. The guilty has destroyed the lives of the guiltless.

The root of sexual addiction is a spiritual condition fueled by an individual's sinful nature and the choices an individual makes. It is dealt with by choosing not to indulge in it, deciding whether to rely on God's help in making that choice, and relying on Him as a guide to find other resources that may be a help. A born-again believer must keep in mind that whatever choice he makes will affect everyone close to him and his relationship with God.

A sex addict may say that after picking up a sexually explicit magazine or turning on the computer, they couldn't resist flipping through the pages of the magazine or clicking to open the pornographic webpage; they say they couldn't control themselves.

But, the fact is, before the page was flipped or the mouse was clicked, there was plenty of time to make the right choice. Was the individual in control when he picked up the magazine? Yes, because he made a conscious decision to pick it up. Was the individual in control when he turned on the computer? Yes. Because he made a conscious decision to push the on button.

Since the answer to both questions above is yes, why all of a sudden does the addict say he lost control after picking up the magazine and flipping through the pages, or turning on the computer and clicking to the sexually explicit webpage? The fact is, he was in control every step of the way, from start to finish, because of a conscious decision.

Unlike an alcoholic or drug addict, a sex addict is not under the influence of a drug or alcohol. Under his control, he takes the time to put himself in a place of temptation, and after that, he chooses to make a bad choice. For born-again individuals, spiritual guidance through the Word of God, fasting, prayer, deliverance, and counseling are all the tools available that can help them overcome their sexual addiction. Philippians 4:8 challenges him to ask himself these two questions daily. What is on your mind? What are you thinking about?

Pornography is far from a good thought. This scripture is only one of many a born-again believer who has a sexual addiction can find in the Bible that will guide him towards deliverance. The Word of God will give him the ability to maintain control over his sexual addiction after deliverance from it takes place.

Your mind is where you make all of your decisions and where a will to commit to God's Word exists, but you must choose to apply His Word and exercise that commitment. An individual who chooses to put himself in a sexually tempting situation, desiring to feed an addiction that never reaches satisfaction, also has the ability and responsibility to choose the ways of God, who always satisfies.

Even after spiritual guidance and deliverance take place, former sex addicts are sometimes faced with a feeling of shame and guilt that constantly haunts them; this is where trained counselors who understand the spiritual, emotional, interpersonal, mental, and physical issues of sexual addiction can help.

A born-again believer may have been delivered from viewing pornography spiritually, but counseling helps uncover what is driving the addiction. Is it loneliness, peer pressure, unfaithfulness, anxiety, grief, rejection, depression, etc.? Deliverance from sexual addiction must continue to be dealt with spiritually, and with professional counseling, or else it may rise and prevail again.

If you are a church member or leader with a sexual addiction or any other type of addiction, you may think you are hiding a secret, but God sees all, and He is waiting and willing to help you make the right choices. What God sees is more important than what anyone else sees. You may be a member, choir member, worship team leader, or even a pastor, but until you abandon your pride and fear, and turn your addiction over to God, everything you do in works and worship is rejected.

Because you have not sanctified yourself or spiritually separated yourself from your addiction, your works and worship are deceitful, untrue, and as the King James Bible Version says, "strange fire." It's unauthorized and profane worship that God rejects.

Read Leviticus 10:1-2 and John 4:23-24 (KJV)

Why sit in service after service offering God dead worship? Why sit and die when deliverance is nearer than the pew you sit on? It is impossible to fight your battle with sexual addiction alone, don't fool yourself into spiritual death.

The events that take place in this book shine a light on the victims of a secret and hidden sexual addiction, the forgotten victims of collateral damage. I pray that after reading this book, sex addicts in the church will choose God over their addiction. I also pray that spiritual leaders will, with compassion and without condemnation, give addicts the necessary spiritual help and guide them to where they can receive professional counseling. Thank you for your support.

ABOUT THE AUTHOR

Joseph Flye is the founder and president of Divine Intervention Publications (divineinpub.com). This cutting-edge business provides a plethora of impactful and anointed teaching for anyone seeking to know God and have a deeper relationship with Him. Joseph has a strong apostolic calling in the teaching ministry and renders the revelation of God's Word through article writing, poetry, and book writing.

For over 40 years, Joseph has labored in the ministry of administration. He is a beloved and anointed Sunday school teacher and has served as a Sunday school superintendent. He has generated creative flyers, built websites, and designed essential church literature that every great congregation needs to produce spiritual growth.

Joseph and his siblings have the testimony of their father and mother planting the apostolic doctrine as a seed within them. This seed became the foundation of the limitless possibilities that he has set his mind to pursue after he was baptized and filled with the Holy Ghost at the age of fourteen.

Joseph's teaching is not only expressed through his writing, but his life radiates with examples of what he teaches. He takes care of his wife, always makes himself available to help his two daughters when needed, and finds time to have fun with his grandchildren.

Born and raised in Fort Wayne, Indiana, his anointing is in high demand as he serves and has served in several areas other than teaching and writing, including deacon, board member, and choir member. You can visit his website at divineinpub.com. On this website, you will find author commentaries on books Joseph has written, Bible courses, blogs, media, and other books and instructional resources he recommends or has written and created for your spiritual development.

VISIT: divineinpub.com

www.ingramcontent.com/pod-product-compliance
Lightning Source LLC
Chambersburg PA
CBHW021152110726
47900CB00002B/537